Investment of the Heart

by

Linda LaRoque

Investment of the Heart

Published by *L.G. Smith Books*
Cover Art by *Diana Carlile*
http://www.designingdiana.blogspot.com

Publishing History
First Edition, 2009
Digital ISBN 978-0-9893792-8-1
Print ISBN 978-0-9893792-9-8

Published in the United States of America

Dedication

To my Aunt Barbara for reading my stories and believing in my ability to weave a good tale.

CHAPTER ONE

Simon Cole despised people who arrived late for appointments. It showed a lack of respect for the other person's time. That he waited for a woman, one he didn't look forward to meeting, did little to soothe his mood.

He rolled his tense shoulders and neck, popped his knuckles, then propped his elbows on the white tablecloth. Leaning forward, he clasped his hands, and with his thumbs, massaged his temples where the beginnings of a headache drummed.

Folks in Granite Springs considered him a fair, considerate man—one always willing to lend a helping hand. Today he hoped Hallie Barron would leave this restaurant believing him to be a real bastard.

He would not, *could not,* let history repeat itself. If his nephew, Justin, married Mrs. Barron's daughter, he feared the boy would end up with a broken heart as had his father. Justin's mother, Loretta, thought ranch life would be romantic. It didn't take her long to get bored. She stuck it out for a long time, then left five years ago leaving the children to be reared on the ranch. When Sidney died in a car crash two years later, protecting Justin and his little sister Whitney, fell to Simon. If Mrs. Barron disliked him enough, she might discourage the match.

Full to capacity, the room hummed with the low

murmur of voices, the clatter of dishes, and background piano mood music. Periodic burst of laughter broke through the wall of restrained conversation.

Simon listened with half an ear, the sounds not much different from the ones of cowboys in the cattle pen, the lowing and whistling often interrupted by a bawling calf or upset heifer.

Draining his first beer, he scanned the gaudy room, taking in the familiar dark red, flocked wallpaper, white tablecloths, and heavy gold drapes pulled back with black tassels. The red velvet swing suspended from the stage was empty. He grinned. Damned if the place wasn't decked out like an old west bordello, an expensive one. The *décor* notwithstanding, they served superb steaks.

He ordered another beer and glanced around the room. His gaze stopped at the attractive blonde sitting two tables away. Dressed in a wrinkled type skirt and a silky close-fitting knit top, she sat with her chin propped on her right hand. With her left, she drummed trimmed bare fingernails on the white linen tablecloth that ended almost at her lap. She sipped her iced tea as she surveyed the room, her attention returning to the *maître d'* near the entrance as if expecting him to walk someone to her table.

Yeah, yeah, I know how you feel, honey. It's hell waiting on someone when you've better things to do.

Hell. He had business in town this afternoon. If the woman didn't hurry up, he'd end up stuck in the city instead of returning to the ranch near Granite Springs. Not a pleasant prospect since he hated the beds in motels. He could call his cousin, Jo Beth. She'd be glad to see him, but her matchmaking was an aggravation he didn't want to deal with tonight.

A flash of color jerked his attention back to the nearby table. The woman swiveled, swinging her arm over the back of the chair, pulling her silky top tight across lush curves. He caught his breath and almost choked on a mouthful of beer. Jaw length blond hair teased her cheek. Straight white teeth worried her rosy bottom lip. Oh, man. What a fine looking woman. Scanning the area behind her, she appeared to check the people at each table before moving on to the next. When she turned back around, her gaze locked on his.

The pretty blonde blinked as he studied her. Heat flushed her face. She didn't back down, and inspected him in return. His eyes crinkled with mischief, and his shoulders shook as he gave in to silent laughter. He held his beer bottle with both hand, thumbs stroking the neck as if it were a woman's neck. Her eyes widened, and her jaw dropped as she observed his movements. When her gaze returned to his face, he grinned and winked. She gasped at his arrogance then she bit her lip to keep from laughing.

He watched as she picked up the napkin she'd dropped when she'd turned. For a minute he thought she'd use it for a fan to cool her still red face. But she stopped in mid motion and laid it across her lap.

Hallie sighed. Where was her dinner date? Most men she knew arrived on time. It was her women friends who were always late. She didn't consider this a date. It was a meeting and since they were both busy people, they'd eat too.

Unable to resist the man's magnetic pull, she found herself glancing sideways to study him. Somewhere in his mid-forties, his plaid shirt, opened at the neck, exposed traces of curling auburn hair. Below the short tablecloth, his faded jeans hugged legs that ended in worn leather boots. His wide-brimmed cowboy hat sat in the vacant chair to his right. She looked again at his face, tanned and lined from exposure to the sun, then back to his hat and boots.

Her mouth formed a silent "uh-oh." Could this man be Justin's uncle, her dinner date? Good grief, she hoped not. If so, she'd burn to a cinder from embarrassment.

He'd said to look for a cowboy in a plaid shirt. She'd been expecting a western shirt, not the casual sport shirt type. This man didn't quite fit the picture in her head of a rancher. Like she knew many ranchers.

Indecision gnawed at her. Should she confront him or head for the door? Tired of waiting, she took another sip of iced tea, then stood, picked up her purse and pushed in her chair.

Simon watched her collect her things. *Damn, she's leaving.* For some unknown reason, he was disappointed. He'd enjoyed the harmless flirtation, not that he made a habit of flirting. Hell, he never did. There was something about her. Intelligence and a sense of humor radiated in her eyes. As she'd studied him, he'd done likewise and could see she wasn't too young for a man his age—in her late thirties or early forties. He'd never understood why mature men chased young women. They were smart enough, he supposed, but what could they have in common, talk about?

What would she be like if they had a chance to get acquainted? When he'd winked at her, she hadn't smiled, but he could tell by the twitch of her lips, she'd been tempted.

As soon as Justin took over the ranch, he hoped to find a woman like this one. At one time he'd thought he and Joanne would marry, but there was no spark between them, at least not on his part. He knew she'd been disappointed, but they'd remained good friends.

Right now, it appeared like his dinner guest had at last arrived. A beaming petite woman, in her mid-fifties strolled his way. She wiggled her fingers in greeting. He stood as she approached and pasted a smile on his face. Without glancing in his direction, she breezed past in a cloud of cloying perfume and kissed the grinning man at the table behind him.

Well hell, it looks like she's not coming. I may as well go ahead and order. When he turned back, the attractive blonde stood beside his table.

This must be my lucky day. Without speaking he enjoyed the view. Small smile lines crinkled around her eyes and mouth, adding to her appeal. Without having met this lady, he knew he could like her. Like, hell. He was attracted.

She smiled. "Hello, I—"

Her voice sounded warm and low, like aged whiskey, soothing. Simon had a strong urge to pull her close to see if her head would fit just under his chin. Not that he would touch her. Hands clasped at her waist, she twisted them as she looked at him and spoke.

"Excuse me," she said. "This is awkward, but I've been waiting to meet a man named Simon Cole, and I wondered if you were him?"

Oh, God, please no.

He nodded. She beamed and extended her hand. "Oh, thank goodness. I was afraid I'd be making a fool of myself. I'm Hallie Barron."

Oh hell, why did this woman have to be Hallie Barron? His neck flushed with heat, his smile froze, and then melted into a grimace. Disappointment hit him hard, leaving an ache in his belly. He struggled to regain his composure, cover his reaction.

Hallie stood waiting for some response. The smiling, teasing man turned sober, frowning at her. Had she made a mistake? After a long pause, he gazed down at her outstretched hand and in slow motion, clasped it.

"It's about time. I thought you'd never get here." He pulled out a chair for her and motioned for her to join him.

"You've got to be kidding," she said, sitting. "I arrived long before you."

He cleared his throat. "You're not what I expected."

She grinned and cocked an eyebrow. "What did you expect? Someone a little older, perhaps?" Glancing at the table behind him, she added. "Wearing a flower print dress and a wide brimmed hat?"

"Maybe." He handed her a menu.

She laughed. "Well, you weren't what I expected either. I watched for a man in a country western shirt— you know, the kind with snaps down the front and on the pockets—nothing like the sporty type you have on."

He glanced down at what he had on then back to her. "Would you like a beer or mixed drink? If you don't mind, we need to order. I've got appointments this afternoon." He turned and signaled the waiter.

"Yes, a glass of white wine would be nice." A busy woman herself, she understood his need to rush. "And a chef salad with the dressing on the side." She clasped her hands on the table. "I also have a busy afternoon,

Mr. Cole, so, shall we begin. What do you need to discuss with me?"

He leaned back in his chair. "I might as well get right to the point. This is nothing personal, but I don't want my nephew to marry your daughter." He released a breath and relaxed.

For a minute Hallie couldn't speak, then blurted, "Well, why not?" She picked up the glass of wine the waiter set before her and took a sip. It was cool and tart on her tongue. "From what I understand, you've never met Elise. How could you object?"

Hands locked tight in her lap, knuckles white and shoulders rigid, she listened in shocked silence. "This has nothing to do with your daughter. I've nothing against her. I'm sure she's a nice girl, but she's not the right one for Justin." The hands that had caressed his beer bottle minutes before now held it in a harsh grip. She expected it to shatter any minute.

Not right for his nephew? Her daughter? "How do you know this?" Angry sparks danced in her head making it difficult to be civil. "Is this some kind of cowboy intuition or something?"

A low growl erupted from him. Jaws clenched, he leaned closer. Hallie straightened her back. "I know because Justin's been sweet on the neighbor's daughter for years. She's what both he and the ranch need. She's familiar with the lifestyle and will bring our two properties together. The Cole ranch needs that partnership to survive."

"He may have been fond of this girl at one time, but now he's engaged to my daughter." The movement of her hair tickled her cheek. She flipped it away in frustration.

He combed his fingers through his hair impatiently. "I don't expect you to understand, being a city woman and all, but your daughter can't be the help to Justin Caitlyn can. Of what use will a woman with a theater degree be on a working ranch? Tell me that."

Ignoring his question, she asked one of her own. "What about love? Doesn't it have some importance? It's obvious Elise is his choice, not this neighbor girl."

He snorted. "Love? These kids know nothing about it. They've known each other for such a short time. They're infatuated. You know—in lust."

His remark was the final straw. She threw her napkin on the table and reached for her purse.

Simon clasped her hand to keep her in her seat. "Please, Mrs. Barron, wait a minute and let me finish."

She pulled from his grasp but remained seated. "I can't imagine what you could add to this delightful conversation. I hope you know if you follow through on this, Justin will end up hating you."

He shook his head, and cleared his throat. "I'd hoped you could help me. Between the two of us, given time, we could help these kids see reason. You know, split them up." The deep blue eyes that had crinkled with mischief, now beseeched her. "I know it'd be hard for them at first, but it'd be what's best for both of them. What do they have in common? I'll tell you what, nothing. Your daughter doesn't have the least idea what it's like to live and work on a ranch."

"That may be true, but if they love each other, they'll work hard to overcome any differences they encounter."

Simon couldn't help but admire the woman. Her defense of her daughter was as it should be. If the situation were reversed, he'd do the same for Justin.

Keeping his voice down, he spoke through gritted teeth. "I've seen first hand what can happen when two people so different try to make a life in ranching. One of them will be hurt, and, by God, I don't want it to be my nephew. For that matter, I wouldn't want to wish it on your daughter, either. Justin's mother put the ranch in financial trouble. Caitlyn would bring land and the money needed to return it to its original prosperity."

"I'm sorry, but not all women are like your sister-in-law. Maybe money can be found elsewhere." She knew a way. Elise would inherit a large sum of money when she married, but she'd promised Elise's father not to reveal the information. "I'll not be party to this plot to break them up."

She stood, turned on her heel, and walked away from the despicable man.

* * *

Simon shook his head. That went well. The look of shock on her face, that pretty mouth shaped in an "O" when he proposed they buddy up to sabotage the kids' wedding plans, had been comical. However, he hadn't laughed. Instead of elation, he felt empty. He respected her defense of her daughter, but he had to make it clear. He'd do whatever it took to prevent this marriage. The ranch's future, as well as Justin's, was at stake.

What had caused his nephew's change of heart this spring? The reason remained a mystery that worried him. At Christmas, love had vibrated between him and Caitlyn like heat rising on the scorching Texas highway. Then in March, he changed.

Propping his elbows on the table, he dropped his head into his hands and massaged his temples. A soft, subtle scent reached his nostrils. Lowering his right hand, the one he'd caught her wrist with to his nose, he sniffed. Her fragrance smelled clean, fresh, and tart like the woman herself. Heat coursed through his body. God, she was something with her face flushed and fire in her eyes. His reaction to her exceeded anything he'd felt for a woman in years. He didn't understand it. What was it about her? It must be her scent—those pheromones or whatever the hell chemicals they say caused attraction these days. Doc better add some *Field and Stream* magazines to the women's magazines to her waiting room reading material.

Damn. He scowled at the sixteen-ounce sirloin he'd been looking forward to. His appetite gone, he forced himself to take a bite of his steak. Having met Hallie Barron and faced her disdain, the food tasted like cardboard. The idea of having made an enemy of her didn't sit well.

She'd left him no doubt what she thought of him. Her dislike made his job easier. One comment had cut to the bone—would Justin hate him?

* * *

Hallie couldn't believe the audacity of that insufferable man sitting in the restaurant.

Jerking open the door to her white Lincoln Town Car, she threw her purse across the seat, then slid behind the wheel. With the door closed it was hot enough to bake bread. She started the car, turned the air conditioner on, and directed the vents toward her flaming face. Laying her head on the steering wheel, she strived for calm.

His comments echoed in her head. Yes, maybe the kids were rushing things. They hadn't known each other long, but to stoop to what he'd suggested went beyond ludicrous. If he hadn't made her so mad, she'd have told him she thought time together before the wedding was a good idea. Let them get to know each other better on the turf where they'd build their life together. Let nature take its course, so to speak. But, to plan and plot against them? No way would she stoop so low. And to think she had been attracted to him.

Before she met him, that is. Yet, she couldn't help but understand his worries. She respected him for trying to save Justin's ranch, but no amount of money would assure happiness. She'd learned that first hand. She'd wanted to tell him Elise would bring money to the marriage but she'd promised her husband she wouldn't. Elise didn't even know about her inheritance. Her father hadn't wanted someone to marry her for her money.

Georgetown was a short drive from Austin. Heavy traffic made it take longer to reach. The cool air tossed her hair, freezing her face and ears. She lowered the temperature and adjusted the vents. What would she tell Elise?

Hallie turned onto the blacktop road leading to her home north of Georgetown. Fruitless pear trees lined both sides of the road, a glorious sight when in full bloom. Her two-story brick Georgian home came into view. It was more extravagant than she and James ever dreamed they'd have. With four bedrooms, four and a half baths, they were very comfortable. James, her deceased husband, had provided well for them by investing in the stock market. The house was paid for and she and both kids had substantial portfolios for the future. Her dress shop, Stepping Up, on the square in

Georgetown provided whatever else they needed, like the new car.

Elise lounged on the padded front porch glider, one long bare leg hung over the armrest while the other kept up the back and forth movement. Smile on her face, she discarded her book and with the grace of a gazelle, met her mother on the sidewalk.

"Hi, Mom. You're back early." Brow wrinkled, she added. "Did everything go all right?"

Hallie put her arm around her daughter's waist and hugged her to her side. They strolled up the walk together.

"Our meeting went fine. I wasn't hungry, so I left before eating. We got our talking done and I wanted to get back."

My God. Lying to her daughter. What would she stoop to next?

Hallie opened the door and entered the cool of the wide entry hall. Dropping her purse and keys on the hall table, she walked into the living room, kicked off her shoes and sat on the *crème* leather sofa with one leg drawn under her. Double French doors drew her eye to the spacious lawn. Crepe myrtle bushes, shaped into small trees, outlined the circle drive. Their delicate pink blooms complemented the accents of the muted mauve and green in her French country *decor.* Like a cool watercolor painting, it was a soothing scene, one she'd enjoyed for years.

At times like this, troubling situations or joyous occasions, she missed James the most. She'd recovered from her grief, but not the loneliness—the joy of sharing with someone you love. Of course, she missed sex too, but until today, no one had stirred her.

"And...?" Elise waited in expectation.

"And what?"

"Mother!" Elise stood with hands on her hips. She plopped down beside Hallie. "You know what. Will he like me? What's he like? Justin thinks he hung the moon."

Hallie smiled at her daughter, took her face in both hands and kissed each cheek. She stroked the long flaxen hair back behind each ear. She wasn't going to let Simon Cole hurt her baby. "He will when he gets a chance to know you."

Elise leaned back and studied her mother's face. "What's that supposed to mean?"

"It means," she changed positions on the sofa to ease the cramp in her hip, "Simon doesn't think you two are suited, that you'll be able to adjust to living on the ranch so far from a big city."

"Hmm. He doesn't, does he?" She stared out on the lawn in thought and sighed. "Well, he has a right to his opinion. I might feel the same if I were in his shoes. Justin's mother couldn't handle it."

Relieved to have the issue in the open, Hallie relaxed. "I'm glad you're not upset."

"What about you, Mom? How do you feel about our marriage?"

"I have some reservations. You haven't known each other long, and though you've been exposed to rural life, you've never experienced the hard work involved." She shrugged. "But, I can't dictate your life. I hope during the next few months you'll explore your feelings and expectations." Hallie stood. "Come into the bedroom with me while I change into something comfortable."

She stepped into her large closet, Elise's chatter following her path. "Justin called a while ago. He's glad you were meeting his Uncle Simon. Mom, he invited us to come stay on the ranch for a couple of weeks."

Hallie froze in the process of removing her skirt. Two weeks on the ranch with Simon Cole? Would either of them survive? She'd never been so mad at a man before. And, mad at herself for being attracted to him.

Stepping out of the skirt, she called to Elise from the closet. "Let me think about it." Elise sounded happy about the prospect.

"Sure, Mom."

The time for Elise and Justin would be beneficial, but could she face Simon after their encounter today? A vacation would be good for her. She hadn't taken one since the summer before James died. Right after school started she'd bought the boutique, remodeled and decorated before bringing in a higher quality clothes. A vacation would be good for her. She snorted. A cruise to Alaska, away from Simon Cole, would be better.

Dressed in denim shorts and white cotton blouse, she sat on the bed to put on her sneakers.

The boutique wouldn't be a problem. Gladys would fill in for her. She'd jump at the chance. But she would need to come back to town for a day or two to meet with a lady from Fredericksburg. The woman wanted to open a Stepping Up Boutique in the small tourist town and wanted her help. If a good credit risk, she might consider providing the funds.

Elise gave her a quick hug. "Let me know when you make up your mind." She started for the door then turned back. "You know, even if we don't go, you need to get away from the store for a while."

"Yes, you're right."

She couldn't tell Elise the full extent of her conversation with Simon Cole. She'd be on the defensive when she met him and not herself. After he met Elise, no way could he not adore her.

If Simon pursued their attraction, would she be able to resist him? The love and companionship of a man hadn't been an issue before today. Now the need lingered in her mind. Their encounter had been an eye opener. Her body wasn't dead after all. Neither was her heart. But loving could bring about hurt and disappointment. She wasn't sure she wanted to expose her emotions again. Love and life with James had been perfect, and his death devastated her. If she decided to get involved with a man, it sure as heck wouldn't be with Simon Cole. "Hell, yes I can resist him."

* * *

Elise appeared in the doorway of Hallie's bedroom. Hair held on top of her head with a stretch band, it bounced as she walked toward the bed.

"Mom, phone for you." She mouthed, "It's a man," and wiggled her eyebrows with a grin.

Hallie looked at the bedside clock. It read 10:25 p.m. Who could be calling at this hour? And what man? Could it be Simon? Her heart leapt at the possibility. Maybe he wanted to cancel the invitation Justin had extended. Laying her book aside, she took the phone from Elise.

"Hello."

"Sorry to call so late but I just got back to the ranch."

Goosebumps rose on her arms at the sound of his sexy drawl. "Mr. Cole?"

Elise stretched out across the foot of the bed.

"Yes, this is Simon." He cleared his throat. "I hear Justin invited you and your daughter out to the ranch for a couple of weeks."

She held the phone to her nightshirt. "Out," she whispered using her toe to urge Elise off the bed.

Elise left the room, closing the door behind her.

"Yes. Elise told me when I got home this afternoon." She pulled at the threads on her chenille bedspread. "I've given it some thought and don't think it's a good idea."

She held her breath waiting for his response, uncertain how she'd feel if he agreed with her then added. "After our meeting today, it would be hard for either one of us to be civil to each other."

"We're being polite right now. Don't you think we could act like mature adults and be courteous regardless of how we feel?"

So, he was still angry too. "Maybe. But don't you think the kids and your mother will feel the tension between us?"

He was quiet for a moment.

"I think it's a good idea for you and Elise to visit. It'll give her a chance to experience ranch life, and give her and Justin time to get to know one another better."

"I can't argue with that." She smoothed out the threads on the bedspread.

"Don't take me wrong, I'm still against this marriage and will fight it tooth and nail, however—"

Hallie laughed. "You've made your intentions clear, Mr. Cole. But, I think it would be a mistake to

16

keep them from having this one-on-one time together to see if their feelings are genuine and lasting."

He coughed. "Mrs. Barron, I'm not a complete ogre and if you decide to make the trip, I'll be nothing but polite to you and your daughter while you're in our home."

She had to give the man credit. He'd called and reinforced the invitation. She could at least do the same. "I'll try not to show my animosity, though after our earlier conversation, it'll be hard."

He chuckled. "I think we both know where we stand on this issue."

* * *

Hanging up the phone, Simon leaned back in the old leather chair, and propped his feet on the desk. Was he doing the right thing going along with this visit? So much was at stake. He sure as hell didn't want to cause a rift between him and Justin. Justin was like his own son. He didn't think Justin loved Elise, not the true abiding kind that lasted a lifetime—like his parents, Anthony and Ruth Cole, had shared.

Remembering the mornings he'd caught his dad grabbing his mom and kissing her in front of the kitchen stove made him smile. She'd tell Dad, "Go on about your business, old man." He'd say, "I am. This is my business." He'd swat her on the rear with his big hand, and popping with her dishtowel, she'd send him jumping out of her way.

That old stove still stood in the kitchen at the original ranch house, his ranch. He looked around at the room—Sidney's office. It was the one room in the dwelling where he felt at home. His brother, Sidney, built this monstrosity five miles west of the existing home place. His wife, Loretta, didn't like the plain old farmhouse. Which worked out well while Sidney was alive. Simon loved the old place where he'd lived with their mother, Ruth, until his brother died. Now he and Ruth were at the new house with Sidney's kids.

Simon lowered his feet to the floor, stood and walked into the large den where his mother sat mending his and Justin's work clothes. He leaned into the doorframe, one foot crossed over the other in what he hoped resembled a relaxed pose.

"Mama, Mrs. Barron and her daughter Elise are coming Monday to stay for a couple of weeks. Will that be all right?"

Putting her sewing down, she smiled at him. "Of course it will. I'll enjoy having some women in the house."

She patted the empty cushion next to her. Simon walked over and sat down. She picked up the shirt and went back to sewing on buttons. He put his arm around her shoulders and hugged. Leaning down, he kissed the silver hair at her temples. She still wore it long and pulled back, twisted into a *chignon*, like Dad had loved it.

"You know I'm against this match, don't you, Mama? They come from different backgrounds. Her mother is pretty, like Loretta, only blonde. Doesn't look like she's worked a day in her life. I can't see the relationship working. It's like history repeating itself."

Her hands stopped their work as she thought about what he'd said. "Simon, you can't know any such thing. You can't judge all women by Loretta. I've always wondered if your dislike and distrust of Loretta is why you never married. You should have a family and kids

18

of your own."

"I do. I've got you, Justin and Whitney. You're all the family I need."

She sighed. "I know you're worried about finances and afraid Justin will make a mistake like Sidney's. But, Justin's a lot smarter than his daddy. He saw how he was hurt, and he's level-headed."

"I hope you're right, Mama. But, I don't know how this ranch is going to survive if this marriage takes place."

* * *

"Hell, son. You sure you're doing the right thing?" Chester, Simon's grizzled cowhand turned chow boss, leaned over his shoulder to better view the map Simon had drawn for the women arriving the following day. Chester scratched his weeks' worth of gray stubble as he talked. "If your mama finds out what's going on she'll skin you alive."

Chester had known Simon most of his life. He'd watched him grow to manhood and been there for him when both his father, Anthony, and Sidney died. Simon hated to think what they'd have done if he hadn't been here to help pick up the pieces. He loved the old coot, as irritating as he could be at times.

"Well then, I'll have to make sure she doesn't find out, Chester. I told Mama they would arrive Sunday or Monday. It depends on how long they survive at the old cabin."

He leaned back in the old cowhide seat chair and folded his arms over his chest. "I'm betting they leave after one day. Then I can tell Mama they called and changed their mind."

Chester hitched up his baggy pants before he

plunked his skinny frame down in the chair across from him. "Simon, you're fooling yourself. Your mama knows everything that goes on around here, and I'm here to tell ya, she ain't gonna like this, that's for dang sure."

Simon's chair hit the floor with a thunk. "It can't be helped, Chester. We've got to do something to keep those two kids apart."

He'd tried his best to come up with an idea of how to make Justin and Elise break their engagement. The best he could do was to make the women so uncomfortable they'd want to leave. Being city ladies, they'd balk at the idea of spending one night, much less two, at the old homestead cabin.

Chester jerked his skinny frame upright in the chair. "We! Whatda ya mean, we? I'm staying out of this tangle. Miz Ruth will run me clean off this place if she finds out I took part in this farce."

He watched Chester run his hand through the few strands of hair left on his head. They were so wispy it took several passes to get them to lie down.

"Anyhow, don't you feel bad lying like this?"

Simon shoved his chair back from the table. "I feel like shit and you know it."

He scooped up his map, walked to the door and stood with one arm leaning against the frame, head down. "I need your help, Chester. Please don't let me down." The screen door slammed shut behind him.

CHAPTER TWO

"Mo-th-er! Can't-you-do-something?" The map in Elise's hands crackled with every bump. The road was one rut or pothole after another. "Oops. You missed one, Mom." Her cheeky daughter couldn't resist the retort.

Hallie threw her a dirty look, taking stock of the grin on her daughter's face. She'd tried to swerve around the larger ones but it was futile. They were all gargantuan. "I'm doing the best I can here, so save the remarks." At this rate, her car would need new shocks by the time they arrived. "Are you sure we're on the right road?"

Elise screeched as the car hit another large hole. Bouncing, their seatbelts locked, keeping their heads from hitting the ceiling of the car. "Ouch!" She loosened the tension in the seatbelt. "I'm sure. We passed a grouping of red boulders that resembled a small mountain and turned right on the road marked Cole. This has got to be it."

From the rearview mirror, Hallie watched the long trail of dust spiraling behind them. "Did Justin ever mention a dirt road to you?"

"No. He didn't. But, we haven't talked about the ranch much. I guess there are lots of details we haven't learned about each other."

They crested a hill. Up ahead, to the right of the

road, sat an older tan pickup in front of a small cabin

Except for the worn dirt area in front for parking, it was surrounded by pasture. A barbwire fence, connected to the one along the road, ran behind the cabin. The grass wasn't tall like in East Texas, but a short stubby type. Clusters of prickly pear, growing in dense knots, dotted the area around the groupings of large rock. Pockets of wildflowers in yellow and white grew with abandon amidst the cactus and grass. A trail of smoke rose from the smokestack.

Hallie patted Elise's bare leg. As usual her daughter wore shorts and a tank top. *Oh to be young and thin.* "I'm pulling over to get directions."

As the car crossed the cattle guard into the dusty yard, a skinny man with a broom in his hand came out onto the porch. A grin broke across his whiskered face.

He walked to the car door, his pace measured as if too much movement pained his joints. Hallie lowered the window. As he drew near, he removed his battered straw hat and held it over his heart.

"Howdy, Ma'am. You must be Miz Barron and Elise." He opened her car door. "Come on in, ladies. You're right on time. I've got coffee brewing on the stove."

He extended a huge, callused hand to Hallie. She slid out from under the steering wheel and placed her hand in his rough, gnarled one. It swallowed hers, but for all its size, it was as gentle as a babe's.

"I'm Chester, ma'am, one of Simon's ranch hands. Used to be foreman when his daddy was alive. Got too old for it though and now do odd jobs around here. Do most of the cooking for the cowhands."

"Pleased to meet you, Chester." She glanced

around and then at the cabin. "Is this the right place? I thought the ranch house bigger than this."

"Yes, ma'am. This is the original homestead."

She turned back to the car, put her head in the window, and whispered. "We're here, Elise. Follow my lead."

Elise looked confused, but when Hallie started around the car with Chester on her heels, she unbuckled and got out of the car.

"Chester, this is my daughter Elise. He works for Simon here on the ranch."

Elise smiled and nodded. "Hi, Chester."

The grin on Chester's face stretched wider. "My-o-my you're a pretty little thing. No wonder Justin's head over heels for you."

Hallie watched Elise blush with pleasure. The old fellow knew how to please the ladies.

Introductions over, he put his hat back on. "Y'all come on in now and let me find you something to eat and show you around."

At the cabin door, an old dog thumped out a welcome with his long tail. Chester bent to scratch its ears. "This here's my old dog, Jezebel. Named her that 'cause she used to be a run-a-round gal in her younger days."

He chuckled and they smiled at his joke.

"Simon thought you might enjoy staying at the original cabin a few days. Discover how folks lived in 1890 when his granddaddy built this cabin. Course lots of conveniences have been added to make it more comfortable."

Elise started to speak but Hallie's shake of the head stopped her. "That sounds like a wonderful idea. I'm glad Mr. Cole thought of it. Elise and I'll enjoy reliving the past."

The interior resembled a page from a history book. A wood cook stove stood in one corner near a cabinet with a single sink and hand pump. A wrought iron bedstead covered with a colorful handmade quilt occupied the other corner. Hallie ran her hand over the blanket, marveling at its beauty. A folding screen stood to the side. Behind it sat a chipped crock chamber pot, and a washstand with white bowl and pitcher.

At the sight of the chamber pot, Elise's jaw dropped. She turned to voice her dislike, but snapped her mouth shut when Hallie nudged her in the ribs.

"You ladies come sit down at the table and I'll pour you a drink. You've got a choice of lemonade or coffee."

Chester brought a small pitcher from the little butane operated refrigerator that stood beside the back door and sat it beside the plate of cookies on the table.

He poured Elise a glass of lemonade and coffee for Hallie and himself. Elise munched away on the cookies.

"Yum. These are delicious."

Chester beamed. "Tea cakes. My mama's special recipe. Not everybody can make 'um like this." He took a bite and chewed, an expression of bliss on his face. "The secret is in the ingredients. You have to use lard. Health conscious folks today always try to substitute shortening for the lard. Shortening won't do."

"Chester, will Justin be coming out soon? He knew I'd be here before noon."

He cleared his throat and looked uncomfortable. "Well, I hate to be the bearer of bad news, but Justin will be working with Simon all weekend. They've got a bunch of fence that needs fixin' and will be on the range. Might have to eat and sleep out there all weekend."

"Oh, rats." She glanced out the door. "I wished we'd known. We could have waited until Monday to drive out." She glanced at Chester. "Wonder why Justin didn't call to let us know."

Chester fidgeted in his chair. "They were in a hurry. Guess it plumb slipped his mind." He dropped his eyes to his coffee.

"Honey, emergencies take place on a ranch all the time. You learn to be flexible." Hallie patted her hand. "We'll find plenty to do right here, so don't you worry."

And they would. Hallie knew Simon's plans to drive Elise away. No way would she let on they couldn't handle the situation.

"Yeah, I know you're right, Mom. I'm just disappointed." She smiled at Chester. "But I understand."

He jumped in with suggestions. "There's a pond about a quarter a mile to the east. It's a good swimming place, the water's clear, just be careful of the moccasins. Be sure to wear sturdy shoes so you don't get stickers from the cactus." Standing, he gathered his hat. "I guess I better be heading back to work. I've stocked the icebox with enough food for the weekend."

His gaze drifted around the room and locked on the wood stove. "Ma'am, you think you can operate this old stove?"

She studied it with suspicion, taking note of the damper and the wood stacked in the wood box on the floor. "I think I can handle it. It'll take some practice to

25

produce anything decent though."

"If you need anything, keep going on this road for another mile and you'll come to the main house. Nothing should bother you out here, but if you need us, shoot off a couple rounds from that shotgun over the fireplace. The echo will reach the ranch and someone will come running."

Hallie looked at the shotgun and the shells on the mantel. She knew Simon had planned this little scenario to make Elise seem weak in Justin's eyes. He didn't know she and her daughter were two tough chicks.

They stood on the front porch and watched as Chester drove off in a cloud of dirt. Thank goodness she'd returned to the car to roll up the window so the seats wouldn't be covered with dust.

Elise waited, arms folded across her chest, questions on her face. "All right, Mother. What's going on here?"

Hallie put her arms around Elise's shoulders and hugged her tight. Releasing her, she laughed. "Let's go on in and get comfortable." Inside, she sat at the table. "I think this is a test, my dear—to see if you're up to ranch life. You know, it can be a hard existence, and sometimes lonely. There's not much entertainment out here you don't make yourself."

Elise stood, hands fisted on her slim hips. "Justin wouldn't do this to me, Mom. Anyway, I know for a fact the ranch has satellite, telephone and a computer. They're not that cut off."

"True, but sometimes the electricity goes off and it may take longer to get it back on out here. You're right, Justin wouldn't test you like this, but Simon would. Try not to be too harsh in your judgment. He's trying to protect Justin and the ranch. Trust me. We're going to have a good time. You'll learn a lot. Let's show Simon how strong the Barron women are."

In fact, Hallie would enjoy the remoteness and the quiet. Since James's death, she'd been immersed in building her business and raising her two children. Some reflection time would be good for her. She'd even enjoy making coffee on that old wood stove. She walked over and bounced the old bed with its exposed, squeaky springs. The feather filled mattress didn't promise a good night's sleep.

Elise had never known isolation, but Hallie knew her daughter could hold up to the challenge. Young people needed a taste of seclusion, and she might enjoy their time alone.

She noticed a set of dominos on the mantel. If Elise didn't know how to play, she'd teach her. They'd both brought books and magazines. And Elise had her portable CD player. They could sleep late, paint toenails, and do girl stuff. Simon Cole would learn the Barron women could handle whatever he dished out.

* * *

Thunderclouds covered the moon throwing Simon, atop his favorite red roan gelding, in total darkness. That and the surrounding scrub oak protected him from view by the occupants in the cabin. Loud music wafted from the interior accompanied by female laughter. An occasional glimpse of the two through the door and window convinced him the women were dancing.

Patting the horse's neck, he muttered. "Well hell, Redman. What do you think about that? So much for trying to make them unhappy. It seems like they're having a party."

The horse snorted in response. Simon leaned back in the saddle and patted him on the rump.

"Yeah, fella, you got that right. Women. You can't even count on them to be miserable when they're supposed to be."

He'd expected Elise to have thrown a tantrum by now and be headed home. She appeared to be having as much fun as her mother. Chester said Elise seemed a little spoiled, but minded her manners. Laughing, he'd added. "Had to bite my tongue to keep from busting out laughing when she got a look at the chamber pot. Her mama didn't think I'd seen the gal's jaw drop and her nose wrinkle in distaste."

Simon wasn't pleased with himself for spying. In truth, he experienced feelings of guilt. It wasn't in his nature to invade another person's privacy but in this case, he felt justified. From the looks of things, his plan wasn't working. A lot could happen in two weeks though, and the women had only been here one day.

Mama would be furious when she learned he'd put the women out here. Nothing could be kept from her. The situation already had Chester mad at him. The women had gotten on his soft side. They must've bragged on his teacakes. Chester was vain to a fault when it came to his cooking. When Justin got wind of the situation, he'd be answering to him, too. What a mess. He'd be lucky if Mama, Chester and Justin didn't string him up.

A dog appeared at the screen door and peered out seeking the horse and rider in the dark shadows. Recognizing Simon it whined as the long tail swished back and forth in greeting. It was Jezebel. The two women had taken in Chester's old dog. Wonder what

Chester would think about that.

The presence of the dog surprised him. He figured they'd steer clear of the mangy looking mutt. No way could you consider Jezebel a pretty dog, though no one dared call her ugly to Chester's face. But there she stood like the "dog of the mansion."

A yip from Jezebel reminded Simon to make himself scarce before they realized they had company. He backed Redman up as far as the thick brush would allow, then turned him around and walked him, with as little noise as possible, in the direction of the ranch.

Hallie moved to the screen door and held it open for the dog. "You need out, Jezebel?" The dog looked up, chocolate eyes full of affection, and wagged her tail. "Well, go on then." Jezebel turned away from the door and walked over to the small rug beside the bed and plopped down.

Hallie peered out into the darkness trying to see what had caught the dog's attention. Pitch black out, she couldn't see a thing. She shrugged then latched the screen door. Must be a rabbit or some other animal.

Elise flopped back on the bed and laid spread eagle. Her face, pink from exertion, glistened with a fine sheen of sweat. "Mother, I didn't know you could dance like that. You're pretty good."

"Ha. Pretty good? I'm darned good, my dear. Your daddy and I used to dance a lot in our younger years. As a matter of fact, it was unusual if we didn't get to a dance at least one night each weekend. Schools had more dances when we were kids."

She shoved Elise over, lay down beside her, and stretched out. "Whew. I'm pooped." Her heart thundered. She grabbed a magazine to fan her hot face.

Both peered down at their bright painted toenails, wiggled their toes, and laughed. Elise's were blue, but hers were orange, the loudest color she'd dared try from Elise's collection in her overnight bag.

"Wish your daddy could have known you as a young woman, Elise. He'd have been proud of you." She smiled up at the ceiling.

Elise rolled toward her mother. "I like to think so. He'd be proud of Ted too, wouldn't he?"

"I know so, hon, and yes, he'd be proud of Ted." She sighed. Ted had been eleven years old when his father died, Elise fifteen.

"Do you still miss him? Daddy, I mean?"

"Yeah, I do. More so at times like this. I can hear him now, checking Justin out. She deepened her voice. 'Son, what are your intentions toward my daughter?'"

Elise laughed. "You're teasing me, Mom. Daddy wouldn't have asked something like that, would he?"

Hallie smiled, but didn't answer. James would have been protective, but he'd have been trusting, too. He'd been such a good father and husband. Yes, she missed him.

"Mom, have you ever thought about marrying again?" She grinned. "You know you're rather good looking for an older lady."

"Well, gee thanks. Can I take that as a compliment?"

"Of course you can. You're pretty. You've got a great figure, nice breasts."

"What?" She sat up and peered down at her chest. "What a thing to say to your mother."

Elise laughed. "Well, you do, Mother. Haven't you noticed the way Mr. Sanders ogles them in church every Sunday? It's like, if he concentrates hard enough, your dress will pop open and he'll have a better view."

Hallie fell back onto her pillow. "You're kidding me, right?"

"No, ma'am. One Sunday Ted got so mad at his gawking he walked up to Mr. Sanders and told him to find someplace else to fasten his eyes. The dirty old man turned blood red and stalked off." She chuckled. "He's afraid to glance your direction now."

"I'll never be able to look at the man again with a straight face."

They lay in companionable silence, each tending their own thoughts. Hallie rolled to face her daughter.

"You know, there's never been anyone after your dad. Guess the right one never came along. Maybe one will someday."

Hallie propped herself on her elbow, head cradled in her hand, and peered at her daughter.

"Elise, I hope you'll take these next two weeks and make sure this is the life you want. Marriage should be for a lifetime, though today few people regard it as such. There's a great deal at stake here. Few things can make life as miserable as a bad marriage. Be sure you know your heart and your mind."

* * *

Hallie woke with a start. The rising sun peeked through clouds. A fine drizzle fell. Jezebel stood at the screen door, wagging her tail and whining.

Another noise accompanied Jezebel's muffled snuffling, but she couldn't make out what it was. There—again, an occasional thud and whooshing. It wasn't a menacing sound as much as a curious one.

"You need out, girl?" She threw back the sheet

she'd pulled up against the chill. Reaching up she stretched, then eased her nightshirt back down over her hips. The old feather mattress on bare springs wasn't the most comfortable of beds. She and Elise rolled into each other all night. Elise, being a sound sleeper didn't suffer, but Hallie woke every time either one of them turned.

Barefoot, she walked to the back door. The unfamiliar noise continued. She stopped to listen. A thumping and swishing sound. Then a rustling, like something in the brush. She sniffed the air and her nose twitched. A new odor floated in the air. Ripe and unpleasant, the smell of manure.

At the door, she stopped and stared in surprise at their visitors. A yard full of cattle, of varying age and description, filled the yard. During the night, it had rained. Now the ground was a mixture of trampled manure-enriched mud. Phew! What a stink!

My car, what about my car? She hurried to the front door. Steers surrounded it and one of the beasts used the side mirror to scratch its ornery hide.

Unmindful of her bare feet, she grabbed the broom propped against the doorframe and stormed out. Yelling at the top of her lungs, she swung the broom clearing a path to her car.

She stopped three feet from the scratching steer and pounded it on the head. "Get your mangy hide away from my car. Go on now. Get! Away! From my car!" She emphasized every word with a whack on its head.

Stunned, the animal sized her up and bellowed.

"I mean it, get out of here." She hit him again, then turned the broom and poked several times at the steer's eyes with the bristles.

It shook its head, bellowed, turned and moseyed ten yards or so away.

Hallie turned her wrath on the other animals and jabbed them with the broom, sending them scattering.

Elise appeared on the front porch. "Mother, be careful. They're mean." She screamed, "Look out, Mother, he's charging."

Elise came off the porch at a run, slipped in the mud and went down on her butt.

Jezebel charged the steer and moved in to nip at its hind shank. It kicked out, one hoof just missing her. Fast, she barked, nipped, and circled in to try again. Hallie ran to Elise to get her out of the way.

Atop his horse, around the corner of the cabin, Simon watched the scene unfold. He laughed, enjoying the view. When he noticed their revealing sleepwear, he sent the three cowboys around to the back of the cabin to start herding cattle toward the break in the fence. He should make his presence known but couldn't stop laughing. If she caught him spying, she'd take that broom to his hide. He sobered. A glorious sight swinging the broom in her anger, she looked like a warrior goddess with her sword. His body responded to her beauty. He shifted in the saddle and tried to focus on her antics rather than the lush curves outlined beneath the fabric of her nightshirt.

A shrill scream filled the air. The beaten steer was returning, and he didn't appear happy. Elise ran to help her mother, slipped and fell. Hallie charged to protect her daughter. Both were in the path of the mad animal.

With a slight touch of Simon's heels, Redman bolted into motion. Simon yanked a rope loose from his saddle and rode to put himself between the steer and the women. Thank God Jezebel worked to distract the animal. Lord, he hoped the dog didn't get hurt. Chester would never forgive him.

Yelling, "Hiya!" he whacked the steer across the nose with the rope, then turned the horse on a dime and hit him again. The steer bellowed and shook his head, then turned back toward the other cattle.

Simon jumped off his horse, concern eating at his conscience. "Are y'all right? He didn't hurt you, did he?" Lord, he hadn't meant for anything like this to happen.

Pulling her daughter up from the mud, Hallie held her close for a minute. She gave Simon a dirty look. "We're fine, Mr. Cole." She pulled back from Elise but kept her arm around her. "Elise, this is Justin's uncle, Simon Cole."

Standing in her underpants and a hip length knit top, the girl screeched and ran to the cabin, slinging mud along the way.

Hallie raised her chin and stared him in the eye. "If you'll excuse us, Mr. Cole, we're not dressed for company. Give us a few minutes to get dressed and I'll make coffee. You can apologize over a cup."

As if in her Sunday best, back straight, she marched toward the house, squishing with each step. Feeling like a heel, he mounted Redman and started herding cattle toward the break in the fence. When they were all out of the yard, one of his men fixed the fence. He tied his horse to the hitching post in front of the cabin and checked on Hallie's car.

He smelled the coffee before he stepped on the porch.

He knocked on the door. Elise asked him in. In denim overall shorts and pink tee shirt, she seemed younger than her twenty-two years.

"I'm so glad to meet you, Mr. Cole."

He looked down at the attractive young blond with hair so much like her mother's, only long. He stuck his hand out. "I'm pleased to meet you too, Elise."

Elise shook his hand then gave him a quick, tight hug. "Thank you for rescuing us this morning, Uncle Simon."

Surprised, Simon stood rigid. She released him before he had a chance to pat her back. "You're welcome. That's what us cowboys do. Save beautiful women in distress." He could see now why Justin cared about her. But, he wasn't going to change his mind.

Elise laughed, delighted at his comment. Hallie's lip curled. Her eyes shot him daggers. He grinned at her disdain.

"Coffee's ready. Have a seat, Mr. Cole."

He pulled out one of the chairs and turned it around to straddle while she poured coffee for all three of them. Dropping his hat on the floor, he picked up his cup and took a sip. He glanced at her in surprise. He took another drink then set his cup down.

"You make a good cup of coffee, Mrs. Barron."

She nodded in acknowledgement of his compliment.

"Look, I'm sorry about the cattle. We have a broken fence and they wandered in during the night seeking fresh grass. I checked on your car and it's not damaged."

He watched as she studied him over her coffee cup, her brow wrinkled.

"Now I see why you and Justin are working so hard on the fences," Elise said. "Though I sure would like to see him."

Her comment made him feel like a heel. Where was the spoiled young woman he'd expected? Maybe Justin would be the recipient of her tantrum.

She was a cute little thing. Little? Hell, she stood several inches taller than her mother. With her peaches and cream complexion, she had a clean scrubbed look. Not all painted like many girls today. Her eyes were almost as blue as his own. Not for the first time he wondered what it would be like to have a child of his own, one who resembled him. He felt a slight ache in the region of his heart. Though Justin and Whitney were his nephew and niece, they were like his own children. It would be different though to watch your child grow within the woman you loved.

Simon cleared his throat. "Maybe we'll finish earlier than we planned. We'll see."

Hallie glowered at him, her meaning clear. "That would be nice."

He returned her stare and smiled. Message received loud and clear. Her brown eyes, enhanced by the blue shirt and white shorts she wore, spoke volumes. Why couldn't she have grown ugly in the past few days? If anything, upon closer inspection, she was even prettier. Her blond hair moved as she talked, tempting him to reach out and touch. Was it as soft and silky as it looked?

Simon realized he'd been staring. Glancing away, he peered around the room. They'd kept the cabin neat, dishes washed and put away. Not the state of confusion he'd anticipated. His cup of coffee was excellent. He glanced at the stove to see if Chester had sneaked in a drip coffee pot. No, there sat the old black and white speckled pot for boiled coffee.

"Looks like you've adapted well to an earlier lifestyle. Stove work okay?"

"Everything works fine. You wouldn't have left us out here if it hadn't, would you?" He recognized the challenge in her words.

"No. But, not everyone knows how to operate a wood stove." He sure as hell hadn't expected her to. Like he hadn't expected to see her swinging a broom in the middle of his cattle. She was gutsy, that's for sure.

"Yes, well, there's a lot about me you don't know, Mr. Cole."

He grabbed his hat and stood. "You think you could call me Simon, and I could call you Hallie?" His smile was engaging. "This Mr. and Mrs. gets tiresome after a while.

"I think I can handle that."

"Thanks for the excellent coffee, ladies." At the door, he turned. "Did Chester show you how to use the shotgun?"

"No, there was no need. I'm sure I can use it if necessary." She walked to the door.

He couldn't help but notice how the few rays of sunlight peeking through the clouds glinted off her blond hair. She had nice legs too, round but firm. Not skinny like those pencil thin models in magazines. He'd noticed that earlier. He'd also noticed the fullness of her hips as they flared from her small waist.

He ran his hand through his hair and eased his hat on, pulling it down a fraction in the front. Damn. He better get out of here.

"Again, I'm sorry about the cattle." He looked back at Elise. "I'll see if Justin can't get loose to come by after supper tonight."

Elise joined them at the door. "That'd be great, Uncle Simon."

Twice now she'd called him Uncle Simon. It felt nice, in an uncomfortable sort of way. It made him feel like maybe things had already gotten out of hand.

* * *

It rained the remainder of the day keeping them indoors. With the cabin open, a cool breeze flowed through the room.

Jezebel, covered with mud, bemoaned her eviction to the porch with an occasional howl of displeasure. They filled the metal tub found leaning against the back porch and bathed her. She submitted with calm acceptance. Elise rubbed her dry with towels, the dog's hind leg beating out a rhythm of pure joy.

She wasn't a pretty animal, but when clean her black and white spotted coat glistened with good health. As to the breed, Hallie was at a loss, some kind of a cow dog. From the way she'd worked the steer this morning someone had trained her well. Too old now to work, she'd become Chester's pet.

They'd just cleaned up the dishes after a supper of ham, eggs, and sliced tomatoes when they heard, "Hello!" in the cabin.

Jezebel barked a greeting.

"Justin's here, Mom." Elise went outside, letting the screen slam.

Hallie waited for them inside. A fresh pot of coffee sat on the stove. She got out cups.

Justin grinned in greeting as they came in.

38

Scrubbed and handsome, he looked too much like his Uncle Simon for Hallie's comfort. He'd brought a bouquet of wildflowers for Elise. She took them from her and put them in a Mason jar with water.

"Hi, Mrs. Barron."

"Hello, Justin. It's good to see you." She gave him a hug.

They drank their coffee on the front porch and ate the last of Chester's teacakes. Jezebel flopped down by Justin, propping her head on his boot. He dropped bites of cookie which she caught before they reached the porch. Hallie suspected they'd shared Chester's teacakes before.

Hallie noticed Justin's horse tied to the hitching post. A cloud of suspicion floated around in her head. "Justin, why'd you ride over here and not come in your pickup?"

A pained expression crossed his face. His tan turned a dark red. "Um, the road's too rough. I didn't want to mess up my truck's front end alignment."

Irritation evident, Hallie said. "I figured it was something like that."

Justin shook his head. "Ma'am, I'm sorry about all this. I don't know what's got into Uncle Simon putting y'all out here. The only other person he's put in the cabin is my mother."

Hallie's anger dissolved at Justin's discomfort. It wasn't his fault they were roughing it, so to speak. In fact, it had been fun in a way. She and Elise hadn't talked this much in ages.

"Don't worry about it, Justin. I think we've had a good time despite your uncle's intentions. He's concerned and wants Elise to understand what she's getting into."

"You want to come on up to the house tonight? I can help you get things ready."

Hallie and Elise looked at each other. Both shook their heads no. Elise said. "I think we're fine right here. We'll wait until tomorrow."

"Good," said Justin. "I'm glad you've not been too uncomfortable. I love it out here. Dad let me start spending the night by myself at twelve." He was quiet for a minute. Voice soft, he said, "It made me feel grown up."

They sat in silence for a while, listening to the night sounds, cicadas and the chirping of birds settling in to roost. The sun sank behind the horizon leaving an orange glow in its wake and a strip of turquoise sky.

She had to ask. "Justin, how long did your mother stay in the cabin?"

A big grin spread across his face. His blue eyes twinkled.

"She stayed about five minutes. Long enough to realize it didn't have a bathroom. We could see her trail of dust high tailing it back to town before we were half way home. Uncle Simon laughed so hard I thought he'd fall off his horse."

"I'd like to see that happen," Hallie muttered.

He shook his head. "Just a figure of speech. That'd never happen to Uncle Simon."

Justin raised his lanky young frame from the chair. Taking Elise's hand he drew her out of the rocker. Putting his arm around her shoulders, he steered her down the porch steps.

"Come walk me to my horse, sweetheart," he drawled.

Elise laughed. "If you'd brought another horse, we could've ridden off in the sunset, cowboy."

He turned back to Hallie. "Mrs. Barron, it's obvious Uncle Simon is trying to break us up. I hope you won't take it personal. He must be worried about the ranch." His jaw tightened, as she'd seen Simon's do. "Guess I better find out what's bothering him. He's had it hard the past few years managing this ranch and his own. Plus, taking care of Whitney and me. It's time I relieved him."

"I'll be inside in a minute, Mom," said Elise.

Hallie smiled. "Goodnight, Justin."

* * *

Something woke her. She looked down and saw Jezebel hadn't moved from her spot on the rug. Nothing to worry about then.

Through the window, the full moon cast a dim light on the grassy field. Big rocks resembled mammoths taking their evening rest. It was quiet and peaceful out here. Her eyes drifted closed, and she eased back to sleep.

A screech split the air jerking her awake. "Oh, My God." Someone or something had screamed. Jezebel stood rigid, staring out the back door. A low growl erupted from her throat.

As the shriek broke the silence again, she jumped up to catch the dog's collar as she barked and lunged at the screen door. The cry rose again. This time it ended with a low growl.

Elise, plastered to her back, clutched fistfuls of her nightshirt in an effort to get closer. "What is it?" The whispered words blew warm air across her neck.

"It sounds like a panther, or something like it." She

41

turned around, took Elise's hand and placed it on Jezebel's collar. "Here, hold her and don't let go."

Jezebel continued to bark. Hallie patted her head. "Quiet, girl." Jezebel closed her mouth, and tried not to bark, but huffing noises continued to escape her throat as she strained at Elise's hold.

Hallie stepped into her shoes, walked to the fireplace and reached up above the mantel. She took down the double barrel shotgun, and laid it across the table while she returned for the shells. Taking two, she opened the chamber and slid one into each barrel, snapped it closed and checked the safety. The sound echoed in the room. With two more shells stuffed in her mouth, she started for the door.

"Mother! What're you doing? You can't go out there." Hallie felt herself slide back a few steps. Elise had a handful of her nightshirt and continued to pull, trying to hold her away from the door. With the other hand, she gripped Jezebel's collar as the dog struggled to get outside. "Please, Mother, shut the wooden doors. Then it can't get in."

Hallie removed the shells from her mouth. She twisted her shirt out of Elise's grip. "It's going to be alright. I know what I'm doing. I promise. I grew up using one of these guns. Hold the dog, and don't worry."

As she opened the door, the big cat yelled again. Something wasn't right about this. She'd always thought big cats avoided people. If there were horses around, it'd be different. With eyes trained in the direction from which she'd heard the cries, she eased out onto the porch and closed the screen door. The sky was clear with no clouds, making it easier to see something moving, but she could only make out trees, rocks, and scrub oaks. Anything could be hiding in their shadows. She waited. A shriek split the air. It sounded louder this time. Closer, about thirty feet away, and a low growl continued. Shaking with nerves, she raised the gun to her shoulder, aimed and fired one barrel at a time before reloading and firing again.

CHAPTER THREE

"What the hell were you thinking, son?" Chester shook his head as he scratched his whiskered cheek and surveyed the pile of rubble on the table. Tape from a cassette, looking like a messed up party ribbon, lay twisted among pieces of plastic and batteries leaking acid. He gaped from the blasted ruins of what had once been a portable cassette player to Simon. The younger man looked stunned—like he'd been cold-cocked as he stared at the remains.

Chester tried to keep a straight face, tried to hold his laughter but he couldn't. He covered his mouth and coughed, then erupted into loud guffaws.

Simon looked up and watched the old man's bony frame shake with laughter. His earlier coughing fit hadn't fooled him one bit either.

"Laugh, you old coot. I'm glad I'm good entertainment."

Chester slapped his leg again and again. "That you are, Simon, that, you are. Best laugh I've had in a coon's age."

Never in his wildest imagination would Simon have believed Hallie knew how to use that old shotgun, much less be able to hit her target. The woman was full of surprises. He had to admire her courage and abilities.

Between sniggers, Chester sputtered. "Wish your daddy could be here. He'd have gotten a kick out of your stunt." He wiped tears from his face.

"Yeah, Dad would've loved ribbing me about this." Hell, knowing his dad, he'd have helped. He'd always enjoyed a practical joke.

Chester's laughter was infectious. Simon found himself responding and grinning like an idiot. "It was a stupid idea, wasn't it?"

He'd led Redman into the barn last night when the summer silence erupted with the report of shotgun blasts, not once but four times. The echo that split the night sent a chill up his spine and left him frozen in mid-stride for several seconds. There was no mistaking the direction of the shots or the source. Mounting his still saddled horse, he raced back to the cabin.

Cold sweat covered his body. Nausea churned in his stomach. Horrific pictures of one of the women lying in a pool of blood flashed through his mind. If he found one of the cattle shot to hell, he'd be relieved.

When he neared the cabin, he focused his attention on a flashlight beam scanning the area north of the cabin. Elise stood on the porch holding a kerosene lamp so Hallie must have been holding the flashlight. Thank God they were both unhurt.

He reined in his horse at the porch. When he hit the ground, his legs shook as he walked toward the light. "What's going on out here? Are y'all all right?"

Elise stepped off the porch to join him as he headed in Hallie's direction. "Oh, Uncle Simon, thank God you came. There's a mountain lion out there. Mother shot it."

He strode in the direction of the arching light, Elise at his heels. A mournful howl rose from inside the cabin. Jezebel didn't appreciate missing the action.

"Hallie. Get over here. If it's a cat, it could still be alive and dangerous." His voice boomed across the yard causing the night insects to stop their chatter for a moment.

The beam of the flashlight turned in their direction blinding him. Her voice echoed across the void. "I don't think we have to worry about the *cat*."

Simon didn't miss the emphasis on the word cat. Shit. Busted. "Open the chamber on that shotgun before you come any closer. You might shoot one of us by mistake."

"Don't get yourself in a dither, Simon. I learned to use one of these things as a kid. If I shoot you, it won't be by accident."

Her voice carried across the darkened space from the eerie white beam that swayed with each step she took. Following the ray of light a white shadow emerged into Hallie's form dressed in that damned nightshirt.

He coughed then croaked out. "You ladies get dressed. I think it best we move you up to the main house. Didn't realize the danger you were in out here."

She stopped a yard from him and cocked her head. "You mean right now, tonight?"

"Yes, as soon as you get dressed." His eyes flicked down to her breasts. The damned things, he couldn't seem to control where they landed when it came to this woman.

When she folded her arms across her chest to cover herself, his eyes jerked back to her face. Blushing, she handed him the shotgun and turned toward the cabin.

"I don't think so. Elise, get dressed." She called over her shoulder, "We won't be but a minute. I'll put on a pot of coffee."

"No coffee. Get dressed and packed. Mom will have the coffee ready by the time we get to the house." Hell, he bet the whole ranch would be sitting around the kitchen table waiting for a news update.

"Look, there's no need to move tonight. We're fine out here."

Elise called from inside the cabin. "You can stay, Mother, but I'd rather leave. I don't think I could sleep out here again."

Hallie sighed. "Okay, we'll start packing."

As he'd expected, the house resembled a well-lit Christmas tree. Mama had every light in the place on. Simon groaned knowing he was in for a torrent of questions. His mother could be worse than a dog chewing on a bone when it came to getting all the facts. As a rule, considerate about staying out of his business—ranch business, she'd consider these two women her business.

* * *

"You don't mean that son of mine did something so underhanded?" Ruth, flustered with embarrassment, shook her head, and then chortled with laughter. Carrying a plate of biscuits to the table, she wiped tears of mirth from her eyes with the hem of her apron.

Hallie and Elise joined in. Justin sat, arms folded across his chest. "I'd like to see the evidence before they destroy it. Chester brought it in early this morning. Where on earth do you think Uncle Simon found a recording of a panther's cry?" He thought for a minute. "Maybe from the Nature Channel. Hope he had to sit up half the night to get it. I bet it's my old boom box that's shot to pieces."

47

Justin exchanged a look with Ruth and her titters started again. He chuckled then hooted with laughter.

Hallie liked this woman. She'd welcomed them into her home in the wee hours of the morning. And, as Simon had said, they'd arrived to find coffee and plenty of food on the table. They'd sat around the big table for almost an hour getting acquainted.

Holding his sides, Justin gasped, "Gran. I can't believe Uncle Simon put them out there in the first place. He said he wanted them to experience ranch life as it was, but Hallie thinks he wants to scare Elise off." Justin shook his head. "I don't understand his reasoning."

"Well, I'm not getting into the details. You need to talk to Simon. You know he loves you, Justin, and wants what's best for you." She hugged him from behind then turned to Elise.

"He likes you too, honey. He wants to make sure you're up to the life we lead out here."

Hallie understood his thinking. She'd had similar thoughts herself, but she didn't like his methods. Something else seemed to bother him. Maybe the problem involved more than they realized.

The talk stopped as they heard boot steps on the back porch. No doubt Simon had heard them laughing at his expense. He opened the door and stomped inside, walked to the cabinet, took out a cup and filled it with coffee. He sat down in the chair beside Justin and grinned.

"Don't stop on my account. Guess it was pretty funny." He blew on his coffee and then took a drink. "Chester's having himself a jolly time so y'all might as well, too. He's been laughing so hard, he may bust a gut."

They all started asking questions at once.

Simon held up his hands in mock defense. "Hold on here. One question at a time."

Before he could point to someone, the back door flew open.

Standing in the doorway with hands on her hips stood the cutest little cowgirl Hallie had ever seen. Hallie glanced around at the others for clues to her identity. Could this be Whitney? She'd pictured her older, ten at least. This child couldn't be more than six or seven. Dressed in jeans, tee shirt and cowboy boots, she reached up and pushed her hat off. It fell against her shoulders, held on by the leather thong knotted at her neck. Her eyes surveyed the room. Then she walked up to Simon and folded her arms across her chest, one hip cocked.

"Uncle Simon. Is it true what everyone's saying this morning?" While waiting for his answer, she eased closer to Simon's chair, and melted into his side as she eyed the newcomers.

Justin nudged his uncle and laughed with glee. "Time to pay the piper, Uncle Simon. I can't wait to see how you handle this one."

Simon put his arm around the child and pulled her closer. "Hallie, Elise, meet Justin's sister, Whitney." He pushed back his chair, lifted Whitney and sat her in his lap. Her arms went around his neck as she put her head on his shoulder. "Can you say hello to our guests?"

She smiled and offered a soft, "Hello."

Hallie melted. Such a precious child, it was evident she loved her Uncle Simon. He looked natural with her in his arms, their resemblance so close they could be father and daughter.

"Hello, Whitney, I'm Hallie. This is my daughter, Elise."

Simon glanced down at Whitney. "Now then, princess, as to whether or not it's true, what did you hear, and who did you hear it from?"

She peered into his eyes and prodded his chest with her small index finger. "Chester. He said you put Justin's boom box outside the old cabin and played panther sounds to scare Justin's girlfriend." Her eyes traveled around the table, lit on Elise and pointed. "And her mama shot it to kingdom come with that old shotgun."

Justin groaned. "I knew it. I knew it'd be my cassette player." He laid his hand over his heart in mock distress.

Nailed by five sets of eyes, he cleared his throat. "I guess I'm guilty as charged." He turned to Justin. "I'll replace it with a new one. It's been out in the barn so long I thought you'd forgotten about it."

Hallie watched as Whitney leaned back to gaze at her uncle's face. Her innocent eyes prodded his hard sapphire ones.

"Why, Uncle Simon? You'd blister my butt if I did that. Is Gran going to spank you?"

Her comment caused a round of laughter from everyone except Simon. The little bugger knew how to make the big man squirm. "No. I hope not, as I'm too old for spankings. As to why, it'd take too long for me to explain." He tweaked her nose. "But I do need to apologize, don't I?"

Her auburn ponytail bobbed as she nodded.

He glanced from one to the other of the women,

but his gaze returned to Hallie. "Ladies, I do hope you'll forgive me. My behavior was inexcusable. I promise not to pull any more stunts while you're here." Simon tugged on Whitney's dark ponytail. "You too, princess. You forgive me?"

She looked at him, face solemn then put her small hands on each side of his face. "Do you promise to never, ever do that again?"

He nodded.

"Then, I forgive you, Uncle Simon." She kissed his cheek. He caught her close and buzzed her neck causing squeals of delight.

She jumped down and ran to stand between Hallie and Elise. "Do you forgive Uncle Simon?"

They looked at the child in surprise. Both nodded yes, but Hallie shot Simon daggers. He shrugged and gave her a wicked grin.

Whitney clapped with joy then grabbed one of each of their hands. "Okay, y'all have to stand up." They both did, not sure what to expect. "Now, you both have to kiss Uncle Simon to make it official. That's the rule, right, Justin?"

Simon laughed and shook his head. "No, pumpkin."

Justin grinned and said, "She's right, Uncle Simon, that's the rule. Stand up for your kisses."

Justin turned to the women. "It's our custom around here, kisses to seal a promise and to forgive."

"Now, Justin, the rule doesn't apply to guests, just family. Come on now. We need to get to work. Time's a wasting." He made a grab for his hat but stopped when Hallie spoke.

Hallie couldn't resist. She walked toward him with

a mischievous gleam in her eye. He needed to squirm a while longer. "I'm sure, Simon, you'd want us to keep up our end of the bargain. After all, it's just a little kiss. What could it hurt?"

Simon stood, his brow wrinkled in thought, his eyes shooting sparks of suspicious. *Oh boy, Hallie, you're probably going to regret this one.*

Elise reached him first. He smiled as he leaned down and she kissed him on the cheek.

Hallie took her time as she approached from the other direction, an innocent look pasted across her face. His frown had returned, but he bent toward her, cheek placed for her easy reach.

She grabbed his face with both hands. Pulling his head to her level, she sealed her lips to his in a searing kiss. Before she released him, she ran her tongue across his lower lip. He jerked back and growled softly, "Baby, you're going to pay for that." Then he left the kitchen as fast as his boots would carry him, Justin and Whitney hot on his heels.

Disregarding his threat, Hallie chuckled and started clearing dishes from the table and glanced over at Ruth. The older woman stood, hands on her hips, questions on her face.

"That was some kiss you laid on my son. Are your intentions honorable?"

"Yeah, Mom. I'd like to know, too."

Hallie stopped in mid-stride. *Oh-my-gosh.* She'd not considered how the kiss would appear to the others, above all to the older woman. How could she be so brazen in front of her daughter and a small child?

Heat rushed to the roots of her hair. "Oh, Ruth. I'm sorry if I offended you. Elise, I did it on impulse as a joke. I wanted to get revenge after the way he'd treated us and didn't think how it would look to rest of you."

Ruth grinned. "No need to apologize, I'm not offended. Just had to get in a little teasing of my own." She started drawing hot soapy water for the dishes. "It's about time someone knocked the wind out of Simon's sails. He's needed it for a long time. The boy's too arrogant for his own good."

"He is that, isn't he?" Relieved, Hallie picked up a dishtowel and started drying.

Elise stepped in to help, grinning at her mother. "I was too shocked to open my mouth. To think my sweet mother would kiss a man like that is shocking. My innocence is shattered, Mom."

"Yeah, right. Ruth, these kids think they invented kissing and passion. Us old folks don't have a clue. Go on." She gave Elise a shove toward the door. "I know you're dying to get outside, so go on. Ruth and I'll get this."

"Thanks, Mom." She leaned over and gave her mother a peck on the cheek. Then, gave Ruth one too. "I'll unpack later."

Hallie chuckled. "Have you ever noticed how kids use the word 'Mom' when everything's agreeable and 'Mother' when it's not?"

Not knowing where things belonged, Hallie dried dishes and stacked them on the table for Ruth to put away.

"You've done a good job raising that girl. She's a sweetheart."

"Yes, she is. Her brother's a blessing too. Though I have to admit, raising boys is a little tougher than girls."

Ruth laughed. "You won't get an argument from

me." She moved to the stove to remove cooking utensils to add to the soapy water.

"Has Simon's father been gone long?"

"He died with cancer almost ten years ago."

"I'm sorry, Ruth. I know how hard losing a spouse can be. My husband died of cancer seven years ago."

Ruth stopped washing for a minute. "Yes, I know. Justin told us. It must have been difficult for you and the children." She returned to scrubbing pans. "Anthony didn't suffer long like your husband did. The brain tumor took him fast."

Hallie used the dishtowel to wipe the cast iron skillet before setting it on the lit burner to complete the drying process.

Ruth watched her with a nod of approval.

"It's nice having someone to visit with over this chore. Glad you girls will be here awhile." She mused for a moment. "I suppose you're wondering about the kids' mother."

Startled Ruth had guessed her train of thought, she took a moment before answering. "Yes. Where is she?"

"She's having herself a good old time in Dallas."

Hallie didn't miss the note of bitterness in Ruth's voice. "I don't understand how anyone could leave Justin, much less that precious little girl."

Ruth sighed. "It's a long story, but in a nutshell Loretta would rather have money and her freedom than stay on this ranch with her children." With a sad expression, she shook her head. "Oh, I guess she loves them in her own way. She comes to see them on occasion, but it's not the same. Justin's old enough he doesn't miss her, but it's hard on Whitney."

"Simon seems devoted to them." She smiled at the

memory of him teasing Whitney. "What happened to their father?"

Tears gathered in the older woman's eyes. "A year after the divorce, Sidney was hit by an eighteen wheeler on his way home from a business trip to Austin. Whitney was two years old."

Hallie put her hands on Ruth's shoulder and squeezed. Ruth patted her hand.

"Now, enough of this." She wiped at her eyes with her arms. "You go unpack and get outside for a while. Feel free to look around if you'd like."

Last night she'd been astounded at the size of the house. She unpacked and stored her bags in the large walk-in closet. Her room opened onto a veranda. She stepped through the double French doors to see that it ran the length of the house and around the east corner. There were three bedrooms, including hers on the front of the house and two on the eastside. They all opened to a gallery overlooking the den. Wow. What a place. She hoped Ruth didn't have to clean it all by herself.

Downstairs, she stopped to peer out one of the windows that flanked the oversized fireplace. A huge pool surrounded by a flagstone patio dominated the back yard. That is, if you could call it a yard. Three wooden picnic tables and a barbecue grill dominated a large area of grass. The patio had two tables covered with umbrellas and several lounge chairs. My goodness! It looked like a country club.

Outside she sank onto an upholstered lounge chair and put her feet up. She glanced around expecting a waiter to appear at any moment. Why on earth did a rancher need such extravagance?

The eaves from the house and umbrellas shaded

her from the morning sunlight. It had been a long night without much sleep. She closed her eyes.

The slamming of the back door woke her. Ruth carried a tray with glasses and a pitcher of iced tea toward her. Hallie pulled a small table closer to the chaise lounges.

"Did you have a good nap? How about a glass of iced tea?"

"It was wonderful, but I didn't intend to fall asleep. And, I would love a glass of tea."

"Sometimes the body knows more than we do about what it needs."

Hallie reached out and took the tea-laden tray from Ruth. As she bent to lower it to the table, pain shot through her right shoulder. Wincing, she cried out. "Ow! I guess I'm sorer than I realized."

Ruth came to stand beside her. "Let me take a look?"

Hallie nodded and pulled her tee shirt back exposing the bruise that covered her shoulder.

"Oh, my. We should've put something on that last night. What was I thinking? Had bruises myself after using that old shotgun." She eased the shirt back in place. "I've got something that will work wonders on the soreness. Can't do much for the color, though."

"It's fine, Ruth. It was the weight of the tray pulling it. Don't trouble yourself."

"It's no bother, my dear. Sit back down. I won't be a minute."

She returned with a jar of medicine Hallie had to admit helped the pain. "Thanks. That's soothing."

"You're welcome. We use this cream a lot around here. Always have sore muscles, banged knees and hands. The men are as bad if not worse than Whitney."

She handed Hallie a tall glass and leaned back in the other lounger with a glass of her own. "Ah. This is nice."

Hallie sipped her tea. "Wonderful. Tastes like mint tea. Haven't had any this good in years."

"I grow my own mint. Fresh always tastes better." She rolled the cold glass over her forehead. "As a matter of fact, it's planted in the beds all around the house. Believe it or not, it keeps the ants out of the house. They don't like it."

"It works for real?"

"Works like a charm. At least, it does for me."

"Ruth, I'm curious. Do you keep this house clean all by yourself?"

"Lands sake, no. A lady comes in once a week and spends the entire day cleaning. I do the cooking, laundry and anything that needs doing in between. 'Course Simon and the kids are good about helping out. Couldn't manage without them."

"I'm glad to hear it. I was about to have a complex thinking you were Super Woman."

Ruth chuckled. "What a scary thought. Me in one of those spandex outfits."

They laughed, then sat in silence and drank their tea. The sound of Elise and Whitney approaching broke their quiet reverie. Hallie smiled at the child's chatter.

"Uncle Simon says I'm lucky being a kid 'cause after my chores are done I can do whatever I want. Poor Justin has to work all day."

"What about me?" asked Elise. "I'm grown and he didn't make me stay and work."

Whitney laughed. "Ha! That's because you're

company, silly."

* * *

"Anyone want a beer?" Simon unfolded his length from the chaise lounge and stood, hands on his hips, waiting for their drink orders. He looked cool and relaxed—sexy—in his denim shorts and a white tee-shirt that emphasized the broadness of his shoulders. As much as Hallie hated to admit it, he was too handsome for words. His rich auburn hair, still damp from the shower, and the spicy scent of his aftershave teased her nostrils stirring a dormant yearning.

Dusk faded into darkness. Beyond the pool, the cloudless sky was black. She enjoyed the cool air by the pool. The glow of the underwater lights gave off enough illumination to see in the direct vicinity of the pool. Ripples fanned out across the surface of the water as an insect dove in for a drink.

She let out a contented sigh, wiggled her toes and let her slides drop to the pavement. An occasional breeze swept over the water rustling the gauzy fabric of her sundress against her knees. Twinkling stars were beginning to emerge in the darkening sky.

Elise and Justin cuddled together, hip to hip on one chaise, talking in low whispers. The shadow from the pool umbrella almost obliterated them in darkness.

Ruth came out and sat down in the glider. With the ball of her foot, she pushed back causing the seat to sway. "Big day for our little cowgirl. She's out like a light."

Simon followed laden with drinks, three beers in the fingers of one hand, and two teas nestled in the big palm of his other.

"Here you go, Mama, tea for you and Hallie." He

smiled, the tilt of his mouth and sparkle in his eye causing a flutter in her stomach. He gave them a mocking bow as he handed them each a cold wet glass, sprigs of mint floating on the top. "I crushed a few mint leaves and stirred it in."

"Thank you, sweet boy."

Hallie almost choked on her sip of tea and restrained a chuckle at Ruth's endearment for the big man.

The tea was delicious, sweet with a hint of mint.

He walked to the overcrowded chaise at the end of the pool. "You two love birds want to break it up long enough to drink these beers?"

Justin sat forward, face emerging from the shadows, to take the tall bottles. "You bet. All this talking makes a person thirsty."

Deep laughter rumbled up from Simon's chest. "Son, back in my day, we called it necking, not talking."

Elise giggled.

"Very funny, Uncle Simon. I'm surprised you can remember back that far."

"I'm not as old as you think, young man."

As Simon passed Hallie's chaise, she noticed his eyes couldn't resist the long expanse of leg and shoulder exposed by the filmy sundress she wore. Did he remember the kiss she'd given him this morning? She hoped so because his perusal made her body heat. Maybe she should've left on the wrap she'd worn during dinner.

His gaze softened as it traveled up to her bare shoulders. His expressions darkened. She didn't know if it was due to arousal or anger at seeing the bruise on her shoulder.

The soft thunder of hoof beats caught his attention. He stood and turned to the open range to the east. "What the Hell!" Hands on his hips, he waited. Hallie didn't envy the rider unless it was an emergency. Simon looked ready to kill.

The horse came to an abrupt stop outside the yard, sending a spray of dust billowing across the pool onto the onlookers.

Hallie closed her mouth and covered her tea with her hand.

A girl jumped off the horse. Hallie's heart lurched at the dangerous dismount. She could tell it was a girl because a long braid flew out from her body when she moved. Petite, not over five feet two inches tall, and dark, she resembled a China doll in western wear.

By the time the rider's feet hit the ground and dropped the reins in the dust, Justin stood beside Simon.

With a squeal of excitement, the girl ran toward the two men screeching. "Justin! Justin! I'm home."

Justin caught her as she flung herself at him, almost knocking him in the pool. With a big grin on his face, he hugged her and twirled her in a circle.

She shrieked and hung on. He sat her on her feet, hands still at her waist. "Caitlyn. What are you doing out here this late?"

"I got home an hour ago, and couldn't wait 'til morning to see you." Throwing her arms around his neck, she hugged him again. As if by their own volition, his circled her back and shoulders returning the embrace. Suddenly, as if remembering his company, he released her and stepped back.

CHAPTER FOUR

"I've missed you guys so much." Hallie watched as Caitlyn bent to give Ruth a kiss on her cheek. Then she turned to Simon and hugged him around the waist.

Simon's face was dark with anger, but he hugged her and patted her back. "Dammit, Caitlyn. What'd you mean riding so fast in the dark? That's the stupidest thing I've seen you do in a long time."

She smiled in apology, a smile that doubtless had won her many battles in her young lifetime. "I'm sorry, Simon. I was careful. And it didn't get dark until about half an hour ago."

"What'd your daddy say about you taking off alone so late?"

"He said to wait 'til morning." She looked sheepish. "Guess I better go call him."

"You do that. Tell him one of us will bring you home in the truck. You can pick up your horse tomorrow."

Caitlyn gave Elise and Hallie a curious glance, and then went into the house.

Justin excused himself and followed her, closing the door behind him.

A few minutes later, the sound of Caitlyn's angry voice, muffled by the closed door, could be heard though the words were indiscernible. Justin's voice remained calm, as if trying to reason with her.

His face was grim when they came out. Caitlyn looked ready to crumble into tears. She rolled her lips in to keep them from trembling.

So, this was the young lady Simon mentioned living on the neighboring ranch. The one Justin had loved for so long.

With his hand at Caitlyn's elbow, he led her to Elise. "Elise, I'd like you to meet a friend of mine, Caitlyn Porter. Caitlyn, meet Elise Barron, my *fiancée*."

Elise stood and greeted her with a warm smile. "Hi, Caitlyn. I'm so glad to meet you at last. Justin talks about you often. You must be close."

Caitlyn, blinked back tears and nodded.

Oh dear, this is not good. The poor girl wasn't prepared for this and is not taking it well. On top of that, what if Elise had no idea Justin and Caitlyn had been an item for years. Hallie felt sorry for Caitlyn and angry with Justin for letting this happen.

Always the peacemaker, she walked over and took her hand. "Hi Caitlyn. I'm Elise's mother, Hallie."

Caitlyn tried to smile, but her full lower lip quivered instead. Her dark brown eyes, large and fringed with dark lashes, brimmed with tears. A fat droplet overflowed her lower lid to trail down her face. It was obvious she was crazy about Justin, her idea of their relationship different from his.

Ruth put her arms around Caitlyn. "Come in the house, Caitlyn. Let's get you a glass of tea."

If looks could kill, Justin would drop dead any minute. Simon appeared ready to blow. His shoulders were rigid, jaw clenched.

Justin looked uncomfortable, his tanned face pinched with concern. But he didn't avoid his uncle's glare.

"Uncle Simon, she knew we were no longer seeing each other. We both agreed to date other people when I left here after spring break."

He looked at Elise. "I'm sorry this happened. I should have found some way to get in touch with her." He combed his fingers through his hair. "I'd planned to go by and talk to her before she came over. She wasn't due back until tomorrow."

Elise, face solemn, went to his side and put her arm around his waist. "I hope she'll be alright. Our engagement must be a shock for her."

A few minutes later, Ruth stepped out onto the patio. "Caitlyn's ready to go home. Which one of you will drive her?"

Justin spoke up. "I will, Gran."

Simon gave him a murderous look and mumbled. "You sure as hell will."

* * *

Justin felt like hell. How could he have been so stupid to think Caitlyn would come home when she said she would? When had she ever been predictable?

"I never meant to hurt you, Caitlyn. Remember we agreed to see other people after spring break?"

Caitlyn nodded but kept her face averted. She'd been huddled on her side of the truck for the past ten minutes. Occasional sobs shook her small body.

He loved Caitlyn. Hell, he had since they were kids. His feelings for Elise were different. Beautiful and smart, he felt the need to protect her. He liked the feeling.

Caitlyn was pretty and smart too, but she was also wild, full of spit and vinegar. Her energy wore him out sometimes. And temper, Lord, she had one. He smiled remembering how sparks could fly from her eyes. She didn't stay mad long—just blew up, got it out of her system and moved on. He admired that about her. Caitlyn didn't hold grudges like most girls did. There lay the problem—he saw her as a girl, not a woman. Stunned at the revelation he glanced over and took another look.

In truth, she'd had the body of a woman since high school. Her jeans molded to well-shaped hips, her t-shirt pulled taut over full breasts. He shook his head to get the tantalizing picture out of his mind. Her behavior prevented him from seeing her as grown.

Why wasn't she yelling at him, getting rid of her anger like she had in the past? She'd always been so independent. She didn't need anyone. Until tonight. This was so unlike her.

It had been devotion at first sight—she was all of five years old and he an ancient seven. They'd been inseparable ever since, their relationship changing from childhood friendship to love in their teens. They'd been devoted to each other through high school and college. In late March, he'd met Elise and his life changed.

Justin could see moisture on her long, dark lashes and beads trailing down her cheek. He knew her eyes would look like luminous pools of rich coffee. The one time he'd seen her cry was when she'd chased after him and his friends, fallen and skinned her skinny knees. From then on he'd slowed his pace so she could keep up.

The sexual attraction between them was so intense he feared it would burn out and he'd end up like his father—alone and heartbroken. He couldn't take that risk. Elise was steady and sure, Caitlyn, flighty like a young untamed colt.

Her words interrupted his thoughts.

"You lied to me about their being someone else, didn't you? You were seeing her in March when you came home."

"I swear, Caitlyn, I met Elise after we were together in March. I've never lied to you." He reached over and covered her clenched fist with his hand. "Please, Caitlyn. I didn't mean for this to happen but I think it's best for us both. I'm ready for marriage and I'm not the man for you. You'd be bored with me in a year's time. There's a good man waiting for you out there."

Hoping she could see what he felt in his eyes, he added. "Caitlyn, I don't want this to break up our friendship."

She flung his hand away from hers. "You've got to be kidding. I've loved you my entire life. You think I can forget that and be friends?" Hysterical laughter erupted from her small frame. "Another man?"

He pulled the truck to a stop in the circular drive in front of her tall house with Greek columns.

"You're crazy! There will never be another man for me."

"Caitlyn, you don't mean that. You're upset right now." He reached over to hug her shoulders.

She recoiled, swung around with her palm open, and slapped him hard on the face. For a minute she looked at him. Shocked, filled with shame and remorse, he stared at the look of pain on her face. She got out of the truck and spoke through the open window.

"Don't you ever touch me again." Then, she spun

on her heel and ran toward the house.

* * *

"Did you talk to Sam?" Tense and tired, Simon sat behind his desk. Papers in neat stacks stood on each side, leaving a clear space in the center where he worked. Right now his clasped hands, knuckles white, occupied it.

Justin stood, hat in his hands, but returned Simon's gaze.

"Yeah, I did." He tossed his hat onto the old leather sofa that lined the wall opposite Simon's desk. "When Caitlyn ran into the house and slammed the door, Mr. Porter walked out onto the porch. I got out and joined him."

Simon exhaled the breath he'd been holding and relaxed the grip on his hands. "How'd he take it?"

Justin dropped onto the sofa and leaned his head back against the cushions. "Not well. He raved awhile about stomping my ass, but after he calmed down, he apologized." He could see the big man in a rage. Sam Porter had a terrible temper, more bark than bite, but was a fair man. He loved his daughter and whatever she wanted, he wanted her to have. Plus, he'd watch Justin grow up and thought of him as the son he'd have one day. He'd been counting on Justin and Caitlyn running both ranches. This was a big disappointment for him.

"Justin, are you sure it's Elise you love and not Caitlyn?

Justin leaned forward and used both hands to massage his neck. He seemed to be fighting for composure. Hell, the kid was struggling with some issue. He'd give anything to know what it was. Maybe he'd had second thoughts about his decision to marry

Elise. Whatever bothered him, he couldn't help him unless he opened up.

Simon studied Justin. He loved the kid so much. Mama often told him Justin resembled him when he was that age. Of course he and Sidney looked as much alike as brothers could. You could see the resemblance in their old high school and college pictures.

"I love Elise. I have since the first moment I saw her. She's more settled and will make a good wife and mother. I love Caitlyn too, but it's so wild and crazy, I don't trust it. Caitlyn is so unpredictable I'm afraid she'd get bored like Mom did."

A fist closed around Simon's heart and Justin looked as bad as he knew they both felt. Why had he not known Justin worried about these issues? There was more to the boy than he realized. Boy? Hell, he was a man, and had been since his father's death. Mama believed Justin was smarter than Sydney, that he wouldn't make the same mistake.

"I can respect that, Justin. But you've got to be sure it's Elise and not Caitlyn you want to marry. Three people's happiness is at stake here, not just yours."

"Yeah, I know."

"I like Elise. She and her mother are good people. I don't know if she can hold up to ranch life or not, but I'm willing to give her a fair chance." He thought for a minute. "I admit I was against you marrying Elise. To my shame and embarrassment, I tried to scare her off. I had my reasons though." He cleared his throat. "I didn't want to tell you this, but the ranch is in financial trouble. If you and Caitlyn married, Sam Porter would help you with finances." He held up his hand at Justin's expression of indignation. "I know you wouldn't take money from Sam, but you might borrow from him or let him invest in your ranch."

Justin looked stunned. "How bad is it?"

"When your mother divorced your dad, he had to sell over half the stock and 100 acres of land to give her the money she wanted. It was either that or sell the ranch."

Sidney had worked hard trying to bring it back—make it solvent—but he couldn't. Though Simon had tried too, he'd just been able to keep their heads out of water.

"That bitch!" Justin stood, face contorted with rage and pain. "God, sometimes I hate her."

"Hold on now, son. I don't like the woman, but she is your mother. We don't allow that kind of talk, in particular about your family, whether they deserve it or not."

Justin shook his head as he paced in front of the desk. "If she hadn't left, dad would still be alive. I think he gave up. I know one thing. If he'd been happy, he wouldn't have been so careless the night of the wreck."

Simon often wondered if stress caused Sidney to let his guard down while driving, thus contributing to the accident that killed him on impact. They'd never know for sure.

Despite their differences and problems, Loretta had been devastated at his death. Good at putting on airs and acting, Simon knew her grief was real. She had loved his brother but couldn't stand ranch life.

God, what a mess.

"Justin, don't take this too hard. We'll work out something. Get a bank loan or sell off more land. When I turn this place over to you, I want it to be in the black, not in the red." He splayed his hands on the desk and opened a folder. "As a matter of fact, I've got the paperwork right here. You take control June first."

He stopped his pacing and faced Simon, pain on his face. "You've been mighty good to us, Uncle Simon." His throat clogged with emotion. "You've given up several years of your life and neglected your ranch to take care of Whitney and this ranch."

Simon stood and walked around the desk, put his hands on Justin's shoulders and gave him a gentle shake. "God, Justin. Don't think like that. I've given up nothing. I love you and Whitney like you were my own."

He pulled the boy into his arms and hugged him hard, slapping his back in comfort.

Justin held tight for a second. "I love you, too, Uncle Simon."

With a nervous laugh, Simon said. "Now, enough of this. We better get to bed so we can get up before Whitney in the morning."

* * *

Morning came too early. He was getting too old for these late nights. Simon stretched, moaning as muscles and bones protested, then rolled to a sitting position on the side of the bed. With elbows on his knees, he dropped his head into his hands and groaned, then flopped back and rolled to face the wide expanse of empty bed. He stared at it for a while before splaying his hand over the vacant area beside him. An ache formed in the region of his heart. It was lonesome waking up to that empty space every morning. A sound sleeper, he seldom moved at night so the other half of his bed remained almost wrinkle-free making his spot easy to smooth out in the mornings.

His mind drifted down the hall to Hallie's room. Was she snuggled up in that damn nightshirt? Did she long to wake up beside someone or was she content with her empty bed? Hell, maybe her bed wasn't empty much. At the thought, his stomach clenched. The picture of a man in her bed didn't sit well with him at all.

What would it be like to wake up with Hallie curled up beside him? He sure as hell wouldn't be laying here feeling sorry with himself. *Don't go there, old man.* No way could anything develop between them. They were too different and had the two kids to think of. The idea of the two "old folks" having a relationship would horrify them both.

Disgusted with the journey his mind traveled, he bounded out of bed and strode to the bathroom, tossing his jockey shorts in the hamper. A damn nuisance to sleep in but he never knew when Whitney would climb in his bed and he didn't want to be caught in the buff. Once had been more than enough. She'd had a bad dream during the night, and crawled into bed with him. He'd thought she was asleep when he eased out of bed. The sound of her voice sent him scurrying for cover. Explaining the difference in male and female anatomy to the child had not been fun. Embarrassed him to death. Didn't faze the squirt, though. She listened and said, "Ok," before heading down the hall to her room. Of course, she'd relayed all her new found knowledge to Justin at breakfast, checking to see if *he* knew all the facts. He'd been mortified. Mama and Justin had struggled to keep a serious face. Damn! The child needed a mother. A long shower was what he needed.

* * *

Hallie lay awake, enjoying those last minutes in the warm comfortable bed. A door down the hallway shut, then the sound of heavy footsteps, muffled by the carpet, passed her door and down the stairs. A second door opened. A scurrying sound followed Simon's procession to the living area below. She heard Simon's deep tones, but not the words, and Whitney's delicious giggle. Smiling, she tossed back the cover and headed for the shower. Those two were a pair, as close as two peas in a pod.

Dressed in jeans, t-shirt, and her old boots she descended the stairs and joined Ruth in the kitchen. Simon had mentioned her and Elise riding out with them today. She wanted to be ready when he decided to leave.

Ruth smiled in welcome. "Simon and Justin will be back in a minute. Want to finish pouring the juice for me?" She bustled back to the stove to dish up scrambled eggs and bacon. A big bowl, lined with a red checked napkin, already decorated the table along with a pitcher of milk.

Hallie poured the juice and grabbed the coffee pot. "Is it too early to pour the coffee?" She glanced around. "Where's Whitney? I thought I heard her down here earlier."

"I sent her back up to dress and make her bed."

Whitney came flying down the stairs looking scrubbed and rested.

"Did you make your bed, Whitney?"

"Yes, Gran." She eyed Hallie with a shy smile.

"Good morning, young lady. Did you happen to hear Elise stirring around in her room before you came down?"

Whitney looked up the stairs, then back at Hallie, shaking her head. "No".

"Will you run up there and make sure she's up and at 'um."

With a big grin, ponytail bobbing she headed for the stairs at a run.

"Don't forget to knock," said Ruth.

She did, giving two quick taps before charging in Elise's room. The sound of Whitney's chatter floated down to them. Elise's replies were soft from the adjoining bathroom.

Ruth smiled. "It's good Elise is comfortable with Whitney. She needs some female attention."

Conversation around the breakfast table was cheerful. Whitney begged to go out to the range with them and Simon explained, again, why she couldn't. She gave up and then batted her eyes at Simon and Justin.

Simon froze and stared at her hard. Was this another method of getting her way? Something was different about her this morning. Then he noticed what it was.

"Whitney, is that lipstick I see on your mouth?" He tried to keep his voice neutral but didn't like the idea of her trying out cosmetics at her young age.

She pursed her lips and blinked her eyes again. "Yes. Aren't I beautiful this morning?"

Justin leaned toward her. "Turn around, squirt. Let me get a good gander at you." He lifted her chin and studied the bow shaped mouth.

"Yep. That's lipstick alright." He leaned in, gave her a quick peck on the lips then smacked his lips.

"Tastes like watermelon." His eyes met Elise's and they both grinned.

He hugged Whitney. "Yes, pumpkin, you are beautiful this morning. Looks like in a few years I'll have to fight the boys away with a stick."

Innocent eyes questioned his. "What's that mean?"

Tweaking her nose, "It means, Miss Priss, I'll have to chase all your boyfriends away. That's what big brothers do."

"You're silly, Justin. You know I can whip any boy around here."

Simon knew right now she could. She'd given Rusty James, a town boy a year older, a black eye at church last month for marking on her dress with colored markers. He'd made her sit in her room the rest of the day as punishment.

Elise turned to Simon. "I hope it's all right I put some on her. She was curious and I hated to say no."

Voice gruff, he said, "No problem. A little lipstick is okay on occasion. Not every day, though, Whitney. You understand?"

She nodded in agreement. "Elise said it was a subtle color. A good one for a young lady."

Ruth chuckled. "And what does subtle mean, Whitney? The word's as big as you are."

"Well, Gran. Elise said it means it's not too much for a little girl. You know, not gaudy." She blinked at Ruth. "Didn't you know that, Gran?"

"Yes, darlin', I knew, but I wanted to see if *you* knew."

In truth, Simon noted, the color was natural. Thank goodness Elise had good taste and hadn't let Whitney come to the table with red or orange smeared on her lips.

"Anyway, Elise said if you didn't mind, we'd paint my toenails and fingernails tonight." She looked smug. "I wanted green but she said it wasn't appropriate for a girl my age so we're going to do them pink. Can I, Uncle Simon?"

* * *

As Hallie approached the barn, Jezebel trotted over wagging her tail and huffed a greeting. She stopped and gave the dog a good scratch behind the ears. "Hi ya, girl. We've missed you. Yes, we have." Jezebel fell over and exposed her belly for rubbing. Hallie laughed and obliged her, setting the dog's right hind leg to jerking in enjoyment. "You been a good girl?"

A loud snort interrupted their greeting. "You're spoiling that old dog, Mrs. Barron."

Hallie recognized Chester's voice and the smile in the words. "Good morning, Chester. Please, call me Hallie." She gave him a dazzling smile.

He yanked his hat off his head, revealing his thinning hair. "I'd be right honored, ma'am."

He stood next to the corral, skinny butt propped against one of the posts. "You know how to ride? Simon wants me to help you pick out a horse for you to ride today."

Hallie walked up beside him and leaned against the upper rail to look over the horses she would choose from. "They're a fine bunch, Chester." They were prime horseflesh. She'd grown up around horses and recognized quality when she saw it.

"You bet they are. Simon stocks the best, though he's tender hearted and keeps some of the older ones on rather than have them put down." He chuckled. "The boy's more tender-hearted than you'd think. Always was a sucker for hurt and old animals, most of all those that have served the family well."

Hallie looked at Chester and nodded. Seems there was more to Simon than met the eye.

She turned her attention back to the horses. "How about the mare standing all by herself over there, Chester?"

His eyes located the mare and pondered a minute. "Are you a pretty good rider? Sadie can be a bit frisky, so if you're not, we better pick out one of the older horses."

"I grew up on a farm, Chester. I started riding soon after I could walk. Of course, not like here on a ranch, but I got plenty of practice."

His eyes gleamed with interest at her admission. She knew Simon thought she'd been raised in the city and knew nothing about life away from department stores and take-out food.

"Elise can ride, too, but I'd rather her have a little older horse to start out on. Which one do you think?"

He decided on Lulu, a horse of indiscriminant age with a slight sway back. "She's a real sweetie. She'll take good care of your girl."

In the tack room of the barn she picked out a saddle for herself and one for Elise. Chester led Sadie into the barn. She went about saddling her and adjusting the stirrups to her satisfaction. She talked to the horse as she worked. Sadie turned around as if checking her progress, then snorted before turning back to the front.

* * *

Simon watched Hallie at work. *Well, I'll be damned. Seems like she knows what she's doing.* He'd never dreamed the lady knew anything about horses, in particular not how to saddle one herself. Loretta could ride but she'd always had Chester or one of the other hands saddle her horse.

He had to admit Hallie appeared comfortable standing there in the barn, right at home. Damn if she didn't look good in her worn Wranglers, blue t-shirt, and scuffed ropers. He'd expected to see her in a pair of those fancy colored boots, like red or some other stylish color.

He walked farther into the barn and stopped a few feet from her. "Did Chester tell you Sadie's a little ornery sometimes?"

She glanced up. "Yeah, he did. But, I think I can handle her."

He walked over and started checking the saddle and other tack.

She laughed. "Don't trust me, huh?"

He grinned back. "Well, I have to admit, you surprised me. But, humor me. I'm responsible for your safety while you're on this ranch."

"No problem. I expected you to double check."

She stood in front of Sadie and scratched her forelock. "Justin is saddling a horse for Elise around back. Chester brought in an older horse from the pasture for her."

He nodded but didn't say anything.

When he finished his inspection, she took her hat and a long sleeved shirt off a stall door and led Sadie out of the barn.

Redman stood waiting for Simon outside, reins folded across his neck. He nickered at Sadie and she returned the greeting.

"You need help getting in the saddle?"

"I don't think so. Though it's been awhile, I think I can manage."

Simon watched her mount, noting after she put her foot in the stirrup she pushed off with her right leg to help her jump up into the saddle.

He mounted and they walked the two horses to the road where Justin and Elise waited.

"Hey, Mom. Isn't this neat." Elise's face glowed with excitement.

"You bet, hon. I hope we're half as excited when we return this afternoon."

Simon knew her butt and leg muscles would be sore. Walking would be a trial for a couple of days. He doubted it would be as hard on the young one.

"Here's your lunches and water." Chester handed Justin and Simon each a saddlebag with two canteens.

Simon handed a canteen to Hallie. "Thanks, Chester." He draped the saddlebag across Redman's neck and looped the canteen strap around the saddle horn. "Think you can keep Whitney busy today so she doesn't drive Mama crazy?"

Chester hitched up his jeans and put his hands on his hips. "You bet, Boss. I'll put her to work cleaning tack."

Simon grinned and saluted the older man.

"Justin, you and Elise take the fence on the north rim; we'll take the west. Jim and Zeke have the east and south areas." He looked over the supplies Justin had strapped across the back of his saddle. "You got everything you need?"

"Sure do. Checked it twice."

"Okay. You two be careful and meet us back here

no later than five this evening."

"Gotcha, Uncle Simon." Both kids waved as they rode out.

Simon gazed at Hallie in question. She nodded and they rode off toward the west.

Simon urged his horse into a gallop, Hallie following on his heels. When they reached rougher terrain and descended into a gully, he slowed and they walked the horses single file along a narrow trail cut by rainwater through a jumble of large boulders. From the red dirt around the massive rocks grew a variety of wildflowers, clumps of prickly pear cactus, and brushy shrubs.

As they climbed out of the ravine, the trail widened. Hallie drew up beside Simon. They rode awhile in companionable silence as Hallie gazed across the wide expanse of land. Simon threw darting glances at her as she viewed the landscape. He didn't want to be caught watching her, above all not the provocative sway of her body in the saddle. She seemed comfortable on Sadie, and after letting Sadie know who was boss when they first started out, she hadn't given Hallie any more trouble.

"Where'd you learn to ride, Hallie?"

She smiled up at him. Her cheeks rosy from exertion enhanced the sparkle of mischief in her eyes. "I grew up on a farm. We had several horses and rode as often as possible."

He threw her a condemning glance. "I thought you were a city girl."

She batted her eyes at him. "Well, sir, you never asked."

"I guess the farm is where you learned to use that

wood stove."

"Yep. My grandmother used to have a similar one. My granddad had one of those old shotguns, too." She laughed and kicked Sadie into a gallop.

"Smart aleck." He kneed Redman and rode to catch up.

They found three breaks in the fence before stopping for lunch. Under the branches of a big oak tree on top of a hill they tied the horses, loosened their girth then let them munch on the grass growing nearby.

Hallie moaned as she walked to ease the tightness of her muscles. "Oh, my aching body. I don't think I'll be able to walk tomorrow."

"Yeah, you will. Take you a hot bath when we get back. Then go for a swim after dinner and then another hot soak. You'll be good as new in the morning."

"I'm willing to try anything." She sat down on a wide, flat rock under the tree. Simon rummaged in the saddlebag and handed her a thick ham sandwich, an apple, and poured her a tin cup of cold iced tea from a thermos.

"Oh wow. This is the best sandwich I've ever eaten." She closed her eyes and chewed, a look of bliss on her face.

He watched her through hooded eyes as she devoured the sandwich and started on her apple. "Save some room for dessert. Chester sent some of his brownies." He tossed her a zip lock bag.

She opened the sack, removed a brownie, and took a bite. "Mmmmmm. This is scrumptious."

Simon opened his second sandwich and started eating. He glanced up to see Hallie eyeing it. He stopped eating, feeling guilty. "Are you still hungry?

I'll share."

"No, you go ahead. If I had room, I'd take you up on it but I can't eat another bite." She picked up their empty sandwich bags and stuffed them in the saddlebag. "Man. If I worked like this every day I could eat anything I wanted."

He nodded and went back to eating.

She studied him awhile then asked. "How come you've never married? I can't imagine the women around here letting you get away."

He stopped chewing, looked at her for a minute then finished off the sandwich before answering.

"Never found the right woman, I guess. Not for lack of trying on my part. I decided I wouldn't settle for anything less than what my folks had."

Hallie nodded in understanding.

"Then, when Sidney died and I took on the kids, there wasn't much time for dating. Oh, there've been women over the years, one from town I considered marrying. I care for her but don't love her." He shook his head. "Wouldn't have been fair to either one of us."

He filled her cup with more ice tea from the thermos. "What about you? Ever think about getting married again?"

"Elise asked me that question the other night." She sipped her tea. "I've not dated since James's death. I've been out with men associates, business lunches or dinners." She gazed off into the distance. "I've been asked out often enough, but wasn't interested in any of the men. James and I had a wonderful marriage. I don't think I could settle for anything less than what I had."

"What about your business? If you married again would you want to keep it?"

"In all probability, yes. Besides the kids, it's all I've had for the past six years. It's kept me sane." She smiled. "All my hard work is about to pay off, too. I may be expanding by opening another store soon."

"Is that so? Congratulations." He finished off the brownies and washed them down with his tea. "The thought of all the money you're making keep you warm at night?"

She flushed. "That's none of your business."

What the hell made him ask her such a question? "You're right. I apologize."

He'd gotten her dander up. She threw him a scalding look, scooted off the rock and leaned against it, laying her head back. "I think I'll close my eyes for a minute."

Simon watched her. Dark eyelashes lay against cheeks still pink from exertion. Her lips parted as she drifted off to sleep. He watched the gentle rise and fall of her chest, then feeling guilty for looking, averted his eyes.

Just as he figured, she was career-minded, interested in money, climbing the corporate ladder.

He stretched out on the hard ground, arms folded beneath his head, and surveyed the smattering of clouds in the sky overhead. -*What would it be like to be married to a woman like Hallie?* He'd longed for a family, but Sidney's marriage to Loretta had soured him. After their divorce, and then Sidney's death, Loretta pursued Simon until he'd told her to "stay the hell away from him". She took Sidney's death hard, was confused and mixed up. *God, I tried to hate that woman but felt sorry for her.*

Hallie was different in several ways. Yes, she was

beautiful as well as intelligent, but she also had a fun sense of humor and seemed to enjoy the ranch. She helped around the house and hadn't complained once while they worked fences this morning. He wanted to get to know her better, but he wouldn't. It didn't take a fool to see she belonged in the city. His life was with the two ranches and his nephew and niece.

The sun passed from beneath a cloud, filtered through the leaves above him, blinding him for a moment. It warmed his closed eyes.

He awoke to the sun's glare, feeling roasted. *What the hell am I doing sleeping during the day?* He rolled to his feet. Hallie still slept. Remembering his earlier thoughts about her made him more irritable.

Hallie jolted awake when he nudged her leg with the toe of his boot.

"Time to get back to work." Simon pivoted on his heel and walked toward his horse. Then he was in the saddle galloping away.

CHAPTER FIVE

Hallie hobbled down the stairs, one step at a time, trying not to extend her muscles. She stopped at the sound of Elise's giggle behind her.

"Mama, you look as bad as I feel."

At the graceful way Elise trotted down to join her, Hallie doubted she suffered at all. "If you're sore, it doesn't appear to be slowing you down."

Elise hugged her and they walked the remainder of the way down arm-in-arm. "No, I'm tender, but it's a good discomfort, like after exercise. It'll go away after I stir around."

Hallie squinted at her daughter. Yeah, she remembered the perks of youth.

Ruth worked at the stove scooping scrambled eggs onto a plate. Beside it sat a platter heaped with bacon. "How'd you two girls sleep?"

"Great, Gran." Elise gathered plates and started setting the table.

Ruth gave Hallie a comforting pat as she passed on her way to the coffee pot.

"I can tell by looking at you it was a rough night."

She returned Ruth's sympathetic smile. "No matter how I turned, I couldn't get comfortable. About one this morning I took a couple of aspirin." She took another drink from the hot cup. "I slept after that."

"In a day or two you'll be right as rain. Get back in

the saddle as soon as you can."

The front door bell chimed then it rang again and again as if someone leaned on it.

Ruth hurried to the door. "Who on earth can that be?"

Voices traveled from the large entry hall.

"Aunt Ruth, it's so good to see you."

"Jo Beth, honey, what a surprise. Is everything okay with you?"

Laughing, she said. "Now, why would you ask?"

"I've never known you to leave the house this early and here you are before 8:00. That in itself is an indicator."

"I got so excited since talking to you yesterday I couldn't sleep. As soon as Paul got up, I packed a small bag and headed this way."

"Without Paul?"

"He'll be here tonight. I couldn't wait to meet Justin's fiancé. Where is she?"

A petite young woman entered the large den in a whirl of the reddest hair Hallie had ever seen. Her wide mouth, devoid of lipstick, emphasized the freckles on her clean peaches and cream complexion. She was beautiful in a natural, unadorned way.

When she spotted Elise, she dropped her small suitcase, rushed over and hugged her as if she'd know her for years.

"Elise, this is Jo Beth, Simon's cousin. She's a few years older than Justin. Those two got into one scrape after another as kids."

Elise hugged her back. "It's good to meet you, Jo Beth. I'm anxious to hear about those childhood escapades."

"You too, hon, and I'll be sure to tell you about the ones that Justin instigated. He kept me in trouble as a kid."

"Ha. Most of them were your fault, young lady, but Justin got blamed." Ruth's voice scolded but Hallie saw her lips twitch.

"Jo Beth, meet Elise's mother, Hallie Barron."

Without a self-conscious bone in her body, the young woman looked Hallie over then extended her hand.

"Hi, Mrs. Barron. Pleased to meet you."

"You, too, Jo Beth, and please, call me Hallie."

"Okay, Hallie, I will."

Shooing with her dishtowel, Ruth ushered them back into the kitchen. "We better get the food on the table. The men will be in soon."

Jo Beth gave Hallie a speculative appraisal. "So, Hallie, is anything going on between you and Simon?"

Ruth popped Jo Beth with the dishtowel. "Jo Beth, where are your manners?"

Rubbing her backside, she danced out of Ruth's line of fire. "I was just asking."

"Well, mind your own business, young lady."

Hallie laughed at the young woman's brashness. "In fact, Jo Beth, Simon pretty much just tolerates me. We don't see eye-to-eye on many things."

"Hmmm. That's too bad."

Footsteps at the back door and male voices announced the men's arrival. Jo Beth stood behind the door and when they entered she yelled, "Surprise!"

"Oh, my Lord, look what the wind blew in. Hey, Red." Justin lifted her off her feet in a bear hug.

"Hey, yourself, Cuz. What do you mean getting

85

engaged without telling me?" She swatted at him.

Justin grinned and shrugged.

She watched Simon at the kitchen sink where he washed up. "Don't you have a greeting for your favorite cousin, old man?"

He looked toward the door. "You mean your brother's here?"

She stomped her foot and turned away.

Circling her waist from behind, he lifted her, flipping her feet high into the air.

Taken by surprise, she screeched. The air whooshed from her lungs. Gasping, she said, "Put me down, Simon. You might hurt me."

Her yell puzzled him. Now concern etched his face. "When has a little horse play hurt you?" He looked her over from head to toe. "You're not sick are you?" Taking her arm, he walked her to a chair and settled her into it.

She gazed around at everyone watching her with concern. "Y'all sit down. I have an announcement to make."

All eyes on her, not saying a word, they found their chairs and sat waiting for her to speak. Ruth's face lost its color, worry etched her brow. Simon's mouth cut a grim line across his face and if Hallie wasn't mistaken, his chin trembled a little.

Jo Beth reached for Ruth's hand as tears gathered in her eyes. Voice thick with emotion, she said, "I'm pregnant. I'm pregnant at last."

Crying, Ruth reached out for Jo Beth. They embraced while crying then broke into joyous laughter.

Simon rounded the table and put his long arms around them both. "Jo Beth, honey, that's wonderful news. But, don't scare us like that again. I thought you were dying, for gosh sakes."

He stepped back so Justin could give her a hug. "What does Paul think about having a baby?"

She laughed. "He's so puffed up he had trouble buttoning his shirt this morning."

Hallie and Elise added their congratulations.

"Oh, thank you. I can't tell you how happy I am, as I've been trying to get pregnant for two years. We'd about given up hope."

Ruth stood, mopping at her eyes with her apron. "I better get breakfast on the table before it's not fit to eat."

Hallie patted Ruth's shoulder. "You sit down and visit with Jo Beth. Elise and I'll bring the food to the table."

"Oh, I couldn't let you do that."

"Yes, you can, Mama. Sit down." Simon's eyes reached Hallie's. His smile conveyed his thanks.

Ruth sat down. "Thank you, dears."

Jo Beth looked around. "By the way, where's Whitney?"

A door slammed upstairs. When Whitney saw her cousin, she ran down the stairs. "Jo Beth, Jo Beth!" She flew into her cousin's arms and was pulled onto her lap.

"How's my girl?"

"I'm good. Did you meet Justin's girlfriend? Isn't she pretty? See my fingernails. She painted them for me but Uncle Simon said only on special occasions."

Jo Beth looked at her nails. "Pretty color. What's the occasion, pumpkin?"

Whitney shrugged. Her "I don't know" made them laugh.

Breakfast was a rowdy affair, the family glad to have Jo Beth with them and basking in her news.

"Paul will be here tonight, Aunt Ruth. Will you have enough room for us to spend the night?"

"Of course we will. I bet Elise won't mind bunking with Whitney or her mother. You can have her room."

Whitney bounced in her chair. "Oh boy, Elise. You get to sleep in my room. Will you tell me some stories?"

"You bet. But, I don't know many so you may have to tell me some."

Jo Beth perused Simon and Justin. "You guys plan to take these ladies to the street dance tonight, don't you?"

The two men exchanged looks. "We hadn't thought about it. Didn't remember it was this weekend," said Justin. He regarded Elise's eager face. "But it you want to go, I'll take you both."

"Simon, you're not going to stay here, are you? If you do, Aunt Ruth won't go. So, you have to come."

Simon knew she spoke the truth. Mama would think she needed to stay to cook him supper. Time away from the ranch would be good for her. Just because he went didn't mean he had to dance with Hallie. He might ask for one dance to be polite.

"Okay, I'll go. Why don't we make a night of it and eat supper in town?"

* * *

Paul arrived before they left. Hallie liked him right off. Tall and lanky with blond hair, his smile for Jo Beth left no doubt as to his love for her. He received lots of ribbing from the men on his impending fatherhood, most of it from Chester.

"We got a mare about to foal next week, Paul. I'll give you a call so you can come out to experience birth first hand." He cackled. "Then you'll be ready for that natural childbirth the women find so important these days."

Paul blushed scarlet but took the joking in stride. It was obvious, though he'd grown up in the city, the ranch hands liked him and respected the fact he could handle their tomfoolery.

Hallie rode with Simon and Ruth in Ruth's car while the kids, with Whitney in tow, rode in the car with Paul and Jo Beth. It was a pleasant drive.

"This road is nice and smooth for a country road." She glanced at Simon and watched his neck turn red. "Nothing like the old bumpy road we drove in on Saturday morning."

He threw her a dirty look. She grinned.

"What!" cried Ruth? "You don't mean to tell me you drove in on the old road to the cabin." She leaned up from the back seat to place her hand on Simon's shoulder. "Please tell me you didn't give her those directions on purpose."

"Guilty as charged, Mama. I've already apologized so don't wring me out about it again."

Ruth scooted back on the seat and mumbled. "Lord, have mercy, what could the boy have been thinking?"

* * *

The town square glowed with old-fashioned street lamps. Colorful lights outlined stands where beer, roasted corn, and other goodies were sold. Sawdust covered the makeshift dance area, a blocked off street, to make shuffling easier. In the center of the dance floor, a tall dead tree was affixed to a metal anchor and from its bare branches hung small coal oil lanterns. Metal benches and sawhorses surrounded the area and the glow from the lit lanterns gave off enough light to give the area an intimate feel.

Simon watched Hallie as she absorbed her surroundings, waiting to see derision on her face. Her comment surprised him.

"This is charming." She beamed her pleasure. "Someone's gone to a lot of trouble to make this a success."

He breathed easier and smiled. "The town has a committee to make all the arrangements." He turned back to the lighted tree, pleased with the group's hard work. "They try to do something different every year."

"Bet they have a good time doing it, too."

The band started warming up as Paul and Jo Beth joined them with drinks in their hands.

Simon took Jo Beth's hand, the one holding her drink, leaned forward and took a sip.

She slapped his hand. "What're you doing? Go get your own."

"Just checking to make sure you're not drinking alcohol."

Jo Beth bristled. "You think I'd do anything to hurt this baby?"

Simon threw his hands up in mock surrender. "No. But, I couldn't help checking. You know I adore you both and can't help but be a little protective."

Tears made her eyes sparkle. She moved to his side and put her arm around his waist. His arm pulled her close. "I love you, too. But, Paul stays on me enough, so cut me some slack, will you?"

Paul put his hand on Simon's shoulder. "She's been mighty emotional, Simon. One of those hormonal things?"

Before he could reply, the mayor appeared on the small stage opposite where they stood.

"Welcome, ladies and gentlemen, to our biannual street dance." Applause accompanied by hoots and whistles echoed throughout the crowd. "Remember the rules now folks. No one under age will be drinking. All young children need to stay in the entertainment area designed for them. There will be no over imbibing or being rowdy. In other words, that means no getting drunk or fighting else you'll be escorted to the jail for a nap." The gathering crowd laughed and applauded.

He held up his hands for quiet. "Now, we want everyone to have a good time tonight, to get home safe and sound. So pick out your designated driver right now." His eyes surveyed the crowd and locked on a group of young men. "Skeeter, who is your designated driver?" The crowd roared as the young man, sheepish grin on his face, pointed to one of his friends.

"Okay, let's get this show on the road. I'd like a big hand for our band tonight, the Texas Kickers."

Simon leaned toward Hallie, and yelled into her ear to be heard over the music and applause. "Can I get you a beer or something?"

Tapping her toe to the music, she smiled and shook her head no. She grabbed his collar and pulled him down to her level to be heard. "You go ahead and get you something. You don't have to hang around me all night. I'll be fine."

Though he wanted to stay with her, he knew he shouldn't. He was too attracted to her. It would be easy to forget she wasn't the one for him. "Are you sure?"

"Positive."

No sooner were the words out of her mouth, and she was pulled into the arms of a cowboy and swung onto the dance floor.

He'd wait a minute to see if she'd need rescuing. Grinning like she was having the time of her life, she kept step with the young man. Her hair shone in the lamplight, flying out as she swung to the music. She was beautiful. Face aglow, her laughter drifted on the night air, and from the looks of the men on the sideline, he wasn't alone in his appreciation.

In the crowd of dancers, he noticed Jo Beth and Paul. Jo Beth stared at him with a knowing smile on her face. Thunderation. He didn't need her thinking he was interested in Hallie. Playing it cool, he smiled and wove his way through the dancers to his cousin.

With his index finger he prodded Paul on the shoulder. "Hey, partner. Can I dance with my cousin a minute?"

"You bet, buddy. But don't keep her long. There are too many single cowboys scouting for a pretty woman to dance with tonight. I don't want to be a wallflower like them."

Simon laughed. "Okay, lover boy. I'll escort her back to you."

It was a slow number and Jo Beth settled into his arms like a comfortable shoe. They'd danced like this many times when she was a teenager. Though fifteen years older, he made sure she always had someone to dance with at these functions. If not him, then a friend he trusted. When she started dating, he watched her boyfriends like a hawk. She was more his sister than a cousin.

"I sure like seeing you so happy, Jo Beth. If I didn't tell you earlier, I'm thrilled about the baby. We need some more little ones to spoil."

"You need to be having some of your own, Simon." She reached up with her left hand and yanked on his hair. "Why aren't you out there dancing with that gorgeous woman?"

"Ouch, that hurt." He yanked his head back then looked around. "What woman?"

"Don't play dumb with me. I saw you observing her with hungry eyes."

"Hungry eyes? Who are you talking about?"

She reached for his hair again but he jerked his head out of the way. "You know who I'm talking about. Hallie, the beautiful woman staying at your house."

"I admit she's beautiful, and hell yes I'm attracted to her, but we have nothing in common. I don't intend to get involved with a woman when there's no future for us."

"What do you mean? No future? She's perfect for you."

The music stopped and they stood glaring at each other, hands on their hips. If one weren't short, the other tall, they'd look like carbon copies. When they both noticed their "I mean business" stance, they laughed.

Simon took off his hat and smoothed his hair back. "Jo Beth, she's a city woman, one like Loretta. I will not get involved with someone tied to the city."

She poked him in the chest with her finger. "Simon, I swear, someone needs to beat you over the head and knock some sense in you. Not every city woman is like Loretta."

"I'd appreciate it if you'd drop the subject and not bring it up again." He grabbed the finger waving in front of his face as she floundered for words.

"I mean it, Jo Beth. Leave it alone."

"Hey, you two. No fussing." Paul grabbed Jo Beth around the waist. "Did she step all over your toes, Simon?"

"Something like that." He waved goodbye and walked toward one of the beverage booths.

Susan Bitters, Susan Calloway last year, was serving. The current gossip said Sam Bitters, her third and current husband, wouldn't be her last.

"Hey, Simon. What'll it be?"

"I'll take a beer."

As she filled a plastic glass from the tap, Simon watched her study him with her painted blue eyes. She'd always worn too much makeup, even in high school. Tonight was no exception.

"You're looking good, Simon. Still not married?"

He noticed the familiar glint in her eye. "Nope. Not in the market either."

"Well, bust my bubble, will you?" Her bright red lips formed a pout. Then she grinned.

He laughed and walked toward the bench where Ruth sat with Paul and Jo Beth.

Jo Beth grabbed his hat to fan herself with. "Shew we, it's hot."

Paul stood, eyes locked on a couple in the crowd. "Simon, I think you better cut in on that guy dancing with Hallie. Looks like she's trying to get out of the choke hold he has on her."

Simon rose to stare in the direction Paul pointed.

Blood rushed to his face when he saw the man's big hand move to her butt and jerk her toward him. His other arm was around her neck. Damned if he wasn't trying to kiss her. Rage throbbed in his head as he plowed his way through the dancers, many moving back to watch his progress. All of a sudden, Hallie was free and the man was bent double using both hands to hold his crotch.

Justin reached Hallie's side before him. Chester and another self-appointed deputy hauled the fool to his feet and off toward the jail. Hallie's face was as red as his felt. He'd expected to see tears but she appeared in control.

"Hallie, are you alright?" Justin examined her.

She leaned in and hugged him. "I'm fine, Justin. Mad as a hatter, but I'll live."

Simon nodded at Justin and took Hallie's arm. "How about a cold drink?" He led her to the long seat where Ruth, Jo Beth, and Paul sat.

A little shaky from fear, anger and adrenalin, Hallie was grateful for Simon's strong arm. "Thanks, yes, I'll have a beer."

Ruth put her arms around her and hugged. "Honey, are you alright? That scared me to death." She leaned toward Hallie, so both women could hear her. She whispered, "But you sure knew how to rattle his balls."

Jo Beth gasped. "Aunt Ruth. I'm shocked to hear you mention a man's balls."

"Well, sugar, they weren't invented this generation. They've been around since the beginning of time." She pinched her cheek. "You kids think we older folks lived a sheltered life."

Jo Beth leaned in over Hallie's shoulder. "Ruth,

did you see the look on Simon's face when he plowed through that crowd trying to reach Hallie?" She glanced behind her to see if Simon was returning. "I thought he might commit murder." With a wink at Hallie, she added, "I think he's sweet on you, Hallie."

"I don't think so," Hallie sputtered. "And I don't want him to be."

"We'll see," Jo Beth added with a scheming grin.

Paul grabbed her hand and pulled her up. "You better stay out of your cousin's business before you cause hard feelings between the two of you."

"Oh, pooh, Paul. Giving them a little help won't hurt anything."

"I mean it, Jo Beth. No meddling."

Simon returned with three beers. "Jo Beth and Paul dancing again?"

"Yes, son. Paul drug her out there before she got herself into trouble by interfering in other people's business." She shook her head and took a drink of her beer.

Simon sat down on the bench with his long legs stretched out in front crossed at the ankles. He watched Hallie tapping her foot while watching the dancers. Several men approached, eyes on Hallie, but one glance at Simon's glare and they turned the other way. He wasn't going to let her go through another groping experience. Ah, hell. That wasn't fair. Most of the men around here were decent and respectful of women. He squinted at his watch in the low light. It was almost time for them to head home. Saturday was another workday for him. Justin might be able to hang out half the night and still put in a full day's work the following day but Simon's body would rebel.

Before he knew what happened, Joe Booker, president of the bank, had Hallie's arm leading her onto the dance floor. He looked at Mama to see her reaction.

"That's about the fourth time they've danced this evening. Joe must find Hallie good company."

Simon stood up and bowed before her. "How about a dance, Mama?"

"I'd love to dance, Son." She put her arm around his shoulder and kissed his cheek. "You're such a good son, Simon. Have I ever told you how proud of you I am?"

"Lots of times, Mama." He kissed her hair. "And, you've told me I'm almost as good a dancer as Daddy was."

"Oh, your daddy could out dance any man in the county. He was the handsomest, too."

Several dances later, Justin tapped Simon on the shoulder. "Gran, how about a dance?"

"I'd love one, Justin." She gazed around. "But, where's Elise?"

"She's dancing with Paul and Jo Beth's with Chester." He asked Simon. "Where's Hallie? I haven't seen her in a while."

"She's still dancing with Joe Booker," said Ruth. "That man's monopolized her most of the night."

Simon looked around until he spotted the couple. Joe had danced with her long enough. As he approached, he noticed Joe held her closer than what Simon considered proper.

Joe saw him coming, grinned and swung Hallie in the opposite direction. Quick on his feet, Simon maneuvered through the throng of dancers and landed a tap on his shoulder. "Excuse me, Joe, I believe this is my dance with Hallie."

He'd been right the first day he met her—her head did fit just under his chin. The scent that reached his nostrils was as he remembered it, clean and spicy with a hint of floral. Her softness sent jolts of heat thundering through his veins causing him to grow hard with need. His body and heart craved what his mind told him to avoid. Unable to resist, he pulled her closer, folded her arm and laid her right hand over his heart.

The song, "Born to Lose", was a slow number, one for lovers. His hand ran up her back to cup her neck before settling it at her waist.

Hallie responded to the desire emanating from Simon, causing an ache at the core of her body. Her heartbeat matched the rapid rhythm of his under her hand. As he sang the words, his voice, low and husky in her ear, a tingle shot through her body. She trembled, longing washing over her. *Oh, God. This isn't good.* She couldn't fall for this man, a man she didn't trust and one who didn't trust her.

When the music ended, they remained close for a minute, and then parted.

Simon cleared his throat. "Are you ready to leave? I imagine Mama's tired and tomorrow is a work day for us."

She nodded.

With his hand at her waist, he escorted her back to where Elise and Justin sat with Ruth. "Justin, we're headed home. Let Jo Beth drive. She's not drinking."

"We will, Uncle Simon." He kissed his grandmother goodnight, then turn to Simon.

"How about we start work a little later in the morning?"

"All right. We'll have breakfast around nine. That'll give us time to visit with Jo Beth and Paul before they leave."

* * *

A short distance away, Corbett Porter watched his younger cousin, Caitlyn, observe the kiss between Justin and his new girl. She turned away in pain. He hated to see her hurting, but he couldn't fault a man for marrying a woman he loved. Thing is, he'd always believed Caitlyn that woman. If Justin weren't one of his best friends, he'd stomp his ass. He might have to anyway. It depended on the answers he got.

He pushed away from the storefront wall and moved toward the couple.

Caitlyn grabbed him by the arm. "Where are you going? Don't go starting any trouble. Please, Corbett."

He patted the hand attached to his arm. "Don't you worry, Cuz. I'm going over to say hello and meet this paragon of womanhood."

She brushed back a tear and smiled at his remark. "Promise there won't be any trouble."

"I promise. Now, quit turning down all those requests for dances and try to have a good time. Don't let him see you crying over him."

When Justin saw him coming, he smiled and stood, drawing the young woman with him.

Justin extended his hand. "Hi, Corbett. I didn't know you were home. It's good to see you."

Corbett returned Justin's handshake. "I'm taking the summer off from school. Going to work with Doc Adams, get some hands-on experience."

"It'll be great having you around." He put his arm around Elise. "Elise, I'd like you to meet one of my best friends, Corbett Porter, Caitlyn's cousin."

Elise smiled and offered her hand. "I'm glad to meet you, Corbett."

The smile dazzled him. She was a beauty, a natural one that didn't need much makeup to enhance her features. Her long blond hair complemented a creamy complexion and blue eyes. Though tall and thin, she filled out her jeans with feminine curves. He removed his hat.

"The pleasure is mine, Elise." He took her small hand in his large work-roughened one and kissed her knuckles. A jolt of electricity startled him. He lifted his eyes to hers.

She jerked her hand back.

"Hey, friend. This lady is taken."

He tore his eyes from hers and cleared his throat. Though Justin's words were teasing, he knew he meant business. "Justin, we need to talk. Can you meet me at the swimming hole in the morning at 10:00?"

"Yeah, I can be there."

"See you there then." He tipped his hat to Elise, then turned and walked away.

CHAPTER SIX

Carrying his boots, trying not to wake the household, Simon walked down the stairs in his sock feet. Soft humming drifted from the kitchen along with the aroma of fresh coffee. Hallie stood at the sink looking out the window.

"Good morning, you're up early."

She jumped at the sound of his voice spilling some of her coffee. Hand over her heart, she gasped. "You startled me." Her smile made her mouth tilt to one side emphasizing a dimple in her cheek. "What about you? I thought you'd take advantage of the extra sleep time." With a paper towel, she wiped up the spill. He poured a cup for himself and sighed as the warm brew hit his stomach.

"Nah. I never sleep late. That was for Justin's benefit. I said breakfast at nine o'clock but it wouldn't surprise me if Mama delayed breakfast until ten. I don't expect we'll get any work done until after noon. "He studied her face, void of makeup, clean and natural. Small lines curved out from her eyes and beside her mouth. Each day he admired this woman more. She knew how to work, didn't complain, and was good company. Without thinking, he blurted, "You look good without makeup."

She flushed. "Uh…thanks."

To cover his remark, he lifted the pot. "You want

to finish this off outside?"

"Yeah. Sure."

Outside, he sat the glass *carafe* on a small table between their two chairs. Still dark out, it was comfortable by the pool—cool, quiet and peaceful. They drank their coffee in companionable silence and watched the sun rise. He studied her when she wasn't paying attention.

He refilled her cup and topped off his. "You have any plans this morning?"

"No, nothing in particular."

"I'm riding over to my ranch this morning to check on things." Nobody ever bothered the place but he liked having an excuse to go. "You're welcome to join me."

"I'd like that. Let me put on my boots and get my hat." She carried their cups and the coffee pot in on her way.

"I'll start saddling the horses."

In less than ten minutes she stood beside him in the barn. Over her tee-shirt, she wore a long sleeved cotton shirt to protect her arms from the sun. Her old straw hat looked well loved. Folks around here called it a "shady Brady." Where it got that name he didn't know. Must be something about the way the brim curled on the sides. It could be reshaped, if necessary, for more sun protection.

"You have any food at your house? I don't know if I can make it there and back without food."

"Yeah. I've got all sorts of frozen stuff in the freezer. Nothing fresh though."

They walked the horses side by side. "It feels good to be out. I need some physical exercise."

"Seems to me you got plenty of exercise last

night."

Her laugh rang out. "I guess I did." Her face echoed her pleasure. "I had a wonderful time. People around here are nice."

"Tell me about this farm you used to live on. Is it still in your family?"

"No. Daddy sold it after we were all grown. He and Mama couldn't work it by themselves any longer and my brothers weren't interested in farming. He got enough money to buy Mama a house in town then split the remainder between us three kids." Her face glowed as she talked. Her memories of life on the farm must be pleasant ones. "It was rich black soil in the north Blacklands area of Texas."

Simon whistled. "Expensive dirt."

"Yeah, daddy got over a thousand an acre in 1980. Both my brothers were struggling in college so the money made their final years much easier. I wanted to get married so daddy gave me money to put away for the future."

"And did you?"

Surprised, she said. "Of course I did. I never touched it, even when I was pregnant with Elise and we needed it so bad. James wouldn't let me. He was in his third year of college and working a full time job. Thank goodness I had insurance with my job or I don't know how we'd have made it."

Most women he knew would have spent the money as quick as the bank cashed the check. It appeared James and Hallie had worked hard for what they had.

"Then, in 1982, James's father died. His brother didn't want to keep their family farm. We didn't have the money to buy him out so they sold it. James never got over losing the land—over a thousand acres. He invested the money. When he died, he left us well provided for."

"Sounds like James was a smart man. One I'd have enjoyed knowing."

"I think he would have liked you, too."

What would it have been like to know James and Hallie years ago? Would he have been as attracted to her if she'd been someone's wife? Lord, he hoped not.

"How about we kick these horses into a gallop? Race you to the top of that little hill over there."

She looked around. "Which one?"

"That—" She was off before the word exited his mouth.

He touched his heels to his horse. Anxious to join the race, Redman shot forward like a rocket. "Go get 'um, boy."

Hallie was bent over Sadie's neck, leaving Simon with a view of Sadie's tail flying, hooves kicking up clods and Hallie's rounded tush. "Come on, boy. We can catch 'um."

In less than a minute he'd overtaken the smaller horse. Simon held Redman back to stay abreast of Sadie then let him move forward to reach the hilltop first.

Simon pulled Redman up beside Sadie. Face flushed with excitement, Hallie laughed out, "That was fun. I haven't ridden fast in years."

"Don't get to ride much in the city, huh?" Nose in the air, she ignored his remark. Grinning, he added. "You're welcome to come here to ride anytime you want."

Cutting her eyes to his to see if he was serious or teasing, she nodded. "Thanks, I'll remember your offer."

"Look below there. That's my home, the house where we grew up. My grandparents lived here before Mom and Dad." Soon he'd be back there. Sidney's house didn't feel like home, even after living there three years. His heart was in the building below. He watched Hallie as she absorbed the view.

* * *

Hallie studied the white farmhouse settled in the surrounding live oaks, mesquite and prickly pear. It had two stories with clapboard siding, tin roof and wrap around porch. Two of the rooms upstairs had dormers.

"Simon, it's charming." She kicked Sadie and started down the slope. "I love the clapboard siding. Our farmhouse had it too." He smiled with pleasure at her comments. He was proud of his home. Hallie liked the old house's character.

They dismounted near the front porch. Simon handed her the keys. "You go on in. I'll tend to the horses. There's coffee in the freezer if you want to start a pot."

The front door opened to a wide hallway that ran from front to back. Each door had a transom above for air circulation. A quick glance told her the living room was on the right and the dining room to her left. Behind it she found the kitchen. Big and airy, a long family table in front of a fireplace dominated the room. The linoleum was old, cracked in places but clean. Centered on the wall across from the fireplace stood an old Chamber's cook stove flanked by counter space. The large sink, the old rounded refrigerator and additional counter space covered the adjacent wall.

Locating the drip coffee maker on the counter, she

rinsed it and within minutes had coffee brewing. Rummaging through the freezer, she found frozen pancakes and frozen precooked bacon. She snickered. Looks like the bachelor didn't like to cook.

Simon knocked on the back door. She let him in. Hanging his hat on the rack by the door, he walked to the sink to wash his hands. "I see you found my emergency stash."

"I did. Are you saying you didn't eat like this when you lived here?"

"No. Mom did the cooking. But, she insisted we learn to cook the basics. I can make a mean pancake. If I had the supplies I'd prove it."

"That's all right. I believe you." From the look on his face, she could tell he wasn't sure if she teased or not.

"I'll get the coffee and set the table while you cook." She couldn't hold in her giggle.

"You wait, I'll prove I can cook before you guys leave." He grabbed plates, filled each with three pancakes and bacon then nuked them one at a time. "Sorry, no butter or syrup."

She took a bite of her pancakes. Not bad at all. "No problem. They're fine by themselves." Hungry, they concentrated on eating. Finished, she sat their plates in the sink and refilled their cups.

"That's a beautiful old stove. My grandmother had one. I think she was prouder of it than the new Frigidaire Granddad came home with. Of course, she cooked for a big family and needed something designed for quantity cooking."

"This one was my granny's, too. Daddy tried to get a new one when he and Mama moved in but she wouldn't hear of it." He looked around the kitchen at the cabinets and appliances. "This room could use a lot of work. But, it suits me fine."

"It's a beautiful room. A coat of paint and new linoleum would do wonders. But, be sure you pick out a floor that's consistent with the time period of the house." She was anxious to see the rest of the home. On her way in, she could see wood floors, rag rugs and turn of the century furniture. "Can I look through the rest of the house?"

"Sure. Go ahead. I need to check the barns and out buildings. Take your time." He grabbed his hat and went out.

The dishes washed and put away, she unplugged the coffee pot and started her tour. Across from the kitchen was a large bedroom, doubtless the master. The bedroom furniture, made of tiger oak, had a headboard almost eight feet tall. Off the large hallway she found a bathroom complete with a claw foot tub. Upstairs she found four more bedrooms and two bathrooms. One of the bathrooms was modernized with a stall shower.

By the time she'd explored the downstairs, Simon was back. They locked the house and mounted their horses.

"Thanks for bringing me with you."

"You're welcome. I enjoyed the company." His smile was sincere. "I've been meaning to tell you, I was wrong to judge Elise before meeting her."

Surprised at his confession, Hallie studied his facial expressions as he continued. "I still think she'll have a difficult time here, but she's not spoiled and knows how to work. Those traits will go a long way in helping her make a place for herself."

"Do you mean you no longer disapprove of their marriage?" For some reason she felt teary.

"No. I don't. I hate like hell Caitlyn was hurt. But that's part of life. Sometimes it can't be helped." They rode in silence for a while. "Justin's ranch is in financial trouble."

His statement wasn't a surprise. He'd briefly mentioned it at their first meeting though she wasn't sure he remembered doing so. She'd suspected this was a part of the reason for Simon's earlier animosity. Loretta bore responsibility for the other half.

"Sidney's divorce sapped it of stock and capital." He shook his head. "I have enough money put back to help Justin but doubt he'd take it. I've been thinking. The best way for him to get operating capital is to sell off some land. I've mentioned it to him but nothing's settled."

"Oh, no. There has to be another way."

He shook his head. "If there is, I haven't found it yet."

"Simon, I have some money put away." He started to protest. "No. Wait and let me explain. It wouldn't be a loan, but an investment. I could have papers drawn up that would protect us both."

"It's good of you to offer, but I don't think it's a good idea. You never know when you might need your money."

"I assure you, Simon, I wouldn't offer if I couldn't spare the money. At least think about it."

"Okay, I'll give it some thought. But, it will be Justin's decision. I can't see him wanting to take help from his mother-in-law."

She hoped Justin would consider it. That way the

ranch could stay intact.

"By, the way, Mama and I are having the annual Cole barbecue next Saturday night. We'll announce their engagement then."

* * *

Justin tossed Jezebel a biscuit as he walked to the stall Thunder occupied. She swallowed the treat whole and rose from the pile of hay to nudge his jeans leg. He hated to see her getting feeble, her arthritis making her slow. "You're welcome, girl." He reached down to give her ears a good scratch then returned to saddling his horse.

Thunder snorted, shook his head then butted him in the chest. Justin chuckled as he stumbled back a few steps. "I didn't forget you, boy." He pulled a couple of carrots from his back pocket and held them in front of the horse. Thunder took half of both carrots in one bite. When finished, he sniffed around his pockets looking for more treats.

"That's it, boy. Can't have you getting fat." He saddled the horse and led him out of the barn. "You ready for a good ride today?"

Thunder stomped his feet in impatience. Justin pulled the reins over his head and holding onto the pommel, eased into the saddle. With a gentle nudge of his boot heels, Thunder shot forward, anxious to stretch his legs.

"Slow down, big fella. Let's warm up first." He slowed Thunder to a canter.

He munched on the biscuit and bacon sandwiches he'd grabbed before leaving the house. Not substantial, but they'd have to hold him until lunch. Another cup of hot coffee would be great but a drink from his canteen would have to do.

Dusting crumbs off his hands, he leaned forward in the saddle. "Okay, boy, let's do it."

Justin bent low over Thunder as they streaked across the strip of pastureland. He couldn't stifle the "Yee haw" of joy that erupted from his throat at the thrill of speed.

He let Thunder stretch his legs and then slowed him back to a canter. Overhead the sun beamed down making it hot. His shirt, damp with sweat, stuck to his back. Removing his hat, he wiped the perspiration from his forehead with his shirtsleeve.

As he approached the tank they called a swimming hole, he slowed Thunder to a fast walk. Memories washed through his mind and he smiled. They had great fun here as kids, swimming, fishing and overnight campouts. One time Caitlyn caught them skinny-dipping. She'd laughed and taunted them threatening to take their clothes. Corbett called her bluff. "You take one step closer, brat, and I'm coming out of the water. And when I catch you, I'll blister your butt." She'd stuck her tongue out and started down the slope toward them. Not a shy bone in his body, Corbett stood up, started toward her. Caitlyn screamed, covered her eyes, then turned and ran. Of course, she was twelve at the time. If she'd been a couple of years older, she'd have run off with their clothes without any warning. For safety's sake, they started tying their clothes to their saddles. If she took the horses, a whistle would bring them running back.

Dismounting, he led Thunder to the water for a drink before letting him graze on the grassy bank. He sat down then laid back, arms folded under his head and looked up at the sky. What would Corbett have to say to him? Wouldn't surprise him if he wanted to deck him in private rather than create a public spectacle last night.

Approaching hoof beats and Thunder's nicker of greeting announced Corbett's arrival. Justin stayed where he was, stretched out on the bank.

"Glad to see you're on time, buddy."

Justin yawned. "Seems to me you were the one always late, friend."

"Yeah, maybe a time or two." Corbett sat down on the grass a short distance from him. "Not often, though."

"I doubt you asked me here to talk about old times. What'd you want to talk to me about, Corbett?"

Corbett sat in silence, thinking. Justin observed as he pulled a blade of grass and watched it spin as he rolled it between his thumb and index finger. With dead calm, he said, "I want to know why the hell you broke Caitlyn's heart."

Corbett's dark brown eyes looked almost black with anger. He'd seen that expression enough times to know he was reining in as much of it as possible. He and Caitlyn favored each other so much—both dark headed with brown eyes. While Caitlyn was petite, Corbett was over six feet and all muscle. Both were cursed with the Porter temper.

Justin shook his head. "Things wouldn't have worked out for the two of us. I told her in March we needed to see other people. She didn't like the idea but accepted it." He leaned up and sat with ankles crossed, Indian style. "I wish I could've talked to her before she got to the ranch. Never dreamed she'd come over so late."

111

"Why'd that surprise you? When's Caitlyn ever done the usual thing?"

"Yeah, you're right. But she wasn't supposed to be home until the following day."

They sat in silence for a moment.

"I always thought you loved Caitlyn, Justin. Hell, I envied your relationship and wondered if there would ever be someone special for me."

Corbett's comment caused an ache in the region of Justin's heart. "I do...did love Caitlyn. But marriage between us would never work." He removed his hat and scrubbed his head with his fingertips to lift the damp hair away from his scalp. "I need a mother figure for Whitney, someone stable and responsible who'll be a good example. Gram and Uncle Simon need to get on with their own lives. Caitlyn is too wild and immature."

* * *

Caitlyn was reckless and impetuous. Corbett couldn't deny that. "Do you love Elise?"

"Yes, I do. She's a special woman, exactly what I need in a wife."

Corbett could see Justin believed he was doing the right thing, but he had to ask. He studied his friend, gauging his answers. "Are you passionate about her? Does she make you so hot you don't think you'll live another minute if you can't make love to her?"

Justin's look was defensive. "There's more to marriage than passion, Corbett, but yeah, she makes me hot."

"Maybe. But, I don't think you desire her with the intensity you felt for Caitlyn." He'd never seen two people more aware of each other than Justin and Caitlyn. The heat that simmered between them was almost visible. "You better be damn sure you know what you want out of marriage."

"I know." He got up off the grass and dusted his jeans. "I appreciate your concern. Was there anything else you wanted to discuss?"

"No." Corbett stood and they walked toward their horses. He offered his hand. "Good luck to you, Justin."

Justin took it and returned his firm grip. "Thanks. Hope you'll come to the wedding."

"I'll be there." He turned to mount, then stopped and turned back around. "Oh, there's one more thing."

"Yeah?"

Before he could complete his question, Corbett slammed his fist into Justin's face, sending him stumbling back into Thunder before landing on his butt.

He watched as his friend rubbed his hand over his jaw to see if anything was broken. "Why the hell did you do that?"

"For hurting Caitlyn. Figured you deserved it." Corbett mounted his horse and rode off at a full gallop.

* * *

"Gran, Gran, come quick. Justin's been fighting and gots a busted face." Whitney jumped up and down. "It wasn't me this time, Gran."

Justin studied the smug look on Whitney's face as she lectured. "Ammmm, Justin, you're in big trouble now. Uncle Simon is going to punish you. He doesn't like fighting."

Ruth walked from the kitchen into the den. She grabbed his chin and turned it so she could better see the discoloring bruise. "Move your lower jaw from side-to-side. Now, up and down." Satisfied nothing was broken, she asked, "Any teeth loose?"

"No, Gran. I'm fine. You can stop worrying about me."

Snorting, she said, "That'll be the day." She walked back into the kitchen.

"Elise, be a dear and put some ice in a dishtowel and hold it on his face for a while to keep the swelling down."

Elise rushed to get the ice then returned to his side. "What on earth did you fight about?"

Justin snorted. "There wasn't a fight. Corbett decked me as we were leaving."

"What on earth for? I thought he was your best friend. That's what you said last night."

"For hurting Caitlyn. And he's still my best friend." He hated to admit it, but he could have handled the situation better—called Caitlyn or written her. "I deserved it. I didn't handle the situation with Caitlyn like I should have."

From the kitchen, Ruth added, "You're right about that. But, that's no reason for Corbett to get violent. I'll be having a few words with the boy next time we meet."

Justin grinned. "Poor Corbett." He leaned in to kiss Elise.

Whitney, finger down her throat, made gagging noises. "Yuck."

He reached for her and started tickling her under the arms. She squealed and laughed with pleasure until he turned her loose. "Get out of here, squirt, so I can kiss my girl without the sound effects coming from you."

She propped her hands on her hips. "I'm going to go tell Uncle Simon what you've been up to so he can be thinking on your punishment."

"I hate to tell you this, missy, but I'm too old to punish."

"Uh-uh. You are not." She stuck her tongue out at him.

"Uh-huh. I am too." He reached out to swat her on the bottom. She darted out of his reach and made a beeline for the back door.

"Justin, from what I hear from everyone, you and Caitlyn were deeply in love. What happened? Why did you break things off with her?"

It was an awkward question, but she had a right to know. "Caitlyn is impetuous sometimes. You saw how she rode over here the other night. She could have broken her neck and destroyed a valuable horse." He picked up her hand and entwined their fingers. "I guess I outgrew her. I was afraid she was too much like my mother, that she wouldn't be happy with the simple life. Her folks have spoiled her by giving her everything she wants." Drawing their hands to his lips, he kissed her knuckles. "When I met you, I fell in love and decided you were what I wanted in a wife."

"Are you sure you no longer have feelings for Caitlyn, Justin? If you have any doubts, now is the time to say so."

"No doubts, Elise."

He stood up and grabbed his hat off the table. "Guess I better get out there and get some work done before lunch." Leaning down, he kissed her, taking his time, teasing her lips until she put her arms around his waist.

* * *

Whitney sat on a bale of hay with Jezebel at her

feet. "But that's not fair, Uncle Simon. I get punished when I fight."

Simon sighed and added more oil to the bridle and rubbed it in. How could he make her understand punishment in adulthood came from within oneself?

"You know how adults don't have to ask permission to do things they want to do?" He glanced over to make sure she followed him. "Say I wanted to go to town. I wouldn't have to ask Gran, I'd say, 'Mama, I'm going to town but I'll be home in time for supper.' And, I'd try hard to be home because I wouldn't want her to worry or have to hold my supper late because it would make extra work for her. That's what we call being considerate."

Her head bobbed. "Yeah, but I'm considerate."

"Yes, you are. But, you're not grown up, yet, and haven't learned all the lessons of life. So, when you do something wrong, you get punished. Then you'll remember the punishment and not make the same mistake again. When a grown-up does something wrong, it hurts them in here." He brought his fist to his heart. "He feels guilty and wants to make things right by apologizing or paying for the property he destroyed. Justin learned his lessons when he was a boy, and since he's a grown man now, he'll be punishing himself."

He hung the bridle up and turned back to her. "Now, when an adult breaks the law, that's a different story. The police issue the punishment and it may be going to jail."

Whitney scooted off the hay bale. "Is it time for lunch now? I'm hungry."

He scooped her up, and lifted her atop his shoulders. "I believe it is, cupcake. Let's go see."

* * *

Justin hugged Ruth, and gave her a loud "smooch" on her cheek. "Great lunch, Gran." He rubbed his belly. "I may have to take a nap now." He winked at Elise to see if his comment would bait Simon.

Elise watched their playful exchange.

"You must be dreaming, son." Simon whacked him on the shoulder. "We've got work to do. You'll have to do your napping at bedtime."

They headed for the door, arms slung over each other's shoulders.

Justin stopped. "Are you sure, Uncle Simon? I'm feeling kinda poorly."

Simon grabbed him around the neck and scrubbed his knuckles across the top of his head. "You're going to feel worse than poorly when I get through with you if you don't come on."

"Ouch! That hurts." He wrestled loose and grabbed Simon around the neck from behind. "Now let's see what you can do, old man."

Whitney squealed with glee. "Take him, Justin. You can do it. Get him in his ticklish spot."

"Whap! Whap!" Ruth popped them both with the dishtowel. They jerked and scrunched their rear ends out of her line of fire.

"Take your horseplay outdoors."

"Yes, ma'am," they chorused.

Whitney followed on their heels. Outside, they each grabbed a hand and swung her forward and back as they walked. Her laughter echoed across the yard.

As she turned back from the window, Elise grinned. "They're so cute."

Ruth tried to be serious but a chuckle erupted from

her throat. "I don't know how cute those two are, but they're pretty crazy about each other."

Hallie started carrying stacked dishes into the kitchen for Elise to rinse and put in the dishwasher. Ruth transferred leftover food to refrigerator containers.

"Those two kids are mighty well-adjusted after all they've been through. You and Simon have done a wonderful job." She shook her head. How on earth could Loretta leave those two precious people? In particular Whitney. Of course, Whitney wasn't grown yet, so there could still be problems.

"Ruth, does Whitney ever ask why she doesn't live with her mother?"

Ruth set the three bowls she'd stacked on top of each other, in the refrigerator, and then turned. "She used to all the time. Simon and I both tried to explain why she needed to be here but our answers didn't satisfy her. Whitney would say she understood, but she'd bring it up again a month or two later." She shook her head. "We were at a loss as to what to do. Then about a year ago, Loretta came, got a room in town at the Cottonwood Bed and Breakfast. Whitney stayed with her. She must have asked her mother that question because since then, she hasn't asked us again."

Ruth started rinsing pots and pans. "When we asked her what she and her mother had done in town, she said, 'We just talked. Oh, and we had ice cream, too.' But, from all the packages she came in with we knew they'd shopped." She chuckled. "Whitney's not as impressed with pretty clothes as she is ice cream."

"Do you think she asked her mother why she wasn't living with her?" Hallie picked up a dishrag and started drying pots as Ruth stacked them in the drainer rack.

"I expect she did. Before she came, Simon told Loretta she needed to explain some things to her." She stopped washing and shook her head. "You know, Loretta let Sidney have the kids, in part because they would hamper her lifestyle, but also because Sidney wanted them to grow up on the ranch. She saw them often, and when Sidney died in that crash, Simon begged her to let him take care of the kids."

She resumed washing, occupied with her thoughts. "Whitney couldn't understand death and kept saying, 'I know my Daddy's dead, but when's he coming home?' She clung to Simon and for days wouldn't let him put her down for more than a few minutes at a time.

"It broke Loretta's heart when Whitney wouldn't let her comfort her. I guess she knew we could give Whitney more of what she needed than she could herself so she agreed to let Whitney stay. It was the least selfish thing she's done her entire life." Her voice choked up, and tears blurred her vision. "She does love those kids and wants what's best for them."

Elise brought over tissues for Ruth.

She smiled up at her. "Thank you, sugar."

"Her actions took a lot of courage," said Hallie.

"Yes, they did." Ruth tossed the tissues in the trashcan below the sink and continued working. "You know, when they returned from town that weekend, Whitney was happy as a lark but Loretta looked bad. It was a rough couple of days for her." She drained and wiped the sink, then removed her apron. "Let's go sit down in the den and put our feet up."

They hung tea towels to dry and started the dishwasher. Elise went in search of Justin.

"Oh, this feels good. My feet hurt like the devil." She took her shoes off and propped them on the coffee table. "We're having sandwiches for supper."

"Sounds good to me." A cold meal did sound appealing in this hot weather.

"I don't doubt for a minute Loretta loved Sidney, she just couldn't live here any longer. She hated the isolation, the dust, and the hard work. And she wants Whitney to have the choice of city or ranch life. I think it's easier to adapt to city life than to ranch life." She leaned back against the sofa cushions and closed her eyes. "I know too, that if Whitney were raised in the city, she wouldn't be happy on the ranch."

Ruth was doubtless right. If Whitney visited her mother in the city, which she'd do more often as she got older, she'd know the advantages of both. Deciding what she wanted to do in life would be easier. Hallie heard Ruth's soft breathing and looked over to see Ruth's closed eyes. She was sound asleep. They'd kept her out too late the night before.

* * *

Justin sat on the same bale of hay Whitney had been on earlier. He might as well go ahead and get the talk Uncle Simon had suggested he have with Whitney over with. "Hey, squirt. Come sit over here with me a minute. I need to talk to you."

She crawled onto the bale and sat cross-legged. "What do you need to talk about? Have you got a problem that needs 'scussin'?"

"Well, I guess you could say that. I need to explain to you about this bruise on my face, about punishments and such."

She looked up at him with wide eyes and nodded.

"Well, uh, Corbett felt I had hurt Caitlyn's feeling and deserved a pop in the face." Dang, this would be harder than he thought.

"Did you deserve it? Did you hurt Caitlyn's feelings?"

"I guess." Oh, hell. "Yes, to be honest, Whitney, I did." He took off his hat and sat it on her head. "But, Whitney, Corbett shouldn't have hit me. Violence never solves anything."

"Couldn't you 'pologize to Caitlyn, kiss, and make up?"

He chuckled. "I wish it was that easy. I did apologize but there's more to it. She's not ready to forgive me." Should he go ahead and tell her everything without too much detail or just the basics?

"You remember how Caitlyn used to be my girlfriend and we thought we'd get married someday?"

She nodded.

"When I came home in March I told Caitlyn I wanted to date other girls and that she should date other guys."

"Why? I thought you loved Caitlyn." She scowled at him in defiance. "I love her."

"I do, uh, did, still do, but not the getting married kind of love." A fist closed around his heart. He prayed God wasn't going to strike him dead for lying to his little sister. "I met Elise, and we fell in love, so we're going to get married." He couldn't deny his feelings for Elise, but he couldn't seem to forget Caitlyn.

Quietly, she looked at him. He could almost hear the wheels turning in her head.

"What about Caitlyn? Will she meet someone else and get married to him?"

He cleared his throat, and his heart dropped to his toes. "Yes, I imagine she will."

"Where will you live?"

"We'll live here. Uncle Simon and Gram will move back to the old farmhouse. I want you to live with me and Elise but they may want you with them."

Her chin trembled.

"Don't cry now. You can see Gran and Uncle Simon almost every day, spend the night with them whenever you want."

"Okay, but what about Caitlyn? Will I see her anymore?"

"Even if she's mad at me, she'll still want to see you." He hoped so at least. Caitlyn was fond of Whitney and wouldn't punish her to get back at him.

"What I want you to understand, Whitney, is that my punishment is the guilt I feel because I didn't call Caitlyn and tell her I'd met someone else. She came home thinking things would be like they'd always been. She was hurt."

She thought about his words for a minute, then placed her palm on his chest, over his heart. "So, you're punishment is in there, right?"

He nodded.

"Will it help the hurt if I kiss it?"

He gathered her close for a hug. "It surely will. A hug will be better."

CHAPTER SEVEN

"I'd be pleased if you'd join me for dinner tonight, Hallie." Joe Booker was the first person to greet her after church services Sunday morning. He grabbed her hand, looped it through his arm and walked her to the Coles' car where he stayed to talk with Ruth. She got a whiff of his sweet cologne, which for some reason annoyed her. Maybe because it was such a contrast to Simon's clean, spicy scent.

Flustered, she glanced around at the others to find an excuse to say no. "Thank you, Joe, but, uh, I'm not sure."

Ruth spoke up. "Go ahead and go, Hallie. Don't stay home on account of us."

Oh, what could it hurt? He was a nice enough man. She'd enjoyed dancing with him. She smiled and nodded.

"That's great, then. How about I pick you up around six?"

Several women stopped Simon as he made his way toward them. Beautiful women, Hallie noticed. One hugged him and he kept his arm draped across the attractive woman's shoulder as they talked. About Simon's age, she wore her light brown hair shoulder length. She wondered if he was involved with her. *It's none of your business, Hallie.*

* * *

As Simon approached his family, he noticed Joe still danced attendance on Hallie. *Why do I care?* Other than the fact he'd monopolized her time again by preventing others from visiting with her, he didn't. Frowning, he wondered what they talked about. Maybe he should warn Hallie about Joe, a born womanizer. He dated one woman after another. Though he considered Joe a friend, he didn't want to see her hurt.

Joe put out his hand. "Hello, Simon. Beautiful day but it's going to be a scorcher before it's over."

"You got that right, Joe. How's business at the bank?"

"It's slow right now. It'll pick up when school starts."

"That's good." He turned to Ruth and Hallie. "You ladies ready to go?"

Ruth spoke up. "I am, if everyone else is. I need to check on lunch."

The others added their agreement.

Joe opened the car door for Hallie.

"See you tonight, Hallie." He closed her door and joined Simon on the other side of the car. "I'm taking Hallie to the country club for dinner tonight. Why don't you invite Joanne and join us?"

Simon closed the door for his mother. "The country club, huh?"

Joe cleared his throat. "I hope that's all right with you, Simon."

"And why wouldn't it be?" His words came out like a growl. To soften them, he added. "Though Hallie is our guest, she's a grown woman. I don't make her decisions for her."

Joe rocked back on his heels. "Just checking,

Simon. From the look you were giving all the men at the dance Friday night, I wasn't sure you hadn't staked a claim." He grinned. "Don't want to be stepping on anyone's toes."

"When I decide to stake a claim on a woman, there'll be no question in anybody's mind."

On the trip home, Justin drove with Whitney between him and Elise. He sat in back with Hallie between him and his mother. Uncomfortable with his arms scrunched to his sides, he laid his right arm across the back of the seat behind Hallie.

When his hand touched her shoulder, she started. "Sorry, there's not enough room for my arms back here," he said.

"No problem." She smiled giving him a glimpse of that cute dimple beside her mouth. "It is rather close quarters."

"Uncle Simon, why don't you get a date and go with Hallie and Joe? You haven't been to the country club in a good while." Simon looked up to see Justin watching him through the rearview mirror, waiting for an answer. Maybe he should go.

"As a matter of fact, I think Elise and I might go too. They have a little band that plays on Sunday evenings. We could dance on the patio."

"I'll think about it." At least then he could keep an eye on Hallie, make sure Joe didn't make a pass. He hadn't been out with Joanne in a good while. She was a good friend but he knew she'd like for their relationship to be more. He enjoyed her company but there was no chemistry between them, and he wasn't about to settle for a marriage without passion. Not that he hadn't tried to make more of their relationship, he had. But it hadn't worked. It might be unfair to ask her. Though beautiful, smart, and a local woman, she was not the one for him.

Hallie's delicious scent reached his nostrils. He leaned toward her to catch a better whiff. He closed his eyes and savored it, so clean and spicy. When he opened them he saw Justin's eyes watching him in the rearview mirror. The kid had the audacity to grin and wink. He looked at Hallie to see if she'd seen the exchange.

* * *

She was in shadow, backlight by the sun beyond the window. As she stood looking out, Simon enjoyed the view. Her sleeveless black dress hugged her figure, her small waist and flaring hips. When she turned, he caught his breath at her beauty. The V-shaped neckline of her dress hinted at the generosity of her breasts, a large diamond pendant at the spot where her cleavage began. It wasn't a provocative dress, but on Hallie it was dynamite. He wanted to move the icy pendant aside and place a warm kiss there. Her shiny blond hair moved with her, keeping time with her hips as she walked toward him.

Her voice warm, as sexy as the dress, she said. "You're mighty handsome tonight, Simon."

He glanced down at his black suit and white starched shirt. "I hate getting rigged up like this." Adjusting his collar, he added. "I'd much rather get a steak at Jim Bob's where I could wear my jeans."

Her laugh was throaty and musical. "I can appreciate that, but it's nice to dress up once in a while."

"You're beautiful." He reached out to take a strand of her hair and test the texture of it. "So soft."

"Thank you."

She gasped as his fingers brushed her breasts when he lifted the pendant. Their eyes locked. Lost for several seconds in the brown depths of her eyes, he forced himself to look down at the necklace. Ten to fifteen stones were set together to resemble one large stone. "Nice."

"It's made from the stones of my wedding rings."

"Ah." He placed the pendant back in its nest.

A horn honked outside.

He walked to the door. "I hope that's my ride and not yours. I know Joe's mama taught him better manners." Opening the door, he relaxed. "It's Justin and Elise. We'll see you there." He stopped and glanced back over his shoulder. "Joe's my friend but you should know he has a reputation with women. Not always a good one. I thought you should know."

"Thank you for the warning. I'll be alright."

The country club was a surprise. Hallie had expected an older white frame building with green shutters—the colonial type seen so often in the south. It was modern red brick with a wide expanse of glass looking out on acres of green lawn and trees. A bridge crossed a creek leading to the golf course.

When they reached their table, Simon and Justin rose while Simon introduced Hallie to Joanne, the woman who'd hugged him at church. A pretty woman with brown hair and a beautiful smile, she was pleasant and welcoming.

The table was set with white linen cloths, fine china and crystal. She leaned toward Joe. "Wow, this is extravagant. How can people afford this?"

"Uh, well…" He glanced at Simon.

"What Joe's trying to say, is this was Loretta's last project before she left. She raised money to build and furnish this place then left the club with a big debt."

Hallie's mouth formed a silent "O."

Joanne spoke up. "The other building was too small to house everyone who belonged. We needed something, but perhaps not the fancy tableware and accessories. She did a great job on this building though."

As she listened, she was glad Joanne wasn't a catty woman who liked to get her digs in at every opportunity. It appeared not everyone hated Loretta and gave credit when it was due.

Joanne turned to Hallie. "Our little town is wealthier than it looks. Some of the ranchers in this county have large operations that are quite profitable. They had a fundraiser to clear the balance due."

The food was delicious and conversation flowed as they ate. Simon, Joanne and Joe had attended high school together. They competed by telling outrageous stories on each other. Laughter flowed around the table.

Justin shook his head. "Uncle Simon, I can't believe you put a steer on the roof of the gymnasium. What did Grandpa do?"

Simon's lips twitched. His warm and boisterous laugh transformed his body. Chuckles rumbled from his chest shaking his shoulders and belly. Hallie was entranced. She'd not seen this side of him. "It wasn't what Daddy did, it was what Mama did. I was grounded for a month." He chuckled. "Daddy laughed until Mama glared at him. With a stern face, he said. 'You're mother's right, son. And the grounding includes your pick-up truck. You can ride the bus to school.'"

"Whoa. That was pretty tough." Justin turned to Elise. "Gran is one tough cookie."

"Yeah, she is. Riding the bus was humiliating." He locked eyes with Justin. "And, your daddy enjoyed every punishment I got. He thought the folks let me get away with too much."

Joanna turned to Justin. "Of course, Simon learned most of the stunts he pulled from his big brother, your daddy."

The band played a slow tune and Justine led Elise onto the dance floor.

"Hallie, would you like to dance."

"I'd love to."

Joe held her chair as she stood. His arm around her, they walked onto the dance floor.

Simon didn't like the looks of Joe's arm around Hallie's waist. Though he had no claim on her, that touch of intimacy irked the hell out of him.

"So, I can see how the wind blows." Joanne's remark startled him. "Don't try to deny it. Your face tells the story."

"You're mistaken. I don't want Joe to hurt her." He took her hand. "Let's dance."

"Whatever you say, Simon, but you're a bad liar."

He sighed. "Okay. I'm attracted to her, but that's all. We're too different. Nothing could ever come of it."

"I know how that goes."

Simon looked down to read her expression. It was solemn. "Ah, hell, Joanne, I'm sorry. I shouldn't have invited you tonight."

She touched his cheek. "No, Simon. I'm glad you did. Seeing you tonight will allow me to close the door on us ever having a serious relationship." Biting her lip, she added. "I hope we'll always be friends."

He hugged her, stroking her back. "Always."

Joe was a good dancer and easy to follow. As they danced, she watched Simon and Joanne. They seemed comfortable together and…intimate.

"Has Simon been seeing Joanne long?" Joe drew back and glanced at the other couple.

"Just about their entire life. I don't think it's ever been serious, though. Joanne would like for it to be but I think she realizes it will never go beyond friendship."

They traded partners and before long Hallie found herself dancing with Simon. Still breathing hard from the fast number with Justin, she was grateful it was a slow song.

Simon took her hand. "Let's dance on the patio. It'll be much cooler."

Hallie was grateful for a chance to see the outside. Lights decorated the trees and the arched bridge that crossed the creek. From the patio the tiny bulbs resembled fireflies. "It's beautiful out here."

Simon gazed into her eyes. "Yes, it is."

The music was soft, muffled by the glass separating them from the band. In Simon's arms their bodies moved to the seductive melody of the song. Hallie paused when he pulled her closer, molding her body to his.

"Simon, this isn't a good idea." She tried to pull back but he held her secure.

"No, it's not. But humor me this once."

She relented and gave in to the feel of his firm body, his spicy scent and the thumping of their hearts. A deep longing rose in her, a need for not just any man, but this man. Why did the differences between them have to be so strong? She tilted her head back and put her lips to the warm softness under the curve of his jaw.

He stilled at the contact, then put his lips to her ear and breathed, "Hallie." The music stopped and he held her a minute before withdrawing his arms.

Inside Hallie looked for Joe. She glanced at Simon in question.

"I convinced Joe to take Joanne home so he wouldn't have to drive all the way out to the ranch." He seemed pleased with himself.

Hallie felt the heat rise in her face. "You had no right to do that. I had a date with Joe and should have ridden with him." Not that she cared but she didn't like to be manipulated.

"Well, hell. Excuse me for trying to help out." He took her elbow and walked her out of the building to the car.

It was quiet on the trip back. Simon drove. Justin and Elise were in the back seat. She stole glances at Simon. He was miffed but needed to mind his own business. At the ranch, he dropped the kids at the front of the house. She released her seat belt and reached for the door. He stilled her hand.

"Ride around to the back with me." She nodded and they drove around to the garage. He took her hand to help her out.

"Walk with me a while?" She studied his face. Gone was any sign of anger.

"Alright."

Still holding her hand they walked toward the barn. Moonlight and a faint glow from inside paved their way. They stopped several yards from the barn. "I wanted to talk to you in private. First, let me say, perhaps I was out of line earlier. If my actions offended you, I'm sorry."

She snorted. "Perhaps?" She yanked her hand from his and stood, hands on her hips. "Okay then, I *sorta* accept your apology."

He laughed. "Thank you." His face grew serious. "Justin and I had a talk this afternoon. He's going to think about your offer, give you a decision in the next few days."

"Good. I'm glad to hear it." While in Georgetown Monday, she'd have a financial agreement drawn up. The contract would give Justin enough money and leverage to start building the ranch to its former state.

Somehow, he'd gained possession of her hand again. He looked down and stroked the palm with his thumb. "I want to assure you about Justin's qualifications. He received a good education in ranch management. Plus, he's had hands-on experience working here his entire life. I believe he'll make wise use of your money and produce a profit. Otherwise I wouldn't encourage him to enter into this agreement with you. For your sake as well as his."

"I appreciate that, Simon. I trust Justin. As I trust you. Since this ranch was a thriving business at one time, it increases the chances it will be again. If it hadn't been, I wouldn't have offered the money. Justin has a strong legacy backing him up."

He tilted his head as he studied her. She thought his expression one of appreciation, but wasn't sure until he spoke. "You're a fine woman, Hallie. Your trust humbles me." He paused and cleared his throat. "I'm grateful."

For some reason his comment embarrassed her.

"Let's visit the horses."

Dim lights glowed from the barn's interior. Welcoming knickers greeted them. Stopping at every stall, Simon talked to the animals, giving them a scratch or pat. Redman butted his chest and snuffled at his pocket looking for a treat.

Laughing, Simon moved out of the horse's reach. "Hey, boy, none of that. This is my good suit." He removed his jacket and tossed it across an empty stall door.

"I think you've spoiled him," she said.

His grin made his eyes light up. She watched has he stroked and patted his horse not sure who enjoyed it more, Simon or Redman. "Yeah, I have." He didn't act at all remorseful. "But he takes good care of me. Works hard. You deserve it don't you, boy?" The horse nickered and tossed his head in agreement. Simon threw back his head and laughed, delighted with Redman's antics.

She watched them together. "Does he understand everything you say?"

"Not everything. But, he's smart and picks up on a lot. Much of it's from my tone of voice." He gave the horse a final pat and reached for his jacket.

As if he did it every day, he put his arm around her shoulders and they walked out of the barn toward the back yard. At the big oak surrounded by picnic tables, he drew her into the dark shadows of its branches where the moonlight didn't penetrate. He tossed his jacket onto the nearest picnic table. They were completely hidden under the umbrella of leaf-covered arms. With his free hand, he cupped the nape of her neck and pulled her face closer to his. Spellbound, Hallie didn't protest. He blew at the wisps of her hair and watched it dance, then inhaled. "You always smell so clean. Your scent haunts me." He ran his fingers through the blonde strands then watched it drop back into place. "I've wanted to touch your hair from the first time I saw you."

"Simon, I don't—" His touch was gentle, mesmerizing. She should put a stop to before it got out of hand. But heaven help her, she didn't want too.

"Ssssh. Let me kiss you. That's all I want is to kiss you." His eyes burned with passion as he looked down at her. "You feel it too, don't you?" He leaned closer and rubbed his check against hers. "The fire that bursts to life each time we touch. I've tried to deny it for days, but it's futile. You invade my mind night and day."

His breath was warm against her ear causing shivers to run up her spine. "Let's see if it's as explosive as I think it is." He kissed the side of her mouth, and then nuzzled her right ear. With his lips, warm and moist, he explored the side of her neck, kissing, nibbling, stroking with his tongue. "Come burn with me, Hallie."

Hallie gripped his forearms to keep her balance. She was sinking, drowning in the feelings he provoked in her body. *Oh God, oh God, help me.* When his tongue traced the tendon in her neck she cried out, and pulled his head up so she could reach his mouth. Her arms locked around his neck.

With a low growl, his lips captured hers and deepened the kiss until her mouth opened for him. His tongue dipped and twined with hers as he explored the warmth within. Hallie's knees sagged. Breaking away, he gasped, "God, Hallie, you taste sweet, so sweet."

While his mouth played on hers, his hands roamed her back, her hips, molding and fitting her body to his.

Hallie moaned in pleasure at his touch, her body alive with the awareness of the maleness of his. Every inch of him was hard as her hands moved from around his neck to his chest and then to his back. She wanted to touch him, to open his shirt and taste his skin, feel the hair against her face.

When he lifted his head, she drew in deep gulps of air. He laid his forehead against hers, his breathing ragged. His hands stroked her back then moved to her neck to pull her head to his chest. The rapid beating of his heart matched the rhythm of hers. For several minutes they held each other while he stroked her hair.

"God, Hallie. I'm sorry. I shouldn't have started that." He dropped his forehead to hers. "For some reason when I'm around you I can't think straight. You move me as no woman has before." Voice raspy, he added. "But our lives are too different for anything permanent to develop between us. Aren't they?"

Though she knew he was right, she couldn't help but feel stung. She pulled back and he dropped his arms to his sides.

"Yes, you're right. My life is in the city with my son and my boutique. Yours is here." Cold comfort, but falling in love was a risk, one she wasn't ready to take. There were no guarantees in this life. If there were, James would be alive. No, those emotions caused heartbreak. She'd had enough to last a lifetime.

Their eyes met and held. For just a moment she saw regret and longing in his eyes, his twisted smile. It matched the ache in her heart. She reached out a hand to comfort him but drew it back. It would serve no purpose. His expression changed to one of resolve. Jaw clenched, he stood, arms folded across his chest.

"Good night, Simon."

Simon nodded and watched her walk toward the house. She'd felt so right in his arms, now they felt empty. He ached for what he couldn't have.

"Good night, Hallie." Had she heard him? She was almost to the back door.

Was that pain he'd seen in her eyes? Had she been thinking about her husband? The thought made him jealous though he had no right to feel that way. He should be relieved she'd agreed a relationship between them was out of the question. But, dammit, he wasn't.

CHAPTER EIGHT

Hallie woke with a groan, the taste of Simon's kisses still on her lips. Lying on her back, she stared at the ceiling—remembering. Lordy, the man knew how to kiss. He wasn't bad with his hands either. A big man, he touched with care, teasing and tweaking to increase desire. If he'd led her to his bed she wasn't sure she would have resisted. She wasn't interested in a one-night stand or an affair. In fact, she didn't think Simon was either. He would view sex as a commitment. Her opinion of him had changed in the days they'd been at the ranch. A good man with traditional values, he loved his family. Their health and happiness was his major concern. Now that she knew of Justin and Caitlyn's prior relationship, she understood his concern about the sudden engagement. Something wasn't right about the situation.

It had been years since she'd desired a man, been desired in return. The prospect was heady medicine and tempting. She missed sex, but more than that, she missed the closeness of sharing a bed, cuddling and talking before falling sleep. Her soul craved companionship. But, the thought of loving and losing again terrified her. In the early months of James's illness, she'd read, researched, talked to doctors, prayed and tried to bargain with God for a cure. Nothing helped. She'd felt helpless. Simon could be snatched from her too. Be thrown from a horse, gored by a mad bull, or be hit by a car. No. She didn't need love again.

Knowing that, why then couldn't she put him out of her mind? Simon had made it plain they had no future together. She agreed. His life was here on the ranch, hers in the big city with all its refinements. She had her friends, her business associates and her church family. They would have to be enough.

She had to get away and think. Checking on her business gave her a good excuse to be gone overnight. While in Georgetown, she'd pick up the prenuptial papers from her lawyer. Maybe she should call ahead and give him the particulars for a loan contract for Justin. Then he could have it ready when she arrived.

"Mama, when will you be back?" Elise sat on her bed while she packed her overnight bag. "Early tomorrow afternoon." That would give her plenty of time to help Ruth with the barbecue planned for Saturday night. Justin and Elise's engagement would be announced then.

Hallie sat on the bed and took Elise's hands. "Honey, have you talked to Justin about his relationship with Caitlyn?"

"Yeah, Mama, I have. He says he's over her, and it's me he loves and wants to marry."

"Do you believe him?"

She looked down at their hands. "One minute I do and then the next I'm not sure. I want to believe him but something keeps niggling at my mind. I don't know what to do about it." When she raised her head, tears pooled in her eyes.

"Oh, Elise. Love and life is hard but you're strong, up to the challenge. Just remember, don't marry if you have any doubts. Promise me that." She gathered her close and rubbed her back.

"I promise, Mama."

* * *

When Simon saw Hallie exit the house with a travel bag and head for her car, he left the barn to meet her. How could she be so fresh and rested when he'd tossed and turned most of the night? Just the sight of her had his body hard again. Dammit, he felt like a randy teenager.

He took the bag from her hand and tossed it on the back seat. "Had your fill of ranch life?"

"No, as I said last night, I have business to take care of at home. I'll be back tomorrow afternoon."

He backed her up against the car door leaving mere inches between them.

"What's your problem this morning? Didn't you sleep well last night?" She stood her ground but Simon could see her heartbeat quicken at the pulse point of her neck. He wanted to place his fingers there and see if it matched his own.

"As a matter fact, no, I didn't. I couldn't get a certain woman with soft breasts and flaring hips out of my mind."

He couldn't keep the grin off his face and when she blushed, he chuckled. He couldn't deny the magnetism between them. Hell, he didn't want to and Hallie could try, but her response was proof positive. The heat radiating from his body echoed the flush of her face. If he got any closer they'd burst into flames.

"How about you? How did you sleep last night?" He reached out and ran his thumb along her jaw.

She poked out her chin. "Fine, thank you very

much."

He smiled. "You can lie all you want darlin' but I saw a light shining under your door at three a.m. when I went downstairs for something to eat.

"What kind of business do you have in town— beauty shop appointment, or do you have a hot date tonight?" He knew his face reflected irritation, at himself for caring who she saw in town. He didn't want her to go and he didn't want to think she might be seeing a man tonight. This feeling of jealousy didn't suit him one bit.

"I do have a business to run you know." She shoved at his chest. "Move back and let me get in the car."

"No."

"No?" Her eyes widened and then narrowed. "Why not?"

He leaned in, eyes locked on hers before drifting down to her lips. His intent was clear.

A squeak escaped her lips. "No."

Voice husky, he replied, "Yes."

She shook her head from side-to-side, as she whispered, "We decided last night it wouldn't work between us."

He gave her a cocky grin. "A man has a right to change his mind." Lips inches from hers, he murmured. "I can't let you go without tasting you again."

His lips captured hers in a hot searing kiss. When her knees sagged, he lifted her to better align her body with his, holding her in place against the car with his weight. Her hands clutched his shirt as one of his arms circled her waist and the other cradled her head.

Dear Lord, thank you for making this woman for

me. Her body was a perfect fit to his. He deepened the kiss, his tongue dipped into her mouth and drew hers into his. Yes, his actions belied what he'd said the night before but he couldn't seem to help himself where she was concerned. Was he in love with this woman? The idea scared him to death. He certainly wouldn't win her this way. He ended the kiss and eased back to allow her to slide down the car and land on her feet.

"Sorry, sweetheart. I didn't mean to manhandle you." He reached up, fanned his fingers through the hair above her ear and watched as it sprang back into place when he released it. What was it about her hair that fascinated him so? Other women's hair had never seemed to catch his attention. Opening her car door, he took her elbow as she slid behind the wheel. "You be careful now."

Up the road, in the shadows of the barn, Justin and Elise stood, transfixed by the scene playing out inside the garage.

Elise broke the silence. "Oh, my, God. Did you see that?" Using her hand, she fanned her face to cool the rising heat. "I'm shocked."

Justin grinned at her discomfort. "I think Uncle Simon has the hots for your mama."

"I think the feeling's mutual." Elise stared after her mother's departing car. It felt strange seeing her being kissed, much less one so full of passion and heat.

Justin was beaming. "From your expression, I take it you'd be happy to see them get together."

"Sure. Wouldn't you?"

"Yeah. I would too. It's about time he found someone to love. Strange, but he's always been prejudiced against women from the city."

Justin had kissed her many times but never with the heat she'd witnessed between her mother and Simon. Oh, his kisses were arousing and Justin's body couldn't hide the fact that he wanted her. But they'd never slept together. Was he being a gentleman or did his passion belong to someone else? He believed she was the woman he wanted to marry. She had doubts. In her opinion, Loretta had confused both of the Cole men about love, marriage and its expectations.

* * *

"Damn the man." He knew what he was doing. Overloading her senses with his kisses left her weak-kneed all the way to the highway. It was hard to push on the accelerator in her condition, but she managed to drive out the ranch gate.

What was she going to do? She couldn't deny her attraction to him. To do so would be a lie. She was happy with her life. Her children were great, the business was going well and she was about to embark on a new adventure by expanding her business. What did she need with a man? Stupid question. Her body reminded her every time she looked at Simon what she needed with a man. Not just the physical needs, but the emotional as well. Sharing with someone you love, a meal, a problem, or a quiet time together. Should she risk her heart? If she fell in love with Simon and he didn't return her feelings, could she move on without scars? No, she didn't think so. But she had more than her share of scars, so what would a few more matter?

* * *

"Justin, we need to talk." Elise tucked her arm through his as they walked to one of the picnic tables shaded by the big oak tree. Hot out, the shade made it bearable. An occasional breeze ruffled the leaves. When it hit the perspiration on their bodies, it felt wonderful.

Elise sat facing the table. Justin straddled the bench so he could face her. "What's on your mind?" She looked at the clean, strong lines of his face and reached up to trace the shape of his jaw with her fingers. Her lips began to tremble and to stop them she caught her bottom one with her teeth.

"Honey. What's the matter?" He scooted closer and pulled her into the shelter of his arms. "Have I done something to hurt you?"

She shook her head no and tried to swallow her tears so she could speak. "Justin, why haven't you ever made love to me? It's not like I'm inexperienced. Not to say I've done it lots of times, mind you. But, we are engaged."

His face registered shock at her question, then resolve as to where the conversation would lead. He cupped her neck and drew their foreheads together. "Elise, honey—"

Touching his lips, she stopped the flow of words. "Here me out, Justin. I don't doubt you care for me, but I do doubt the depth. Your love for me doesn't include passion." The memory of her mother and Simon's kiss earlier came to mind. "I want a passionate love from the man I marry. The kind I think you have for Caitlyn."

There, she'd said it. She breathed a sigh of relief.

Justin looked ill. Tension drew his mouth into a grim line. "The passion I *had* for Caitlyn. Passion rarely lasts a lifetime. Elise. I can't deny how I once felt for Caitlyn." He searched for the right words. "Or the fact I loved her no matter how hard I tried not to."

"Are you sure you're over her?"

His shoulders sagged. "It doesn't matter. I can't marry her. She's such a free spirit. She'll never settle down. We'd end up like Mom and Dad, divorced and broken."

"You don't know that for a fact. She deserves a chance. You're letting your father's experience color your thinking."

"Maybe. You might be right. I'm saying *might*, mind you."

"You can settle for a loveless, passionless marriage but I don't intend to. I deserve more, Justin, and you insult me by offering me less. You deserve more too."

"I do love you, Elise."

Tears choked her voice. "I know you do. But you don't desire me, ache for me like you do Caitlyn. I won't settle for a bland relationship. Our engagement is off."

"God, I've created one hell of a mess, haven't I?"

"You didn't do it alone. I did my share. I wanted to meet Mr. Right, so I made you into him."

They sat not speaking for a while, his arms around her, her head on his chest. Thinking.

"Justin?"

"Yeah?"

"You've got to talk to Caitlyn and explain your fears about your relationship. Make things right with her. You've let your mother cloud your judgment too long." She drew back and looked up at him. "Not everyone who grew up rich is spoiled, self-centered and irresponsible."

"Maybe. I don't know. Caitlyn grew up rich but she's always worked on the ranch." His gaze drifted as if remembering something from the past. "I'll think about what you've said. Maybe I've over analyzed the situation."

"Don't take too long. A love like you two have is rare. Some people search their whole lives for such a one and never find it. Someone else may snatch her up while you're thinking."

"Why do you care about my happiness after the way I've messed things up?"

"Darned if I know, but I do."

He nodded, then his eyes jerked back to hers. "I doubt Caitlyn will ever speak to me again. If she does, it won't be any time soon."

"You'll never know unless you talk to her."

* * *

Hallie parked in front of the courthouse in downtown Granite Springs. She had Elise's pre-nuptial agreement and Justin's financial contract. Her meeting with the lady from Fredericksburg had gone well. A bright, energetic young woman, she would do well in the business. When she learned she wouldn't be investing money, just consulting time, Hallie's mind turned to another investment opportunity.

As she got out of the car, she put on a wide brimmed sun hat to shade her from the blazing sun. With it and the sunglasses, maybe she wouldn't be recognized if she ran into some of the people she'd met at church and the dance. She didn't want to explain what she was doing. It was important she know herself first.

The sidewalks held potted plants, benches for tired shoppers and trees in large wine barrels. She crossed the street and sat on one of the seats. The courthouse was magnificent. Three stories of pink granite, topped with a copper dome, stood watch over the surrounding businesses and buildings beyond. Stonework steps, stretching across almost half of the front, narrowed as they approached the second level. Four gray marble pillars supported the three entrance arches. Each was enhanced by gray marble keystones, as were the windows on the second level. Huge oak trees surrounded it, their branches spreading wide enough to protect several hundred people from the scorching sun. Nestled among them was a white Victorian gazebo with red granite steps and foundation.

She got up and walked around the four-block area making mental notes as she did so. There were several gift shops, antique stores, a beauty parlor, barber shop, pool hall, insurance business, two restaurants, an ice cream shop with a bed and breakfast above, two dress shops and a sweet shop that displayed their famous margarita cupcakes. The bank covered half of one block and had several businesses on the upper floors.

Standing in front of the more upscale dress shop, The Gingham Bustle, she debated whether to go in or not. What the heck, she might as well since she was here.

Cool air greeted her as she walked inside. The owner had a nice decorating flair. Old West memorabilia strategically placed separated sections of the store. The clothes were displayed to catch the eye but they weren't the quality she carried in her shop. Interesting.

A young woman approached. "Can I help you with anything?"

"No, thanks. I'm just looking today." Most of the

clothes were casual, though a few dressy items filled a small corner. "You have a charming shop."

"Thank you. I'll tell Mama you said so. She loves to hear what people think." She went back to straightening clothes on the racks.

Outside, she traced her steps back to the bench where she'd started, and read the *For Sale* sign in the window of the vacant building. Using her cell phone she called the number of the realtor.

* * *

Jezebel met her as she parked in the vacant space of the garage. "Hello, girl. I'm glad someone's glad to see me." She squatted to give her a good scratch.

"What makes you think she's the only one?" The warmth of Simon's husky voice washed over her causing a little shiver. Would he grab her, kiss her again? She couldn't decide if she wanted him to or not. *Liar.*

Standing up she greeted him with a shaky smile. "Hi."

He stood there, looking too darn good, hands on his hips and smiled back. "Hi yourself. Did you have a good trip?"

"Yes, I did. I got a lot taken care of." He nodded and opened the rear door to grab her bag. Gripping her elbow, he escorted her into the house and sat her bag on the table.

"Justin and Elise want to talk to us after dinner. Tonight's as good a time as any to go ahead and sign the prenuptial agreements. That alright with you?"

"Yes. That'll be fine. Thanks for bringing in my bag."

His smile reached all the way to those beautiful

blue eyes. He winked. "You're welcome, darlin'."

* * *

"You guys go ahead. I'll do the dishes." Ruth started gathering dishes to haul to the kitchen.

Hallie joined in to help clear the table. "No, you won't. Elise and I'll help then we can talk."

"Anyway, Gran," said Elise. "We want you to hear what we have to say"

Ruth observed Hallie with questions in her eyes. She shrugged. When Simon said the kids wanted to talk, she'd figured it was about the wedding or something of that nature. Maybe, it was more involved.

"Elise, honey. Would you get Whitney in the tub and ready for bed for me?"

"Sure." She tugged on Whitney's pigtails. "Come on, squirt. I think you need a shampoo too."

Whitney's smile turned into a frown. "Do I have to? I want to watch television."

"After your bath. You want to use some of my special shampoo?"

"All right. It smells real good."

Hallie watched them run up the stairs. "I have no idea what this is about."

Ruth appeared thoughtful. "Yesterday morning after you left, they sat at one of the picnic tables and talked for a long time. I think Elise was crying. Justin didn't look happy either."

Everyone was seated when Hallie walked into Simon's office. Elise and Justin sat on the leather sofa, close but not touching. Ruth sat next to Elise. Hallie chose the chair next to Simon's desk, opposite the end he was perched on.

Justin cleared his throat. "There's no easy way to

say this. Elise and I have decided to not get married."

The room erupted with, "What," "How come," What happened?" They all tried to talk at once.

Simon raised his hands and glanced from one to the other. "What changed your minds? Justin?"

He watched Elise. "Elise brought some things to my attention. Things I tried to ignore, or maybe I should say deny." He bowed his head. "My feelings for Caitlyn." He looked at Elise and took her hand. "I do love Elise, I always will, but as a friend. It's not the kind to base a marriage on."

With her fist over her mouth, Hallie bit back the sob that threatened to escape her mouth. *My baby, my poor baby, her heart must be broken.*

Elise went to her mother and knelt before her. "It's alright, Mama. I'm hurt, yes, but I began to see it wouldn't work soon after we arrived. This is what's best for both of us. It's what I want."

Hallie hugged her, somewhat comforted by Elise's words, but the tears could not be turned off. Why she was crying like this she didn't have a clue. Simon handed her a handkerchief. She mopped at her eyes to have them fill up again.

Justin approached. "Please forgive me, Hallie. I never meant to hurt her."

She stood and hugged him. "I know that, Justin. Of course I forgive you." But she continued to cry.

Simon put his arms around Elise and held her close. "You're a rare young woman. The man that marries you will be a lucky son-of-a-gun." He pulled Justin over and included him in the embrace. "I'm proud of you both."

Sniffling, Ruth left the room with, "We all are."

Elise looked with concern at her mother. "Mama, is something else wrong? I'm okay. I promise."

Hallie tried to smile while shaking her head no. She mouthed, "I'm fine."

"Go on with Justin. I'll watch after your mother."

Justin closed the door behind them.

"Come here, Hallie." He led her to the couch where he sat down and pulled her onto his lap. Wrapping her in his arms, he stoked her back. "Go ahead and cry, honey. Let it all out."

At his words and gentle touch, Hallie's tears turned into sobs. Not just for Elise, but for herself, her need to be loved again and her fear of loving and being hurt.

* * *

Simon let her cry. But when she didn't stop, he grew worried. Setting her in the corner of the sofa, he moved to the desk and pulled out a bottle of brandy. He poured two fingers into a glass. Hell, he needed a shot too, so poured the same amount into another glass.

"Here, Hallie. Drink this. It'll help calm you." She pushed herself to a sitting position, took the glass and raised it to her lips. The small sip had her gasping but she took another and then leaned back.

"I'm sorry for behaving like this in front of you." She closed her eyes. They were red and puffy. "You must think I'm crazy."

"No. I don't think that at all. I think you're hurting for Elise."

"Maybe. But, I felt this might happen. Elise did too."

He sat beside her. "I think this," he caught a tear on his finger, "involves more than Elise. What's the real cause of these tears?" He wiped moisture from the outer corner of her eyes. Tilting her chin, he kissed her on the lips. "Come on. Tell me."

Voice choked with emotion, she said. "I hurt for Elise. But, I hurt for myself too." Her face twisted with emotion. "Wanting to love again, yet fearing that love will be ripped from me." She finished her drink. "I don't think I could bear it. James's death almost killed me. I can't take that chance again. I'd rather be alone."

Jaw rigid, he asked. "Is this your way of telling me to back off? You don't want to pursue a relationship?"

Her red-rimmed eyes were huge as she looked up at him. "Yes, it is. As you said the other night, nothing can come of our feelings for each other."

"I thought things had changed between us in the last couple of days. They have for me. I'm willing to change my thinking and take a chance. Why can't you take a chance as well?" He walked to the desk, splashed a generous amount of brandy in his empty glass and drank it down in one gulp. Slamming it down on the desk, he ground out, "Do you believe I'll commit then stop loving you? Just like that." He snapped his fingers." Dammit, Hallie. When I love someone, it will be for a lifetime. You insult me to think otherwise."

Her answer was a whisper. "No. I don't think that. That's what makes it so hard. You're a good man, Simon." She shook her head from side to side as she bowed her head. "But, you could die. I couldn't bear it."

His heart fell to his knees. He ached for her. He knew the suffering involved in losing a loved one. With little warning, his father, then his brother, Sidney, was taken from them. Would his mother have wished those two lives had never been entwined with hers rather than experience the hurt of losing them? He didn't think so.

"Hallie. Sweetheart." He sat down and drew her into his arms. "I'm not going to die."

Twisting away, her eyes shot sparks at him. "Can you write me a guarantee? Tell me." She slapped his chest with the flat of her hand. "Can you?"

"You know I can't." He took her hand and placed the palm against his cheek. God, he would if he could. "Hallie, there are no guarantees in life. You know that."

Her hand was so soft. He kissed her palm and then placed his lips at the pulse of her wrist. "Hallie, I think I'm falling in love with you. I didn't want to like you. I kept telling myself you were like Loretta, but I was a fool to think so. You're beautiful, inside and out. My body swells with desire for you, but my heart aches for the love and gentleness you can give it. It will shrivel up and die if I can't have you." He grinned. "No pun intended."

She choked out a teary laugh.

"Please, Hallie. Take a chance, move here, live on my ranch or in town. Give us time to get to know each other better."

"I can't, Simon." She held her free hand over her mouth to still her trembling lips.

"Why? Your children are grown. You can manage your business from here." His throat clogged with fear, despair twisting his features. She didn't return his feelings. "Do you care for me at all?"

Her gaze took in his tortured expression. "Oh, Simon." Chin trembling, she brought his palm to cover her mouth and nose. She nuzzled it with her lips. Tears choked her voice. "I think I love you, too."

Joy sang through his body. *Thank you, God.* "Then

marry me. Make me the happiest man on earth. I have all a man could ever want—family, my ranch, friends—everything but you. I'd begun to think I'd never find you."

"Simon. I can't." Her eyes pleaded with him. "Please understand. I'm not ready for such a commitment."

Frustration made his voice harsh. "Do you have any idea when you might be ready? Maybe it'll be tomorrow, or next week, or ten years from now."

"I'm sorry. Please understand."

He sighed. "Alright. You let me know when you're ready. Don't take too long. I won't wait forever."

"Then don't." She slid off his lap, straightened her clothes, and left without looking back.

* * *

She couldn't sleep. Images kept running through her mind. Simon's smile, holding Whitney on his lap as she kissed his cheek, his arm slung around Justin's shoulder and dancing with his mother. No one could doubt his adoration for his family. The evidence was everywhere and reinforced the honesty of his declaration of love. Why couldn't she thrust aside her fears and commit to him?

Wasn't looking at property in Granite Springs evidence of a step in that direction? She thought so but wasn't quite ready to reveal her plans to Simon. Thinking about the deposit she'd put down on the building sent her thoughts reeling in another direction—money. If she decided to marry Simon, what would he think about her money situation? Would he feel threatened by her wealth?

Turning onto her side, she beat the pillow until its

shape fit her head. Simon made it clear he wouldn't wait forever. She was so confused. Since she thought she loved him, would she hurt any less if something happened to him and they weren't married? No. Agony was the same, married or single.

A sound disturbed her meanderings. It was a child crying. Whitney must be having a bad dream. She tossed the covers back and walked barefoot down the hall. Whitney's door was open so she took a step inside. Her heart jumped in her chest. A knot formed in her throat.

Simon reclined on Whitney's bed with the girl in his arms. Voice soothing, he whispered to her childish murmurs. Dressed in jeans pulled on in a hurry, he was nude to the waist. His bare skin glowed in the rays of the nightlight. He was beautiful. She wanted to sit behind him, run her hands over his warm skin and place a kiss between his shoulder blades. A sigh of longing escaped without warning.

He turned, looking over his shoulder. His gaze locked with hers, and with lazy abandon traveled lower taking in the whiteness of her skin above the sheer aqua of her nylon gown and her bare feet. She gulped as heat flared in her body. Realizing how exposed she was from the hall night-light, she turned and hurried back to her room.

* * *

Breakfast hadn't been the tense affair she'd expected. Whitney described in living color her dream from the night before. A witch had come into her room and tried to chew on her neck. "See, I have a mark." She pulled her collar aside so Justin could see the bite marks.

"Those are nothing but mosquito bites, squirt." He leaned toward her making biting noises. "Let me show you what real chewing feels like."

She squealed and hopped up and down.

Simon caught her before her feet hit the floor. "Stay put, Whitney. Finish your breakfast."

Ruth spoke. "Hallie, Elise, I hope you don't plan to leave right away. Just because the wedding is off doesn't mean we can't still enjoy your company. Simon, Justin and I talked about it earlier. We'd like for you to stay the rest of the week."

Hallie exchanged glances with Elise and Simon.

"I'd like to stay, Mom, one more day if you would," said Elise.

"Thank you," said Hallie. "We will then, if you're sure."

Ruth patted her hand. "We'd like that."

Simon's gaze locked with hers. "We're sure." He turned toward Ruth. "What should we do about the barbecue?"

"Let's postpone it a week. I'll get the word out to the community. We want you two to come back that weekend and join us."

* * *

Simon saddled Redman and walked him out of the barn in time to see Hallie drive away. Dust billowed out behind the white car. Where was she going at such a fast clip? She could run all she wanted, but she wouldn't get away from him. His heart was committed, and he would pursue her until she was in his bed and wore his ring. It was unimportant in which order.

CHAPTER NINE

Elise drove Ruth's Ford Taurus into the circular drive in front of the Porter home. She could see how Caitlyn might be spoiled growing up in a place like this. The house was a large southern plantation style with four massive columns supporting the balcony above. Black shutters framed the windows and four sets of French doors led out onto the front porch. The porch ran the width of the house and held an array of white wicker lawn furniture. Ferns in hanging baskets hung above the porch rail broke the starkness of the wide expanse of white. Scarlet O'Hara would look right at home relaxing on the veranda.

Before climbing the front steps, she gazed toward the barns and other ranch buildings located to the right, about the length of a football field from the house. Someone had spotted the car and walked toward her. They must have recognized the car as Ruth's. Caitlyn recognized her about the time she recognized the figure as Caitlyn. The break in her stride was slight. Elise waited on the front walk until Caitlyn reached her.

"Can I help you?" Caitlyn's face was neutral, giving no hint to her thoughts. Though her clothes were dusty and sweaty from working in the barn, she was beautiful.

"Hello, Caitlyn. I'm sorry to pop in with no warning, but I was afraid if I called, I'd lose my courage." Caitlyn's eyes showed surprise at her confession. "Can we talk a minute?"

Caitlyn studied her a minute. "About what? Is everyone okay at the Coles'?"

"Yes. They're all fine."

"Then I can't imagine what we'd have to talk about."

"Caitlyn. Don't be rude and keep your guest standing in the hot sun. Bring her up here for a glass of lemonade."

It was easy to see what Caitlyn would look like in twenty-five to thirty years. Dressed in jeans and sleeveless blouse, Mrs. Porter was slim and pretty. Dark hair, similar to Caitlyn's, was beginning to gray. Rather than detracting from her appearance, the subtle streaks accented her dark blue eyes.

"Mom, she's leaving." The look she gave Elise said, "Get lost."

"I'd enjoy some lemonade, Mrs. Porter." Elise ignored Caitlyn's glare and started toward the porch steps. Caitlyn removed her hat and used it to knock some of the dust off her clothes before walking up the steps. Her boots left an echo reminding Elise of her anger.

"Mom, this is Elise Barron, Justin's *fiancé*. Elise, my mother, Shelia Porter."

Elise held her hand out to Mrs. Porter who didn't seem at all shocked to learn her identity. "It's nice to meet you, Mrs. Porter."

The older woman took her hand, studied her a minute and then smiled. "You too, Elise."

She poured two glasses of lemonade and handed one to each of them. "Now you two sit down and visit.

I've got work to do in the house. Elise, give Ruth my love."

"Yes, ma'am, I will."

Caitlyn waited to make sure her mother was out of earshot. "Now, what do you want to talk to me about? Please don't ask me to be a bridesmaid. I'm afraid the answer would have to be no."

Elise choked back a laugh. "Don't worry. That's not why I'm here." She drank some lemonade. It was refreshing, cold and tart on her tongue. "First, I need your promise you won't tell Justin I came to see you."

"Why would I want to?" Face rigid with tension, her brown eyes spoke volumes. Realizing they betrayed her, she dropped her head and studied the stitching on her jeans. Elise hoped to erase some of the hurt reflected in them. It wouldn't be possible to erase it all. That would be up to Justin.

"In the past week and a half, I've learned something about Justin. He's still in love with you." Caitlyn's head came up. She studied Elise to see if she was lying. "Justin has some issues to deal with, issues that confused his thinking about women and love. I don't feel at liberty to discuss those with you. In time, he will." She leaned forward in her chair. "I need that promise from you, Caitlyn."

Caitlyn studied her before speaking. "I promise."

"Justin and I are not getting married. Our feelings aren't the kind to sustain a marriage. We'll always be good friends." This hurt, though it was true. Her lip quivered. "Though he's tried to deny it, you own Justin's heart." Voice cracking, she managed to croak, "You're the woman of his heart, his soul, and his body."

Crying now, Caitlyn reached out to grasp her hand as she continued. "With all honesty I have to admit, my love for him wasn't passionate either. Otherwise, I wouldn't be here today." Smiling, she wiped tears off her cheeks. "You give him hell for a while. Make him work to win you back."

Caitlyn nodded. Voice hoarse, she said, "I will."

Placing her empty glass on the side table, she stood. Caitlyn reached out to her, embarrassed and not sure of what to do. "Thank you, Elise. I know this couldn't have been easy for you." Then she hugged her.

They walked down the steps together. A pickup turned into the drive. At the car door, Elise called out, "One more thing, Caitlyn." Then lowered her voice so whoever was in the truck couldn't hear. "Justin and I were never lovers. I thought you'd want to know."

Caitlyn gave her a radiant smile then burst into tears. Turning, she ran up the steps into the house.

Before she could get the car door open, Corbett appeared at her side and took her arm in a firm grip. "What the hell did you say to her? You had no right to come over here and upset her." He shook her arm. "What'd you do?"

"Ouch." She yanked her arm from his grip and rubbed it. "Get away from me." Face twisted with restrained tears, she choked out, "I told her Justin and I aren't getting married."

* * *

Simon scraped his boots on the boot cleaner before entering the bunkhouse. No need to get Chester's back up by dirtying his floor. The six hands he'd hired to help on both ranches were already seated eating. At his entrance, they all looked his way and nodded in greeting. "Hey, Chester. Did these guys leave enough food for me today?"

"You bet, Simon. Take a seat. About time you visited with us for a change."

He took a seat by Smitty and chatted with the men.

Chester placed a plate of thick beef stew with two slabs of buttered cornbread in front of him. "Anyone wants seconds, there's plenty on the stove." Several men moved to help themselves.

"Mighty good meal, Chester," said Smitty, the youngest of the hands. Grunts of approval reinforced his comment.

"Got peach cobbler for dessert so save a little room." He sat down by Simon. "Got a whole bushel of peaches while in Fredericksburg yesterday. Their crop is a good one this year. Took a bunch up to Miss Ruth so we can make cobblers for the barbecue."

Simon halted his spoon midway to his mouth. "Chester, men, the barbecue's been postponed a week." He took a bite, chewed and swallowed before continuing. "Justin and Elise aren't getting married. So, we'll have it a week later. Hope that doesn't mess up anyone's plans."

"No's" and negative headshakes moved around the table.

"Well, I'll be darned. Did you see it coming, Simon?"

"Didn't have a clue. The two up and decided together to cancel. Both seem okay with the decision."

"When'd this take place? I saw them this morning and everything appeared to be normal." He scratched his bristled chin as he thought.

"Guess that's because they still care about each

other, as good friends they say. Hallie and Elise will be staying another day before heading home."

"You don't say. Young people these days are a strange bunch." He went to the counter and brought two bowls of cobbler back. "How about a cup of coffee, Simon?"

The men carried their plates and dessert bowls to the counter, yammered out praise for the meal then left the bunkhouse in a shuffle and stomp of boots.

"You got any aspirin over there, Chester?"

"You bet." He handed a large bottle to Simon and looked at him in concern.

"God, my head is killing me." He shoved his hat back and dropped his face into his hands.

"How come? You never get headaches, Simon." He felt of his forehead. "You comin' down with something?"

"Yeah, a bad case of love." The knot on his head was sore as hell. "I was daydreaming, walked into a low beam in the barn. Hit it so hard almost knocked my feet out from under me." Hell of a thing for a grown man to admit—mooning over a woman. He took his hat off and placed it in a chair.

Chester examined the growing knot on the forward part of his crown. "Thought you were wearing your hat at an odd angle." He chuckled. "Didn't want the boys to see it, huh?"

He threw him a dirty look.

"That woman leading you a merry chase, is she?" His face reflected his humor of the situation.

"You don't miss a thing, do you, old man?"

Sipping his coffee, he said. "Nope. Knew you were a goner the second day they were here."

"I love her, Chester. So bad it hurts. But she won't marry me. Says she's afraid of getting hurt."

Chester scratched his whiskered jaw. "Scared, I bet she is. Give her some time to get used to the idea. She'll come around."

Simon touched the growing knot with care. "I wish I could believe that." Where the hell had she gone anyway?

"Do you have any idea where she went today? Saw her head out of here a couple of hours ago."

"Got me. The young one left too in Ruth's car. Guess they weren't going to the same place."

"Women. They know how to keep you guessing." Lifting his mug, he noticed it was empty. Rising, he walked to the stove. "Want some more coffee?"

"Sure, I'll take a little dab. You know, Hallie could have gone into town."

"You mean Austin?"

"No. I mean Granite Springs. She was there yesterday before getting back to the ranch. Saw her myself when I stopped by the bank."

Simon's heart lurched. "She was there to see Joe Booker?"

"Hell, no. She was sitting on a park bench looking at the courthouse. When I came out, I saw her going into that little dress shop." He studied Simon. "You don't look so good. Drink that coffee and then lie down over there on that unused bunk and rest a while." Tossing a clean pillow on the bed, he muttered. "Quit your worrying." He lowered his voice. "That woman's as crazy about you as you are her."

Simon walked to the bunk and stretched out. "What'd you say?"

"I said 'quit your worrying.'"

In the kitchen, Chester made a makeshift ice pack using a cup towel. He walked to the bunk and laid it on Simon's wound.

Simon jerked up. "Yeow, old man. That's cold."

Chester snorted. "'Course it is. That's why they call it an ice pack."

He closed his eyes. Women were a mystery. All those clothes available in her shop and she was shopping for clothes in their little town. He sighed. If he could close his eyes and rest a minute, he'd feel a lot better.

* * *

Hallie drove by and waved at Chester and Whitney as they stood on the stoop of the bunkhouse. Before she could get in the house, Whitney came racing up. "Hi ya, Hallie. Where you been?"

She couldn't resist stroking the auburn hair pulled back in neat braids. "I've been to town seeing the sights. What are you doing out here without your hat."

Her hand came down on top of her head. "Oops. I forgot. I was in a hurry to get down to the bunkhouse 'cause Uncle Simon didn't come to lunch. He ate with the men. He does that sometimes."

"He does? That's good." No doubt Chester enjoyed his company, the men too.

"But Chester told me he's got a bad, bad headache. Gots a big knot on his head from a run in with a board in the barn." She lowered her voice. "He's asleep. Chester told me to be real quiet when he let me peek at him. I gave him a little kiss," she pointed to her cheek, "and he said 'thank you, sweet pea' so he was pretending to be asleep."

She giggled. "Chester said a kiss from his woman was the medicine he needed to feel better." When you waved he said, "You go tell Hallie she needs to come down here right now." Her face turned serious. "Are you Uncle Simon's woman, too?"

"Uh, well, here." She handed her purse to Whitney. "Would you put this in my room for me?" Whitney skipped to the house. The big shoulder bag, over her neck and arm, hung to her knees.

It was dim in the bunkhouse. The hum of the window air conditioner muffled her footsteps as she walked to the occupied bed. Simon's boots, still on his feet, were propped on the end rail. He lay on his back, one arm draped across his eyes. A cup towel filled with ice was perched on his head above the hairline. She sat, facing him, on the side of the bunk and laid her hand on his chest. He covered it, entwining their fingers, with his free hand.

Eyes closed, he said. "Did you buy something pretty in town?"

"No, just looking."

He brought her hand to his mouth and kissed her palm. "I wondered where you'd gone. Saw you drive out."

She drew her hand from his and with her fingers traced the lines alongside his mouth. It was pinched with pain. Easing aside the arm covering his eyes, she started massaging his temples. He groaned in pleasure. "I went to town, checked out some of the shops. Didn't Ruth tell you?"

"No. I haven't been up to the house."

"By the way. After the announcement last night I forgot to show Justin the loan agreement papers. Let's get together with him after supper tonight."

"Hallie, under the circumstances, are you sure you still want to do this?"

"Yes, I do. He's a good kid."

"Okay."

"Be quiet now. I'm going to massage your scalp, neck and shoulders." He jerked making her laugh. "Not your sore spot. It'll help you relax enough to go to sleep for a while."

"Lean down here and kiss me first." His hand cupped her head, drawing her face down to his. Her lips touched his in a chaste kiss. Before she could move back, he held her head in place, inches from his. Startled, she stared at him. Eyes darkened with desire, he studied her expression then eased her mouth back to his. His lips nibbled, pulled before devouring hers in a soul-searching quest. Hot stabs of desire shot through her body. She pressed closer to him, wrapping her arms around his head. His free arm came up and locked around her waist, pinning her to him. When she moaned, he broke the kiss and released her head.

She stared in shock at his closed eyes. *Lord 'a mercy. If he could turn her on like that with a kiss, what would happen when the rest of his whole body was involved?* A shiver ran through her at the thought.

His eyes popped open. "Are you cold, sugar?"

Breathless, she sat up. "No. Well, maybe a little."

He ran his hands up and down her arms to warm them until she halted them with hers.

"Now, relax and close those eyes or I'll think your head doesn't hurt at all." He gave her a cocky grin but closed his eyes. He sighed as her fingers worked on the muscles and tendons of his neck.

Five minutes later his breathing was deep. The lines around his eyes, mouth, and on his forehead were relaxed. She sat a while longer admiring the strong features of his face. His cheekbones were high, from possible Indian heritage, his jaw was strong, his lips full. Auburn hair curled a little around his face from wearing his hat and sweating. Her eyes strayed to the hair curling above his shirt buttons. Unable to resist, she laid her hand there to feel its texture. Soft, it curled around her fingers. He jerked in his sleep and she yanked her hand back unseating the ice pack. She grabbed it before it hit the floor.

Satisfied that he was resting, she eased off the bed and tiptoed to the door.

* * *

Hallie handed a copy of the loan agreement to Justin and one to Simon. "Justin, I hope you've decided to do this."

He rubbed the back of his neck. "I don't know, Hallie, it doesn't seem right. It might be better to sell some of the land."

Ruth started around the table pouring coffee. "Justin, you never sell land unless it's a last resort. You want to keep it intact for your future children."

He snorted. "Kinda hard to have kids without a wife."

Simon grabbed his neck and gave him a light shake. "Be patient. Things will work out between you and Caitlyn."

"Hallie, you may need your money. What if I can't pay you back right when you need it?" Simon and Ruth added their agreement.

"Listen to me a minute. I need something to invest

my money in. Why not a ranch?" She shook her head. "No. No, don't interrupt. Hear me out. I'm not trying to be glib or brag when I say I have plenty of money. But, I do. And I'd rather do something useful with it than let it sit in the bank until I die." Squeezing Simon's hand, she peered into his eyes and added. "James would be proud to know some of the money he left was being returned to the land and a family who loved it." Her eyes pleading, she smiled at Justin. "Please let me do this."

She meant every word she'd said. Simon didn't doubt that one bit. What a woman. Here she was, the mother of Justin's ex-*fiancée* and concerned about the future of his ranch.

Ruth sat her coffee cup down and studied Hallie. "Will this loan take all of your savings?"

Shaking her head, Hallie said. "No, Ruth. I promise you it won't. I'll have plenty available for emergencies."

Simon cleared his throat. "It's your call, Justin. I think she's a pretty successful businesswoman and knows what she's getting into." He didn't think Hallie would offer to help if she didn't have faith in Justin's ability to restore the ranch.

They waited in silence for Justin to make up his mind. Hallie breathed a sigh of relief when he spoke. "Alright, I accept, Hallie."

Ruth walked around the table and kissed Hallie on the cheek. "Bless you, Hallie." Patting her on the shoulder, she added. "I think I'll check on those girls in the pool."

Hallie took out her checkbook. "What do you think it would take to get back in top operating business?"

She looked from Simon to Justin.

Justin rubbed his chin and looked at his uncle. "I could do a lot with $100,000.00, but I can work with less." Simon nodded in agreement.

She wrote and signed the check and passed it over to Justin. "Take this to Joe Booker. Tell him he's to handle it himself. No one in the bank, or town for that matter, is to know where the money came from."

Justin looked from the check to Hallie. "My God, Hallie. This is more than twice what I asked for." He handed the check to Simon.

"Why so much, Hallie?" asked Simon. He waved the check. "It won't take this much."

"It will for what I want him to do." She started making notes. "First, I want you to get the cleaning lady to come two days a week to help Ruth. Of course you'll be hiring extra hands so find someone to help Chester out with the cooking. After buying stock, supplies—whatever it takes to operate a ranch, invest what's left. The interest you earn will help to pay me back. I'm charging ten percent interest and payments aren't due for five years." She offered her hand to Justin. "Do we have a deal?"

Taking it in a firm grip, he said. "Deal."

* * *

Hallie knew Elise was hurting. She'd spent the afternoon and evening with Whitney. The two frolicked in the water. Being around Justin was awkward for her. Justin sat watching them, remorse written on his face.

"She'll be alright, you know," said Simon.

Hallie sighed. "Yeah. I know." It was dark at the picnic table under the big oak. "What about Justin? Do you think he'll be able to make things right with

Caitlyn?"

"It's hard to say. You know how you women are." Chuckling, he leaned down and kissed the side of her face. "She might want him to suffer awhile." Her back was against his chest and when he laughed, she felt the vibrations.

"Yeah, it's no more than fair. She's suffered so now it's his turn. But, the main thing is he has to build her trust again." She couldn't help but feel sorry for him. Loretta had screwed up both Simon and Justin's thinking. Not that she had any room to talk. She had hang-ups of her own to deal with.

Elise needed to be at home. The stress of being around Justin was showing on her. She put on a good face, but couldn't hide anything from her mother.

"What are you thinking about?"

"It's good we're going home tomorrow. I'd like to stay longer but Elise needs to distance herself from Justin." She turned in his arms. "I'm sorry, Simon. I hope you understand."

"Of course I do." With his finger, he traced the shape of her brows. "Stop frowning, sugar. How about if I come see you this weekend?"

"You mean like for a date?"

"Yeah. Like for a date."

She rested her head against his chest. "Hummm. It might be fun. Where does a country fella take a city girl when he comes courting?"

He tilted her chin up for his kiss. "How about dinner and a movie?" His lips traveled along her jaw to her ear. "Or, we could go dancing." She giggled when he nipped her ear with his teeth. "Maybe we could sit on your couch and make out."

"I'd love to go dancing."

"No necking on your couch then, huh?"

"We'll see, cowboy."

"Dancing's almost as good as necking anyway."

"You're crazy, Simon."

He growled in her ear. "Crazy about you, baby."

Wrapped in his arms she felt safe. He was comfortable yet exciting. As they sat watching the stars and listening to the cicadas, she didn't feel pressured to keep up a steady stream of conversation. But, when he embraced and kissed her, her heart and body sang.

"Can I spend the night at your place or do I need to get a motel room? I could stay with Paul and Jo Beth, but she'd keep me up quizzing me about you."

"Oh, you poor thing. You can stay with us. I'll get the guest room ready."

He nuzzled her ear. "You mean I don't get to sleep with you, darlin?"

She reached up and pinched his neck. "Stop that." Then laughed. "You'll have to ask Ted what he thinks."

"Ouch! You mean your son will be there this weekend?"

"I think so. If nothing's changed his plans. It will be nice for you to meet him." She chewed her lip, thinking. "He might not be too sociable. I've never had a man friend over, much less one to spend the night."

"Oh boy. I bet he watches us like a hawk." He hugged her. "I can appreciate and respect a young man looking out for his mother." The vibrations from his chest shook her again as he gave in to silent laughter.

"What are you laughing about?" she asked.

"It'll be hard to make out on the sofa with a chaperone."

At the thought she laughed too.

"Don't worry. Ted and I'll get along fine," he said.

"He's not going to be happy about Elise being hurt." Ted was crazy about his sister and had a temper she'd worked years to try to tame. They'd made progress but on occasion he lost it. "I hope he doesn't take his anger out on you since Justin won't be there to take the brunt."

"I can handle whatever he wants to dish out. Let's talk about something else. Where are you taking me dancing? Can I wear my cowboy boots and jeans? Please don't make me put on a suit."

Hallie laughed. "No suit. I promise."

* * *

They left after breakfast. Simon watched their car until the dust trail behind them settled. The house seemed too quiet. He missed her already. Odd how in such a short time Hallie had become an integral part of him. She'd moved in and made herself at home in his heart in ten days. And, damn. He loved it. Grinning, he rubbed his chest. His heart was so swollen he thought it would bust.

Justin and Elise's parting had been tense. She'd tried not to cry. Justin didn't know what to do or say. He'd hugged her, and to her credit, she'd returned it.

Better get cracking. He'd get ahead on his work and have the entire weekend with Hallie. In the office he grabbed his hat. An unfamiliar paper stuck out from under a short stack of bills. It was Elise's prenuptial agreement. Pulling it from under the stack, he glanced over it and smiled. She had stated that in case of divorce, the Cole Ranch would remain intact but any children born to the couple would be future heirs. She respected and loved the land as he did. Here was proof.

Laying the paper down, something about money caught his eye. In case of divorce the money will be paid back with interest over time. What money? He searched the document and found what he looked for. "Shit!"

He dropped into the chair behind the desk. On her marriage or when she turned 30, Elise would inherit one million dollars. Hallie had said her late husband James had provided well for them. But, one million dollars? That meant Ted would get that much too. His stomach felt sick. Oh, God, no…Please don't let it be so.

Reaching for the phone, he called Joe Booker at the bank. Joe was the only person he could think of off-hand who could get the information he needed. He hated to pry but had to know. It took several minutes before Joe picked up.

"Simon. Good to hear from you. What's up?"

"I need you to do something for me, Joe. And I need you to be discreet. No one else needs to know about this."

"Okay. It's not illegal, is it?"

"I don't think so." He paused, thinking. "Elise inherits one million dollars when she marries or turns thirty."

Simon yanked the phone back as Joe's whistle pierced his ear. "That's a bunch of money, Simon. Justin can do lots for the ranch with that kind of capital."

"Justin and Elise are not getting married. It's a long story and I don't have time today. What I want you to find out is if Hallie is a millionaire too." There. He'd said it.

On the other end of the phone, Joe was silent. When he spoke his tone was terse. "I'm disappointed in you, Simon. I never knew you to be money hungry. Is that why you're so attracted to her, you want the money?"

"Hell no. I want the woman, but I sure as hell don't want a bunch of money."

"I have a friend in Austin who can find out. I'll call you back in a few minutes." He laughed. "You're pretty much a goner, aren't you, old buddy?"

"Hell, yes, old friend."

Ten minutes later the phone rang. "You're not going to like this, Simon. Are you sitting down?"

"Oh, God. It's bad, huh?" He leaned forward, elbows on the desk, and dropped his head into his hand.

"Yeah. Fifteen million bad. Looks like she's a pretty savvy market trader."

"She learned from her late husband. Thanks, Joe. Remember, this is confidential."

"Good luck, Simon." He hung up.

That sweet, unassuming woman was a millionaire. Yet she worked, and didn't appear extravagant. Elise didn't seem preoccupied with money. That was due to Hallie's influence and rearing. What a woman.

What was he going to do? He didn't want people to think he married a woman for her money. Why couldn't she be poor, or average, like everybody else he knew? Money could cause problems in a relationship.

"Fifteen million dollars. Shit!"

CHAPTER TEN

They were quiet on the ride home, both deep in thought. Hallie reached over and patted Elise on the leg. "You going to be okay, sugar?"

A tentative smile lifted her lips. "Yeah, Mom. I'll survive. My ego's dented, but it's for the best." Turning in the seat, she added. "I've been thinking. If the region service center will let me enroll late for their teacher certification program, I'm going to do that this summer."

"That's a good idea, Elise. Are you sure you're up to it though? You said it was an intense program."

"Yeah, I think I can handle it. And, it'll get my mind off this mess I helped create. I can't blame everything on Justin."

"I'm grateful you both realized you were making a mistake before the wedding." So much had happened since the meeting in Simon's office there hadn't been a chance to tell Elise about her inheritance.

"Elise, I need to tell you something. Before I do, you need to understand your daddy made certain arrangements for you and Ted before he died. Remember him telling you about the land he grew up on?"

"Yes. He seemed hurt when Uncle John wanted to sell it to get the money."

Hallie nodded. "Yes, he was. Your daddy insisted

we never touch that money. It's been invested for years—in a trust fund for you and Ted. An account was also set up for me. The money has grown and now you and Ted have over a million dollars each."

Elise stared open mouthed. "A million dollars? Mother, that's a fortune. Why didn't I know about this?"

"I promised your daddy not to tell you before your marriage or your thirtieth birthday."

"But why?"

Hallie sighed. "For one thing, he wanted you kids to grow up with a respect for money. He didn't want you to be spoiled rich kids. And, he didn't want a man marrying you for your money."

She snorted. "He must have thought I'd be blinded by a man's good looks and sweet talk. Not much of a compliment."

"Don't look at it like that. He didn't know how smart you'd grow up to be." She reached for Elise's hand.

"Elise, if it's still your dream to try to make it on Broadway, you have the money now. I don't want you to regret not having the chance." It's all she'd talked about as a teenager and during college. Of course, she didn't want her to go but didn't have the right to make her choices for her.

"You'd let me use the money for that?"

"Yeah. I would."

"Thanks, Mom, but I don't think so. I think the best thing for me right now is teacher certification." She laughed. "After my first year of teaching I may grab the money and run."

How did she get such a levelheaded daughter?

"The money will be there if you change your mind."

Leaning her head back against the seat she closed her eyes. "You know, Mom, Simon reminds me a lot of Daddy. It's a shame he didn't have kids of his own. He'd make a good father."

"Are you trying to tell me something?"

"Mom, if you love that man as much as you're hot for him, you better marry him soon."

She hit the brake, and then released it. Thank goodness no one was riding her bumper. "Elise. I can't believe my ears." Her face was on fire.

Elise sat chuckling beside her. Unable to restrain the urge, nervous twitters escaped her mouth. Her response sent Elise into a fit of laughter. When she could talk without laughing, she asked. "Does that mean I have your approval?"

"Yes, it does." She twisted in the seat. "Mom, he's head over heels in love with you. And, on top of being a fine man, he's a hunk. Justin said he's never seen his uncle so taken with a woman."

"I'm pretty crazy about him too."

"But?"

"What if something happens to him, like with your daddy?"

"Mother. You've taught us better than that. Tomorrow you could walk across the street and get hit by a car. For that matter, we could have a wreck on the way home and die. You're not going to let fear keep you from being happy with a man. In particular a man like Simon."

"I don't know." She gnawed at her lip as tears stung her eyes.

"Has he asked you to marry him?" Hallie tried to

smile through her tears but knew her smile looked more like a grimace, and nodded yes.

"Mom. That's wonderful."

Hallie shrugged.

"You told him no, didn't you?" She nodded. "Oh, Mom." She reached over and squeezed her shoulder. "I bet one no won't keep him from asking again. He seems determined."

She reached for a tissue and wiped her eyes. "So, you won't mind if he comes this weekend?" Heavens, that was only two days away. "I'm putting him up in the guest room so he doesn't have to suffer Jo Beth's quizzing."

"No. By all means, save him from the inquisition. That Jo Beth is something else. I like her though."

"You know, Ted will be home this weekend. Do you think he'll mind Simon being there?"

Her mouth tilted in a wicked smile. "No. He won't mind. Just be sure and tell Simon not to look at your boobs."

Hallie shrieked. "One of these days, girl, I'm going to turn the tables on you." She joined Elise's laughter. She could see Ted telling Simon to "watch where you put your eyes."

* * *

They were home before noon. Hallie spent the remainder of the day cleaning house. She baked a red velvet cake for Ted and made chicken salad to have on hand for his between meal snacks.

Friday morning she opened the shop early. Gladys, a longtime employee, stuck her head around the office door.

Both hands over her heart, she gasped. "Lord a

mercy, Hallie, you scared the dickens out of me. I was about to run next door and call the police. What're you doing back so soon from your vacation?"

Hallie glanced up from the ledger she was studying. Gladys was dressed in bright prints and large jewelry as usual. Not many women could carry it off, but on Gladys with her height and graying dark hair it looked wonderful. She smiled. "We decided it best to come back early. Elise and Justin called off their engagement."

Her eyes rounded with shock as she covered her mouth with both hands. "Oh, my, God, that poor child. Is she devastated?" She hung her purse on a hook behind the door. "What happened?"

"They decided their feelings were more friendship than lasting love."

Gladys snorted. "What you mean is, he cheated on her and she found out. I hope you gave him and that uncle of his a piece of your mind."

Hallie couldn't help but laugh. Gladys looked ready to do battle. She didn't have much faith in the male species. That's what she called them—the "male species."

"No Gladys, he didn't cheat on her. But, though he tried to deny it, he still cared for his childhood sweetheart. Elise realized there were problems and they broke up. In time I think they'll be friends."

She snorted again. "Friends, my ass," she mumbled as she started a pot of coffee. Hallie heard words like, "turds" and "deficient species" along with the clatter of dishes and running water.

"Gladys, the books look great. You've done a good job."

The banging stopped. She beamed. "You like that profit balance, do ya?"

"Yes, I do." She studied the page again. "You have a real knack, Gladys. Have you ever considered having your own store?"

"Every day. But, can't put together enough money for a down payment on my own place." She waved her hand and turned back to the coffee maker. "Anyway. I wouldn't want to cut in on your profits."

There was that. Gladys wasn't modest when it came to her belief in her abilities. If she ever decided to sell the store Gladys might be the person to sell to.

She left at 4:00 so she'd be home when Ted came in dragging his dirty laundry. At 5:00, he blew through the door. That's how it felt when he came and went—like a gust of wind rushing through the house that left her swaying in its aftermath.

"Mom, I'm home." She heard his books hit the hall floor.

She met him in the hall as he made his way to the laundry room. "Hey, hon, it's good to see you." He gripped her in a bear hug and she breathed in the scent of him, no longer that little boy "wet dog" smell but the scent of a man wearing aftershave.

"You too, Mom. Got anything to eat? I'm starving."

"Sure, you want a sandwich until dinner time?"

"Mom, do you mind if I grab a bite and go out with the guys tonight?" He looked apologetic. "I hate to run out on you."

"No problem. Save a little time to visit with your old mom before you head back to school." Thank goodness she'd already baked a ham and marshmallow topped candied yams.

"Thanks, Mom, you're a peach."

"Empty your laundry bag while I fix you a plate." He grabbed it and started pouring clothes out in the floor. She raised her voice so it would carry to the next room. "While you're in there, go ahead and sort them for me, would you?"

"Sure, Mom."

She sat with him while he ate. "How're your classes?" He was bright, like his father, so she didn't expect any problems.

"They're great. I like my philosophy class. The professor is cool." He filled his mouth with a forkful of sweet potatoes. "Ummm. These are good, Mom."

She patted his arm. "Glad you like them. Met any girls?"

"Man, you wouldn't believe all the pretty girls on campus. Thing is, they're smart too. Neat, huh?"

Smiling, she nodded. "Ted, I need to talk to you about something."

He stopped eating and peered at her with concern. "Are you alright, Mom?" He looked around. "Where's Elise?"

"Stop worrying. Everyone is fine. Well, Elise isn't too happy right now. She and Justin broke up." He bristled. "She's fine, Ted. It's a long story, one I'll let her tell. They both agreed so don't think it's all Justin's fault.

He sighed. "Dang, he's a nice guy. I'm sorry it didn't work out."

"Do you remember me telling you about Justin's uncle, Simon Cole?" He nodded while he chewed. "He's coming tomorrow and will spend the weekend."

His fork stopped in midair. "What for?"

"To see me." She couldn't help the blush heating her skin.

"What for?" Lowering his fork, he watched her with his daddy's eyes. A hint of guilt niggled at her.

"Uh, well, Justin, we're seeing each other."

He arched his brow. "In seeing, you mean like dating?"

"Yes, that's it. We're dating. I hope you'll be nice to him." Standing, she brought the cake to the table. "Have room for a piece of cake?"

He licked his lips and rubbed his belly. "You bet. My favorite." She cut a large slice and set it in front of him.

The back door opened and Elise walked in. "Hey, bro. I see you've started in on the cake already."

He stood and grabbed her in a bear hug. "Hey, sis."

Hallie glanced at the heavy sack she carried. "Did you find everything you needed at the book store?"

"Yes. I did. They had all the required books stacked together so I didn't have to run around searching for different titles." She emptied her sack onto the table.

Ted looked through the books. "You going back to school?"

"Uh huh. For the summer. I may have a teaching job for the fall. Depends on if there are any vacancies."

He hooted. "You're kidding, right? You, a teacher?" He pointed his fork at her while laughing with a mouth full of cake.

Hands on her hips she glared at him. "Yes, me a teacher. What's wrong with that?"

He washed his cake down with a swallow of milk.

"I can't imagine you in a classroom of kids." He shrugged. "I thought all you wanted to do was act in the theater."

She stuffed the books back in the bag. "Sometimes things change. Not that I'm giving the theater up altogether."

He nodded. "Good. Sit down and tell me about your trip to the ranch. Looks like you got a little sun."

Hallie put the cake and an extra plate and fork on the table. "You two help yourselves. I'm going to start Ted's laundry and go upstairs for a while. Do you plan to be out late tonight, Ted?"

"I'll be home around 11:00."

"Okay. Be careful."

* * *

It was Friday evening and Simon's frustration hadn't receded. He brushed Redman and mumbled to himself. For the past two days, he'd worked like crazy trying to get caught up with work so he could spend time with Hallie. But his mind kept returning to one thing. She was a millionaire. Damn. Could he marry a woman with so much money? He wasn't a male chauvinist, but dammit, a man was supposed to make more money than the woman. It wasn't a written rule, but that's the way it was.

Of course, there were exceptions, like Joe Hadley in town. His wife, Doc Hadley, brought in the money while Joe ran the house. Joe had taught at the high school until the babies started coming. Since her income was more, Joe stayed home with the baby while she went back to her practice. They both seemed content with the situation. Staying home with the kids didn't appear to detract from his masculinity. They kept having babies. By his count, it was three now.

Maybe his thinking was screwed up, and he was making too much of her money. He stood thinking, holding the brush still on Redman's side. The whip of Redman's tail sent him back to brushing.

Dammit, she should have told him. Would he have told her if he had that kind of money? Hell no. He wouldn't want some woman marrying him for his money. Is that what she thought about him? That he'd marry her for her money? How insulting. He'd call her later and get this out in the open.

Having made the decision, he felt better. He put his grooming supplies away and headed for the house. Maybe now he could concentrate on the books.

The phone rang on the other end. Simon leaned back in the desk chair and propped his boots on the corner of the desk.

"Hello, Simon." Her voice was like balm to his soul, easing the muscles in his back and shoulders.

"Hi, darlin'. Wish you were here."

"Me, too. Or you were here." God, he hoped she missed him as much as he missed her.

"What would we be doing if I were there right now?" Visions of cuddling on the sofa with the lights low made his heart race.

"We'd have finished Ted's laundry and be sitting down for a slice of red velvet cake and coffee."

"Mmmm. My favorite."

She laughed, a deep throaty laugh. "Ted's favorite, James's, too."

"After our dessert would we sit on the sofa and make out?"

"Until Ted got home. Then you'd better be on your

best behavior as he'll be checking you out."

"Did you tell your kids I was coming tomorrow?"

"Yes, I did." He waited for her to elaborate. When she didn't, he asked. "And... What did they say?"

"Elise is delighted. But she had some advice for you." He could almost hear her grin through the telephone. "You're not to let Ted see you looking at my boobs. It makes him mad when men do that."

Simon froze at her words. Then laughter rumbled from his belly up through his chest and out. It consumed him and for a full 30 seconds he couldn't talk. Wiping tears from his eyes, he spoke into the phone. "I'm sorry. That was the last thing I expected to hear Elise say." In a choked voice he asked, "Did she say what he'd do it he caught me?"

Giggling, she said. "Something like telling you, 'you better find another place to focus your eyes.'" She cleared her throat. "It seems a man at church had been sizing them up and Ted confronted him one Sunday. Elise said the man was red enough to have a coronary."

He started laughing all over again. The kid had grit and he could appreciate a man looking out for his mother. When he could talk, he said. "You've got fine kids, Hallie. You've done a wonderful job with them."

"Thank you, Simon. I think that's the nicest thing you've ever said to me."

He sobered and cleared his throat. "Hallie, we need to talk about something."

"What?"

"Is there anything you want to tell me about yourself?"

She laughed. "You mean like I'm a serial killer or a street walker by night?"

"That's not funny, Hallie."

"Okay. It's not funny. I don't know what you're talking about then."

"You left the prenuptial agreement on my desk. Being curious, I read it. You never said anything about Elise inheriting a million dollars." Simon waited for her to say something.

"Yes, you're right." She sighed. "James made me promise not to reveal that information until Elise married or turned thirty, whichever came first. Can't you understand?"

"Of course I can. What I can't understand is why you didn't let me know you're a multimillionaire."

"I told you all I had plenty of money. What was I supposed to say? 'Hey, Simon. Guess what? I'm a multimillionaire.'?"

"Hell, I don't know. But you could have let me know somehow."

"Why? I don't see how my money can be a problem." He could hear her strumming on something on the other end. Sounded like fingernails tapping on the table. "How'd you find out anyway? You went snooping in my business, didn't you?"

"Yes, I did. I know it wasn't right but I wanted to know what I'd be getting into if we got married. All that money makes me uncomfortable. I wouldn't want people to think I married you for your money."

"You remember the *if* in all this. I haven't said I'd marry you, and at the rate we're going tonight, it'll never happen."

His boots hit the floor with a loud thud. "Now, hold on a minute. Are you threatening me?" His voice was louder than he intended. She didn't answer him.

Lowering his voice, he added. "Hallie, answer me please."

"I might be." He could hear her moving around in the kitchen. She turned on the water and then the disposal. "Simon, I can't help the fact I have money. It's not important to me. It was to James. It's for the children's future and for me if I'm ever in need. Or to give away if I want to."

"I understand, Hallie. But we need to be able to talk things over like rational adults. I've worked through this in my mind and realized your money is not a problem. I need to be able to talk to you about my feelings."

"I'm sorry, Simon. You're right."

* * *

Hallie had hung up the phone when the doorbell rang. A nice looking, dark haired young man in jeans and cowboy boots stood at the front door. "Yes, can I help you?"

"Mrs. Barron, I'm Corbett Porter, Caitlyn's cousin. Is Elise in?" Hat in his hands, he smiled showing beautiful white teeth.

"Yes, Corbett, she's here. Come in." He stepped inside the entry hall. She waved toward the living room. "Have a seat. I'll tell her you're here."

Upstairs, she studied her daughter in consternation.

"Mother, I don't want to see him. Please tell him what I said."

Hallie looked her daughter over. Her face was flushed, her mouth set in a thin line. "Elise, I'm not going down there and say that. You go down and tell him yourself."

Elise brushed past and went down the stairs. When

186

she entered the living room, Corbett rose.

* * *

"Elise."

"Corbett." He flinched at the chill in her voice.

They stared at each other, neither speaking. She wasn't happy to see him. Corbett didn't blame her. He cleared his throat. "I'm sorry to drop by like this but I have to get this off my chest." Elise didn't speak. "I've come to apologize."

She pointed to the sofa. "Oh. Would you like to sit down?"

"If you don't mind, I'd rather sit out on the porch."

"All right." Outside, he sat beside her on the glider.

"I'm sorry for the way I acted the day you came to see Caitlyn. I overreacted and was rude. I hope I didn't hurt you when I grabbed your arm." He'd worried about her ever since it happened. "I was so concerned for Caitlyn I wasn't thinking straight."

She set the glider moving with her foot. "It's good you care about your cousin so much. Family is important."

"Yes, but I shouldn't have grabbed your arm. Is it bruised?" He reached over to inspect it and she jumped at his touch and pulled it away. "It's fine. The bruise is small, almost not noticeable."

"I'm sorry."

"You're apology is accepted."

"That was a fine thing you did for Caitlyn, for Justin too."

She nodded.

He chuckled. "She's taking your advice and making him suffer awhile. He's invited to dinner tonight but Caitlyn doesn't know. It was Aunt Shelia's doing. I expect to see fireworks in the sky in the direction of Granite Springs any minute now. Should be an interesting evening."

She laughed. "I bet."

He got up. "I better go."

"Thank you for stopping by." She stood with him and started walking with him to his truck.

Her long straight hair gleamed white in the moonlight. Tall and slim, she resembled a wood sprite he'd seen in a book he'd read as a child. His pulse thundered. She had no idea the effect she had on him. He desired her, yes, but he wanted to get to know her, see if they might have a future together.

They stopped at his truck and he turned toward her. "Elise, that night at the dance, you jumped when my lips touched your skin."

She folded her arms across her chest. "You shocked me. What'd you expect?"

"Shocked, huh?" How was he going to explain this? "I was so shocked my heart almost jumped out of my chest. What I'm trying to say is I believe there's chemistry between us. Oh, hell. Let me show you."

He titled her chin, looked into her eyes, then slipped his other arm around her waist and pulled her close. Though tall and thin, her body was soft. Taking it slow, giving her a chance to rebuke him, his head descended and captured her lips. He took his time, teasing, coaxing until her lips softened and returned his kiss. Forgetting this was an experiment, he poured his soul into the kiss. When her arms wrapped around his neck and she pressed her body closer to his, he came to his senses and broke away.

Breathing heavy, he kissed her temple and

whispered. "I knew there was magic between us from the moment I saw you. I know you're not ready for another relationship right now, but when you are, I'll be back."

* * *

"Mother. What's he doing here?" Justin flinched at the harsh tone in Caitlyn's voice. Guess she wasn't ready to forgive him. Corbett said she knew he was no longer engaged. Every time he'd call her she'd said, "I'm not ready to talk to you."

"Come in, Justin. Caitlyn, mind your manners. Bring Justin on in the den." Shelia Porter was pretty and sweet as usual. She was an older replica of Caitlyn, but the eyes were different as was her temperament. Shelia forgave without difficulty. Caitlyn as a rule did too. Of course, this was different.

Sam sat in his ragged leather recliner reading the paper. His large frame overwhelmed the chair. Tall and stocky, Sam Porter was a large, compact man. He looked up. "What the hell are you doing here, Justin?"

He threw up his hands. "I don't have a clue, sir, other than I was invited. I'll leave if my presence offends you."

"You'll do no such thing. Sit down here on the sofa." Shelia turned to her husband. "You mind your manners Sam Porter. Justin is my guest. If you don't like it, I'll take him in to town to eat and you can manage on your own."

Red faced, Sam mumbled under his breath and drew the paper up where his wife couldn't see his face. All that was visible were reddish brown tufts of his hair. Well known for his explosive temper, Justin had never seen him lose it with Shelia. "Have a seat,

189

Justin," sounded from behind the paper.

"Caitlyn, sit down and keep Justin company. It seems your father is hiding again." Shelia smiled and left the room.

Justin shifted on the couch. This was damned awkward. "How've you been, Caitlyn?" She sat on the far end and wouldn't look at him. She wore her dark hair down tonight, caught up on the sides with a large barrette. It showed off her smooth skin, the long column of her neck. She had on shorts and a t-shirt instead of her usual jeans and long-sleeved shirt. It was hard to keep his eyes off the long expanse of tanned leg.

"Fine."

If conversation flowed like this all evening it would be a long night. "Good. I'm glad to hear it." Silence. He glanced toward Sam to see the man duck his head back behind the paper.

"I hope you and your folks will come to our dance and barbecue next Saturday. Should be lots of people there."

"Will Elise be there?" This time, she glared at him as she waited for his answer.

"Yes. She'll be there with her mother. Her brother Ted may come too." Sam had let the paper descend, exposing his dark brown eyes over the top. "Uncle Simon is visiting Mrs. Barron this weekend." He grinned over at Sam. Sam looked at him but didn't smile. "If he has his way, they'll be married before the fall. Not that he's said anything to me, but I can tell he's a goner when it comes to Hallie."

"How does she feel about him?" Caitlyn's eyes were bright with curiosity. Sam folded the paper and set it aside.

"I think she's crazy about him too, but I don't know, seems something else is going on there." He wished he knew what it was. Uncle Simon deserved a loving woman and he didn't want to see him hurt.

Sam spoke for the first time. "Bet she's got another man in town, one with lots of money."

"I don't think so. And from what I heard from Uncle Simon today, she's got plenty of money of her own. Upset him something awful. All that money makes him uncomfortable. You know how people around here can talk."

Sam nodded. "People will talk regardless. If he loves her, forget the money and marry her. If she'll have him, that is. Anyone who knows Simon knows he wouldn't marry for money."

"Come to supper now." Shelia took his arm and led him across the hall to the dining room. He sat to her right, across from Caitlyn, Sam sat at the other end of the table. When they finished their salads, she filled their plates with roast beef, potatoes, carrots and onions. Rich brown gravy drizzled across the meat and vegetables. Gran made a mean pot roast but Shelia's outdid hers. It was the best in the county.

"This is delicious, ma'am." She beamed her thanks. Sam finished chewing and wiped his mouth.

"Sure is, hon, you've outdone yourself tonight." He surveyed Justin and his earlier frown returned. "I hope it wasn't all for this fickle young man."

"Sam!" "Daddy!" Shelia and Caitlyn spoke at the same time.

Justin put his fork down and wiped his mouth with the linen napkin. "It's all right. He has a right to say that. I've been confused about some things."

"Damn right, it's alright." Waving his fork at Caitlyn, he added. "He broke your heart, then went and broke that other girl's too."

He put his napkin on the table. "Sam, could we go outside and talk for a minute. I need to explain some things to you." He stood and waited. Sam looked him over then threw his napkin on the table and pushed his chair back.

"I'm going too," said Caitlyn.

"No, you're not, young lady. You stay in here with your mother. This is between the two of us."

"Come on, honey. Help me get the coffee and dessert ready." She gave her husband a meaningful glower. "I better not hear anything breaking out there." Taking Caitlyn's elbow she ushered her into the kitchen.

Sam watched them go, then turned and walked out onto the front porch. He sat in one of the rockers while Justin leaned against the porch column.

"Well, get to it, son. We don't have all night." The older man was enjoying his discomfort.

"I've loved Caitlyn ever since I can remember."

Sam snorted. "Funny way you have of showing it."

"My last semester in school, I started getting worried. I wanted to get married, make a home for Whitney so Gran and Uncle Simon could get on with their lives." He cleared his throat. "Caitlyn is so beautiful and kind. I've loved her for so long I can't remember when it started." He was quiet for a minute, thinking. "But she's wild and impetuous. I was afraid if we married she wouldn't settle down to the boredom of everyday life on the ranch. I don't have the money to give her the things she's used to, won't for a number of years." Voice choked, he turned to look out at the sunset. "My biggest fear was Caitlyn would regret marrying me and leave like my mother did."

Sam sniffed, and then blew his nose. "Damn allergies."

"When I met Elise, I thought, here's the ideal woman. She's settled, responsible and she'll make a perfect wife. I thought I loved her. Hell, I care about her a lot, but as a friend. I had doubts about my feelings, but I tried to ignore them. Elise wouldn't let me any longer." He laughed. "We happened to witness Uncle Simon kissing Hallie, and I'm here to tell you, there was so much heat between those two we're lucky they didn't burn the garage down."

"Is that so? In the garage, huh? Making out in the garage." He laughed and slapped his knee. "Good for Simon."

"That kind of passion is what a man and woman should have for each other when they marry. Elise and I didn't have it. All my passion belonged to Caitlyn. God knows, I can't get close to Caitlyn and keep my hands off her." He shot Sam a glance to see if he was angry. "It's not just lust. I love her and want to marry her."

Sam cleared his throat. "Passion enhances a relationship if love and respect are present. Without those two factors it's worthless." His voice sounded thick like he had a cold.

"I want a chance to prove my love to Caitlyn and to make things right between us again."

Sam was quiet. "Caitlyn is spoiled. I can't deny that or the fact it's my fault. Will she settle down when she marries? I don't know. The question is are you willing to take that chance?" He looked at Justin.

"That's what this is all about, right?"

He nodded. "It is. Before, I was afraid to take that chance. Now I know I couldn't bear it if I don't. I have to because the alternative is unbearable. The thought of her marrying someone else tears me up."

The sun was a thin strip of light on the horizon. Justin watched as darkness rolled up and enfolded the grazing cattle across the road. Quiet, he waited for Sam to speak, praying he understood and would forgive him. Having told the older man what was in his heart was a relief. More relaxed than he'd been in a while, he started when Sam spoke.

"Go on in and have your dessert, Justin. Tell the women I'll be in before long."

They waited until Sam joined them in the den. His eyes were red rimmed and puffy. "Daddy, are you alright?"

He hugged her. "I'm fine, sugar. These damn allergies bother my eyes." He eyed Shelia. "Where's my dessert?"

"I didn't know you had allergies, Daddy."

"You don't know everything about me, Missy."

Caitlyn brought him a small serving of peach cobbler and a cup of coffee. "Is this all I get? Look at the bowl Justin's got. I want one like his."

"Sam, you know you can't have that much dessert. Justin's young and can burn it off. It would keep you up all night."

"It's heck to get old."

"Oh, Daddy. You're not old. You're in your prime."

"In my prime, huh? Some days I feel plumb elderly." He finished his cobbler and drained the last of his coffee. "Delicious, as always, Shelia."

"Glad you enjoyed it, Sam. Justin, would you like some more?" Sam gave her a pleading glance and she laughed. He shot Justin a dirty glare that dared him to accept.

"No, ma'am. I've had plenty."

Sam rose and stretched. "I think it's time for me to turn in." He picked up his bowl and cup. "You ready, darlin'?"

Puzzled, Shelia gathered dishes and walked with him to the kitchen. Caitlyn's face registered confusion as she watched them leave. From the kitchen their muffled voices were teasing. Caitlyn turned to him with an arched eyebrow. He shrugged.

"I better be going. Will you walk me to my truck?" It was dark out, the only light came from the stars and the soft glow that flowed from the lighted rooms in the house. Caitlyn kept her distance but at least she walked out with him.

He stopped at the door of his truck and turned to her. "Tell your mother thanks for dinner." Should he say more? Try to apologize, explain what happened?

"She knows, but I'll tell her anyway." A breeze blew her hair across her face. She brushed it back with a wave of her hand. "Goodbye, Justin."

"Goodbye." He watched her as she walked toward the house. Each step carried her further away from him. "Caitlyn?" She stopped and looked back. "Can we talk a minute?"

Rather than the chair where her father sat, she chose the glider, her foot setting it in motion. From the same column he'd leaned against earlier, he told her what he'd shared with Sam. She didn't interrupt, but he heard her sobs when he expressed his fear of her recklessness. When he finished, he pulled a chair up facing her. Her tears broke his heart. He wanted to reach out and hold her but knew he'd be rebuffed.

"Caitlyn, please don't cry anymore. I'm sorry I hurt you. Please forgive me and give me another chance." He dropped his head into his hands and massaged his temples. Tears gathered in his eyes and with his head down, he brushed them away. "I love you, Caitlyn. I've always loved you. For weeks I tried to pretend I could live without you, but I was wrong. If you tell me to leave and never come back, I'll respect your wishes and leave, but it will break my heart. I know that's what I deserve, but please, Caitlyn, give me a crumb of hope."

She wiped tears with her fingers. Her lips trembled. "I forgive you, Justin. But, it will take time for me to trust you again. My feelings are still an open wound."

His heart lurched with hope. And twisted with concern. He'd been such a fool. He reached for her hand and brought it to his lips. She pulled it from his grasp and stood up.

"I better go in now." She moved toward the door.

"Goodnight, Caitlyn."

"Goodnight." Standing at the door until she was inside, the deadbolt lock was shoved home with a note of finality.

CHAPTER ELEVEN

Simon turned onto the drive leading to Hallie's house. It was a beautiful lot, a large portion of it kept in its native state. Close to the house a portion had been set aside for lawn. A short wall of native stone divided the two areas. Flowerbeds filled with ground cover, small shrubs, ornamental grasses, flowers and natural stones separated the wall from the carpet grass. The effect was relaxing and soothing. A big oak tree grew in the area formed by the circular drive. Under it hung a double swing. He could imagine sitting there on cool mornings listening to the buzzing of bees as they feasted on the nectar of the pink crepe myrtles lining the drive.

Modest little house, huh? It wasn't what he'd consider humble, but it wasn't extravagant either. Rather than park in the front, he pulled around to the back. The triple garage door was open so he parked behind Hallie. The other two spaces housed a four-year-old Toyota Tacoma pickup and a five-year-old Dodge Saturn. His respect for Hallie grew. Both kids could have been driving new sports cars. James's reason for keeping quiet about their inheritance began to make more sense. He didn't want his two kids to grow up spoiled and without a healthy respect for money and the work involved in earning it.

Hallie came out the back door before he could

unload his things. "Hi, Simon. I see you made good time." His heart thumped at the sight of her. Her blue shorts and red sleeveless blouse showed off the tan she'd acquired around the pool, making her brown eyes sparkle. He admired the curve of her hips flaring out from her small waist and the generous expanse of bosom above.

"Yes, I did." He sat his duffle bag on the front seat. "God, you look good." Looking up from her face he scanned the back door and windows. "Do we have an audience? Can I kiss you or do I have to wait?"

Her eyes lit with mischief. "Oh, they're watching but one little kiss won't scar them for life." Grinning, he moved closer and lowered his mouth to her upturned face. Capturing her lips, he kissed, nibbled, and kissed again. "Mmmm. You taste good."

She laid her hand on his chest. "Okay. That's enough. Ted will find an excuse to come out if we don't go in." Reaching in the truck cab, she grabbed his duffle bag and waited while he unhooked his garment bag. He draped his arm over her shoulder as they walked across the pavement to the door.

Elise was waiting for them. "Hi, Simon." He laid his garment bag across a kitchen chair and gave her a quick hug. She picked up the garment bag and took the duffle from Hallie. "I'll run these upstairs for you."

"No need, I—" He tried to take them but she sidestepped him and started down the hall. Her son, dressed cargo pants and a Texas A&M University t-shirt, leaned against the counter trying to appear nonchalant. Simon wasn't fooled by his relaxed pose.

"Simon, this is my son, Ted." The young man pushed away from the kitchen counter and walked over.

"Ted, this is Simon Cole."

Simon extended his hand. "It's good to meet you, Ted. Your mother's told me a lot about you." Ted gripped his hand in a nice firm handshake.

"You too."

Hallie was flustered. She ushered Simon to a chair. You two sit down. Elise put on the coffee earlier. Let's have a cup with a slice of cake."

Ted poured a big glass of milk. He peered at Simon. "Would you like a glass of milk, Mr. Cole?"

"No, thank you, Ted. Please, call me Simon."

Trying not to be obvious, Ted studied him as they talked. He didn't blame Ted. If his mother started dating someone, he'd be checking him out too.

Elise returned and joined them at the table. "How did Justin's dinner at the Porter's turn out last night?"

Simon thought Hallie had mentioned it to her but from the surprise on her face, she must not have. "How'd you know about that?"

"Corbett mentioned it when he was here last night."

Simon was confused. "Corbett came to see you last night?"

Elise glanced from her mother to Simon. "Yes. He came to apologize." They waited for more but that was all she intended to say.

Hallie studied her daughter. "Did you accept his apology?"

"Yes."

"Well, good. He seems a nice young man." He caught her look and raised eyebrow. It appeared that's all they were to know about the situation.

"He's one of the best kids around. He's working

with our local veterinarian this summer to prepare for his internship next year. Doc Adams wants to retire in a few years. Corbett will finish school in time to work with him a year or two before taking over Doc Adams' practice." He finished the last of his cake.

"Hallie. That was delicious."

"Would you like some more?"

"No. Thanks. But I would take another cup of coffee." When Hallie settled back in her chair, Ted rose and excused himself but carried his dishes to the sink before leaving the room.

"Now, about Justin. He said Sam had a fit when he showed up at the door but Shelia told him 'to mind his manners or she'd take Justin to town for dinner and he could fend for himself.'" Hallie and Elise laughed. "During dinner Sam made a comment about Justin being fickle so they went outside to have a man-to-man talk. Justin told him everything, his fears and worries and he hoped Caitlyn would give him another chance. He thinks Sam is willing to forgive because he went up to bed and left him alone with Caitlyn so they could talk. Caitlyn said she needed time."

Elise nodded and smiled. "Good. I hope they can work things out."

He didn't doubt for a minute Caitlyn would one day forgive Justin. He didn't blame her for taking her time taking him back. Poor Justin. He'd had no idea what was going on in his mind. Thank God he met Elise and not some young woman out to get married at all costs. He felt sure Justin would have realized his mistake before going through with a wedding, as would have Elise.

Hallie stood and started gathering dishes. "Tell

Simon your plans for the summer while I put these in the dishwasher."

While Hallie straightened the kitchen, Elise told him of her plans to become a teacher. Her blue eyes flashed with excitement over the prospect of a possible teaching job in the fall. She would be a good teacher. He'd watched her react with Whitney and she enjoyed children.

Today her long hair was pulled back with barrettes. The style emphasized the bone structure of her face. She was a beautiful young woman. When had she met Corbett?

"Elise, when did you meet Corbett?"

"We met at the street dance in town. Right after you guys left to go home. Then he came out to the ranch one day to see about one of the horses because the doc was out on a call." Her brows furrowed. "I didn't like him at first, in particular after he hit Justin." She shrugged. "It was nice of him to come by to apologize."

Simon rubbed his chin. *Hummm. Wouldn't that be interesting if those two got together?* "I guess it would be inappropriate for us to ask what he did that required an apology."

"Yes. It would."

Well, hell. That made him more curious. He couldn't imagine what Corbett had done. Known for a temper like Sam's, Corbett found himself in scrapes all the time growing up, but he'd never hurt anyone, above all a girl. The boys were always suffering with bruises and black eyes from one misunderstanding or another. He looked Elise over with care. She wore shorts and a tee-shirt. An inch below the sleeve of her right arm appeared to be a small bruise. Could that be a thumbprint? He reached over and with care, lifted her arm and rotated it a little. "How'd you get this bruise?" Underneath were fading finger marks. His jaw clenched. Could Corbett have done this? From his own experience, he knew men didn't realize how much strength they had in their hands.

Hallie lifted her arm to take a look. "Elise! Did Corbett do that to you?"

"Mom, he didn't mean to. Caitlyn and I were talking. She was crying so he thought I'd said something ugly to her. He grabbed my arm, as I was getting in the car, to keep me from leaving without explaining. It was a mistake. He didn't realize the strength of his grip." Her expression was pleading. "Believe me, Mom, he's punishing himself enough about it." Hallie looked at Simon in question. He shook his head no. Don't pursue the issue.

"Okay, Elise. I'll trust your judgment. You're a grown woman and know the dangers of abusive men. If you believe Corbett doesn't fall in that category, I believe you."

"He doesn't, Mom. It was an unfortunate mistake."

"Okay. End of discussion."

* * *

At 7:00 that evening, they were dressed and ready to leave for Austin. Simon couldn't restrain a delighted grin when Hallie came out of her downstairs bedroom dressed in tight jeans, a short sleeved red and white plaid blouse and scuffed red ropers. Red earrings, bracelet and bandana completed her outfit. A low wolf whistle hissed through his teeth.

"Wow, Hallie. You are stunning." He wanted to

express how great but her two kids were observing them. Ted didn't appear too appreciative of his wolf whistle so he'd better cool it.

"Thank you, Simon. You look mighty handsome yourself." He looked down to see what he had on. Not used to paying a lot of attention to what he wore, he'd bought a new blue western dress shirt for the occasion. His jeans weren't new but washed and starched with a sharp crease down the front. He'd been tempted to wear his newest ostrich boots but rejected that idea because they weren't broken in yet. Nursing sore feet while dancing was not in his plans for tonight.

"I'm glad you approve of my attire, madam, and grateful you didn't pick some place where I'd have to wear a suit."

"Well, if you wore a suit, I'd have to wear heels. Now we can both be comfortable." She turned to the kids. "Are you guys going out tonight?"

Both shook their heads no. Hallie's gaze moved from one to the other. "Is that right?"

Ted rocked back on his bare feet. "Yeah, Mom. I'm going by the video rental store and then pick up a pizza. Elise is going to study for a while then we'll watch movies. We've not had time together in a good while."

Hallie shrugged. "Okay. That's good. Don't wait up as we're going to the Dancing Steer and they don't close until 1:30."

"The Dancing Steer?" Ted asked in amazement. "That's downtown on Lamar. I thought the 6th Street area was off limits because of the drinking and wild university crowd. Fights break out down there all the time." He looked from one to the other. "Which one of you will be the designated driver?"

Simon had to restrain a chuckle. She wasn't used to being questioned by her son. Seems the shoe was on the other foot.

Hallie sighed. "Ted, the Dancing Steer is family oriented. I doubt the atmosphere will be wild like some of the other places downtown. I will be the designated driver. We'll be fine." She reached up, patted his cheek then gave it a pinch. He stood his ground, arms folded across his chest.

Simon laid his hand on Ted's shoulder. "Don't worry. I'm not going to let anything happen to your mother. We'll have breakfast and coffee before we leave and we'll be eating as soon as we get there."

Ted nodded. "We'll be glad to come get you if you have too much to drink."

"Ted, I swear..."

Simon hooked his arm around her waist and hurried her to the back door. "See you guys later."

Ted nodded and Elise waved. "Y'all have a good time." She turned to her younger brother. "Ted, what is wrong with you?"

In the truck, unable to resist any longer, he leaned over and gave her a quick kiss on the mouth. He'd enjoyed being in her home but wanted her to himself for a while.

Hallie apologized for Ted's behavior. "Don't worry about it. It's natural for him to worry. Harassing you might ease it some." He chuckled. "He's got your speech pretty much memorized, doesn't he?"

Her eyes got big and she covered her mouth with her hand. "Oh, God. I hope I don't get the birth control and sexually transmitted disease talk in the morning."

He glanced over to see if she was kidding. She shrugged. "I wouldn't be surprised if he included you in the lecture."

"You're kidding me, right?" Her silence wasn't reassuring. He rubbed his chest. Oh, man.

"I wouldn't put it past him. It appears to be payback time. When Elise had her first serious relationship, I sat her and her boyfriend down and talked to them. Elise was so mad she didn't speak to me for several days."

He reached for her hand and squeezed it. "You did the right thing."

"The boy never called her again. Dropped her like a hot potato. She cried for days. But, a year later she told me I'd saved her from making a bad mistake. Seems the boy had been pressuring her to have sex."

Downtown was packed. He gave up on finding a parking place and pulled into a valet parking garage. "Do you mind walking a few blocks?"

"Not at all. It's nice out tonight."

It wasn't quite dark, the air hot and steamy as they walked toward the Dancing Steer. Crafts and artists booths lined the street, merchants trying to catch last minute customers. Offerings of paintings, sculptures, clothing, and food—all sorts of goods—were hawked as they passed.

The Dancing Steer was cool, dark and loud. Simon clasped Hallie to his side and cleared a path to a vacant table.

"Have you been here before?" He pulled a chair out for her and moved his closer.

"Never have. Friends told me about it." She leaned in so he could hear her over the music. "Isn't the music great?" The country western band was good but having her close better. Arm around her shoulder, he hugged her to his side and kissed her hair.

"You want to dance or eat first?" His stomach grumbled. He was starving.

"How about we eat first." As if on cue, a waitress appeared with menus. They both ordered a beer and she took off while they looked at the menu. "I've heard their hamburgers are awesome."

The hamburgers were huge, almost as big as their plates. A mountain of spicy French fries sat in the middle of the table. Hallie laughed at the look on Simon's face.

"You said you were hungry. Eat up, cowboy." Between bites, they talked about anything and everything. Hallie quizzed him about his high school girlfriends. She told him about falling in love with James when she was fifteen.

Simon set his plate aside. The mountain had been dented but not by much. "That's the best burger I've ever eaten." Half of Hallie's was still on her plate.

"Also the biggest I've put away." He leaned toward Hallie. "Darlin', you've got a little spot of ketchup right here." Tilting her head he wiped it off.

"Thank you." She dabbed at her mouth with her napkin.

The band started playing a Schottische. The crowd went wild, yelling and clapping as they filled the dance floor. "You ready to join 'um, sugar?"

"You bet. This is one of my favorites." He clasped the hand she had around his waist, and she held the one he had over her right shoulder. They stepped and hopped to the Bavarian melody, laughing as the tempo increased in speed and they struggled to keep up. Before they could catch their breath, the band started a country waltz. With Hallie held close, they spun around the room to the three-quarter step beat. They danced well together, both comfortable with the steps of the dance and with each other. Hallie no longer tensed when he touched her. Her hair, soft against his cheek, smelled of citrus and flowers. He dropped his lips to her cheek. Placing a kiss there, he moved on to taste the softness in front of her ear.

She leaned her head back and gazed into his eyes. Did they reflect the love and desire that burned in his body? Her brown eyes looked unsure, then they darkened with longing and desire. She smiled as he lowered his head to hers for a fleeting kiss that promised more to come.

Oh, God. He prayed her feelings were as strong as his. She'd said she loved him, but love had many depths. No longer did he worry about her being from the city. She was strong in character and would make a home wherever fate put her. That strength was evident in the way she'd raised her children. He hoped now she would use some of her strength to have faith in the future they could have together.

Time passed in a hurry. They danced, talked and laughed, ate cold French fries, drank beer, and then danced again. When Simon thought to check the time it was 12:30 am.

At 1:15 a.m., Simon parked his truck behind Hallie's car and turned off the engine. Hallie glanced at the lit window in the upstairs bedroom.

"Ted is waiting up. Drat his hide." She wrinkled her brow and chewed her bottom lip. "I guess we have to go inside." Her face cleared. "Let's check in and I'll tell him we're going to sit out front on the swing."

He pulled her close. "Just in case, I want to kiss you before we get out of this truck." He framed her face in his hands and with his thumb traced her lips. Turning her head, she kissed one palm, then the other. The sensation of her lips on his skin was electrifying. Grasping her hair at the nape of her neck, he pulled her head back to expose her neck. He kissed and nipped the sensitive path from her ear to her pulse point.

She grasped his head and held him close as his lips moved up her neck to her ear. Liquid heat coursed through his body making him ache for her. He lifted his head and looked in her eyes.

"Hallie, honey. I want you so much." His hands slid from her waist up to cup the sides of her breasts. Her low moan was silenced when his lips captured hers. When his thumbs brushed her nipples, she jerked in response then pressed closer as his hands soothed her. Her mouth opened and his tongue explored as—

"Mom. Are you guys out here?" The back door slammed as Ted's voice echoed across the yard.

"Shit!" They jerked apart at the sound of Ted's voice, Hallie settling herself on her side of the cab. Simon growled, "Damned if I don't feel like a teenager."

She giggled then opened the passenger door. "Yes, Ted. We're out here and will be in soon. Go to bed. We're adults, for gosh sakes." She stoked his cheek. "I'm sorry, Simon. I think he's doing this to aggravate me."

"Hummm. You think so? This is new territory for him. He's not used to some horny old man chasing after his mom." He stroked her back. "Give him some time."

"Okay." She glanced toward the house. "I guess we better go in."

"Yeah, we better." They said goodnight at the foot of the stairs.

As Simon moved down the hall to the guest room, Ted's door stood ajar, the light casting a shadow across the hall carpet. In his room, Simon sat on the bed and pulled his boots off. A cold shower should help him regain control of his body. When he turned out the light and lay down, a sliver of light shown under the door. Ted was still up.

He pulled on his jeans. Might as well get this over with so the boy can sleep. He tapped on Ted's door. He was sitting up in bed with a large textbook held upside down. His face registered surprise at his appearance.

"Ted, can I come in a minute?"

"Sure." He tossed the book aside and sat up.

Simon pulled out the desk chair and sat down. "I figured we might as well have this talk and get everything out in the open." Ted didn't say anything but nodded. "I love your mother. I want to marry her and live with her for the rest of my life. She won't accept my proposal because she's afraid of being hurt again. Of me dying like your father did."

He had Ted's full attention now. "She adored your father. Losing him was difficult for her. But, she had you and Elise to ease her grief. You're so much like your father. That pleases her a great deal." A slight smile curved Ted's mouth, but lines still furrowed his brow.

"I'm going to do everything in my power to convince your mother to marry me. If she does, I promise you I'll move heaven and hell if necessary to make her happy. Our home will be your home. You'll always be welcome, as will your friends."

He thought for a minute. "There's one other thing. I'd give anything in the world to be with your mother in that bedroom downstairs. But, she hasn't invited me, and I would never enter uninvited."

Ted's frown eased.

"Is there anything you want to say to me or ask?"

"No. I think you covered all the bases." Ted offered his hand. "Thanks for being straight with me."

Simon grasped his hands and they shook. "You're welcome. Thank you for being such a fine son to your mother. Your father would be proud." He rose from the chair. "Now, will you turn out the light and go to sleep?" At the door he turned. "And, please, don't forget to give your mother the birth control and venereal disease talk in the morning."

When he reached his room, he could still hear Ted laughing.

Hallie could hear voices from upstairs but not what they were saying. From the low timbre, it must be Simon and Ted. What could they be talking about? Maybe Ted was giving Simon the birth control talk early. She snickered. What was she going to do with that son of hers?

Simon was fun to be with and a wonderful dancer. During the slow numbers, he crooned the words in her ear. At every opportunity, he touched her—her waist, her hair, her face and her hands. With each song, every caress, he made love to her. She shivered. Remembering his kisses and his hands on her breasts rekindled the fire he'd started earlier. Lordy, the man didn't have to touch her to turn her on. Turning to her side, she smoothed the pillow next to her, James's pillow. Did she want Simon's head on that pillow, his body next to hers in this big bed? Of course, not while the kids were home. James was the only man who'd ever known her body. The thought of Simon seeing her without clothes was unsettling, yet arousing. Even more exciting was the idea of seeing him without his clothes. She groaned into her pillow.

* * *

"Mom. Wake up. Breakfast is almost ready." Elise sat a cup of coffee on the nightstand. The clock read 9:00.

"What're you doing up so early?" Sitting up, she stacked pillows behind her. Giving her hair a quick scrub with her hands, she smoothed it, and then leaned back. Her first sip of coffee was divine. "Yummm. Good coffee."

"Getting ready for church. Simon's been up several hours. You better get a move on." Her eyes sparkled. "Did you have a good time last night?"

"Yes, I did. A great time." She took another sip of coffee and smiled. "Simon's a great dancer." Dancing was one of his many skills. He was a great kisser too and considerate. Those little touches of his hands when he escorted her made her tingle. Were they spontaneous or were they designed to make her want him. She didn't think they were planned. He just liked to touch. And no question, she wanted.

A knock sounded on the door. Simon strolled into her bedroom as if he did it every day. He sat a tray across her lap and then bowed. "Breakfast, madam." His face was serious, but then he winked and leaned down to kiss her cheek. "I told you I knew how to cook so thought I'd prove it this morning."

What was he doing in her bedroom? Her hair was a mess, she didn't have on any makeup, and she flat out wasn't ready to have him in this intimate setting. Heat rose in her face. She bit back a retort ordering Simon from her room as she looked from him to Elise for a clue as to what each was thinking. Elise appeared nonplused. Simon waited for a response from her. When he didn't get one, fury flamed in his eyes. Then he gazed around the room. Pictures of James, alone and with her and the children, were everywhere. A suit coat still hung on a coat caddy, his cologne and jewelry box sat on his dresser. Simon's condemning stare seared her. She wanted to defend her response, but sat silent, body rigid.

Her irritation with him, as well as with herself for being upset, further confused her. Things were moving too fast and she wasn't the one driving.

His face was rigid, anger held under tight control "Dammit, Hallie. Excuse me for invading your privacy and your holy shrine." He turned and stalked out of the room.

Elise watched him go and whirled on her mother. "What is wrong with you?" She waved her hand toward the breakfast tray. "He did this for you and you may as well have spit in his face."

Hallie groaned. Her behavior was inexcusable. She'd known it at the time, but couldn't seem to stop her reaction. It was like a demon inside her raised its ugly head. Last night she'd been longing to have him sharing this bed with her. What had happened to make her change her mind? Fear.

Had she buried herself in a shrine to James? Yes, yes, yes! How would she have felt if she'd been in his shoes? Her heart ached at the pain she must have caused. And to make matters worse, she'd done it in front of Elise. *Oh God, Hallie, how petty and stupid can you get?* She threw back the covers. *Hurry so you can apologize before we leave for church.*

He sat at the kitchen table reading the Sunday paper. Dressed in a dress slacks and shirt, his jacket draped over another chair, he appeared absorbed in the front page. His white shirt stretched across his wide shoulders, shoulders tense with anger. He looked up as she walked in, paused, and then returned to his paper.

When she touched his shoulder, his muscles jerked. Weaving her arms around his neck she put her face next to his ear. Voice low, she pleaded. "I'm sorry. Please forgive me, Simon."

His hair was soft against her cheek. She rubbed against it, feeling its texture. His subtle aftershave mixed with his male scent enveloped her, bringing pangs of longing to her heart. Why was she so afraid to commit to this man? "Please, Simon. The only excuse I can give is that I'm afraid. Things are moving too fast."

The tension little by little receded from his shoulders. He reached up to stroke her arms. Loosening them, he drew her around from behind him. "I forgive you, sweetheart, but a man can only take so much rejection before you run him off." His thumbs stroked her hands. "I love you, Hallie. But never again will I let you ignore me and dismiss me like you did this morning. Above all in front of your daughter or anyone else for that matter. You can yell at me and tell me anything you please, but don't ever dismiss me." His

213

jaw was set, eyes fierce. She backed up a step, pulling her hands from his.

Her chest and throat ached. "I was wrong to act the way I did. I don't know why I did." But she did know. He'd come into her bedroom, the room she'd shared with James.

"I think you do, Hallie. I trespassed on James's territory. And you didn't like that." She sat sideways in the chair where his jacket hung and put her face in her hands. "James is dead, Hallie. You need to face the facts and move on."

He stood up and put on his jacket. Taking her hands he pulled her up from the chair. It was then she noticed his bag beside the chair where he'd been sitting. She lifted her eyes from it to Simon's, searching for an answer. He dropped his forehead to hers.

"I think it's best if I go on home." She nodded in silence. "Will you walk me out?" Again she nodded, biting her lip to keep from crying.

* * *

At his truck Simon held her close. His heart was breaking for her—her confusion and fears. But, he wouldn't cater to them. She either loved him or she didn't, and if she did, then she had to put her fears aside and make a commitment.

He kissed her forehead and then her lips, drawing in her taste and fragrance as he did so. If she didn't want him, he would without a doubt die. He kissed her one last time then looked into her eyes.

"Hallie, I need a decision about where our relationship is going. If you can't give me one soon, you'll never be able to."

CHAPTER TWELVE

Hallie sat in the glider on her front porch. Filled with pillows, it made a comfortable place to lick her wounds. With her back against the armrest and one foot stretched across the seat, the other set the glider in motion. The movement soothed her somewhat, like rocking did a baby when it fretted. It wasn't having the same effect on her, however. Her nerves, wound tight, threatened to uncoil at any minute. If they did, she'd shatter. She'd been such a fool this morning. Her actions may have turned Simon away from her. Who would want a woman who acted loving one minute and cold the next? No one.

She loved Simon, she wanted to marry him, but she feared changing her life. No longer would she be James's wife, his widow. Except for her kids, that part of her life would be behind her. It was hard giving it up, cutting herself off from what she'd been for so many years. She glanced up at the stars in the clear Texas sky. One blinked every so often, teasing her to try to catch it blinking. There…it did it again.

James would want her to remarry and be happy. Not live alone for the rest of her life. She knew that deep in her soul. He'd said as much when he was dying. Did she think because he had suffered, she should suffer too? She didn't believe she was that messed up. It was difficult to say goodbye to a previous lifestyle.

Linda LaRoque

Was she strong enough to do it? If not for herself, then for Simon? Or would she sit around, deny herself the happiness she and Simon could have together? God couldn't have made a better man. He was loving, tender, dependable, and damned sexy. Not just in features, but also in the way he talked to Whitney, horsed around with Justin, and put his arm around his mother. One look from those blue eyes, with their crinkles at the corners, made her stomach flip and her heart race. And when he grinned, she was lost in a swirl of sensations. She'd heard the eyes were the doorway to the soul. His soul had to be beautiful.

The phone rang jerking her thoughts back to the present. Jumping up, she started for the door.

Elise hollered, "I've got it, Mom."

Simon wouldn't call her tonight. Why would he? He'd made it clear what he expected and wouldn't call her to further complicate the issue. The ball was now in her court.

* * *

By 7:45 a.m. she had the car packed and was ready to leave. "Elise, be careful when you drive down Saturday." She grabbed her purse and keys.

"I will, Mom. You be careful, too." They embraced and walked to their cars. This would be Elise's first day of classes at the service center. Her arms were full of books.

"Call me tonight and let me know how classes went." She blew Elise a kiss and got in her car. Ted had left the day before. He would ride down with Elise on Saturday for the barbecue at Justin's ranch. It was odd to think Simon would no longer be there, but at his own ranch several miles away. Ruth had convinced him she should handle Whitney, that he needed to tend to his own ranch now that Justin was home.

Ted didn't understand what had happened between her and Simon. But, thank goodness he had the good sense not to pursue the issue. However, that didn't keep him from voicing his disappointment the older man had left earlier than planned.

Simon had planned to take them to eat at his favorite steak house. Steak to a growing young man was like manna from heaven. Ted had geared himself up to put away a big one. A fondness for steak wasn't his only likeable quality, though. "He's a straight shooter, Mom. I like him." As to their conversation in the wee hours Sunday morning, he wouldn't reveal the details. He said, "That's between the two of us, Mom." Then he'd grinned and said, "Simon did mention to be sure I gave you the birth control talk."

Elise had been downright mad and didn't speak until she realized her cold shoulder made her mother feel worse. After church, she'd joined her on the crème leather sofa. "Mom, I don't know what was on your mind this morning, but I don't think you were fair to Simon. He wanted to do something nice for you."

Mouth pinched, she shook her head. "And as for him coming into your bedroom, this isn't the dark ages, you know. Your behavior was a lot more shocking than it would have been to walk in your bedroom and find you two curled up in bed together."

"Elise, you know I'd never do that with you and Ted in the house."

"Do what, Mom? Sleep with the man you love and who wants to marry you?" She tossed her long mane of hair back over her shoulder. "I know you wouldn't. I respect that. Simon does too."

"I know, hon, I've made a mess of everything. All I can say is I need to work through some issues."

Elise's brow wrinkled with concern. "Mom, I know you love him. Don't take so long on those issues you lose him."

Traffic on I-35 was a mess, as usual. When she turned onto the Texas highway that led southwest, traffic almost disappeared. Still early in June, the weather wasn't hot yet. The roadside was filled with green grass and wild flowers. In another month or so, the heat and dryness would leave the foliage looking scorched and thirsty, a serious fire hazard. Years ago, when the temperatures soared to 100 and above, glass cola bottles could get so hot they burst. The heat ignited the grass and it would spread in a hurry if not isolated and put out. Thus, the *Don't Mess With Texas* laws. In the rural areas, farmers, ranchers and their life stock as well as their homes were in danger. Fortunately, bottles were now almost obsolete.

When she pulled into Granite Springs it was past ten o'clock. She and the realtor, Helen Posey, walked over to the bank so Hallie could transfer the money for the cash sale.

Joe Booker handled the transfer. Hallie could see curiosity was killing him. "Hallie, what do you plan to do with that property?" She bet he couldn't wait to get on the phone to Simon to see if he was aware of her investment.

"I plan to open another *Stepping Up Boutique* like the one I have in Georgetown." She put her receipts in the small, flexible briefcase she carried and shook Joe's hand. "Thanks for your help, Joe. I'd appreciate it if you'd call the carpenters right away and have them meet me at one o'clock today at the property."

"Anytime we can help out, Hallie, let me know. I'll start making those calls right now." A teller brought him a check, which he handed to the realtor. "Here you go, Helen. Bet that was the easiest sale you've ever made."

She winked at him. "Not the easiest, my friend, but the fastest. The easiest was selling you that pile of rubble you call a house outside of town."

He feigned offense. "What, my beautiful home? It's a masterpiece and you know it. I'm sorry if you can't recognize artistic beauty when you see it."

They left the bank and started walking to the title company. Doing business in a small town was a breeze. It would have taken her all day, if not two to handle a transaction like this in Austin or any other big city. "What was that about? You don't like Joe's house?"

"Like? It's the most God-awful house I've ever seen." She stopped walking and pointed in the direction opposite of how Hallie had entered town. "You can see it on the left about a half mile from the convenience store." Walking again, she added, "It's been added onto multiple times, not by a professional, mind you. It's a hodgepodge of architectural styles. I've never seen an uglier house and I've seen more than my share." She shrugged. "But he seems to love the place. Go figure."

By noon Hallie was the legal owner of the property at Number Five Front Street. She made a quick trip to the electric and water companies and they promised she'd have service before the end of the day. At one o'clock she met with workman. She asked the Farmers, a young couple in business together, for an estimate for painting the interior and exterior of the building and restoring the original woodwork. Since the water wasn't on, she didn't have a clue what shape the plumbing was in, but Fred Posey, Helen's husband, would be there the following morning to check things out. He'd bring an electrician to check the wiring. The hardwood floors had been refinished so didn't need attention. Neither did the roof.

* * *

Simon finished his thick ham sandwich and sat his plate in the sink to wash later. He'd been home less than a week and already missed Mom's cooking. Tonight he'd cook extra at dinner so he could have leftovers for lunch. Grabbing a handful of cookies, he started for the back door when the phone rang.

"Hey, Simon, Joe Booker here."

Damn. He'd been hoping it was Hallie. "What's up, Joe?" He leaned back against the kitchen counter and studied the toes of his boots.

"Saw your woman in town this morning." Joe paused for him to respond but Simon remained quiet and waited for him to continue. "So, I guess you knew she was here, huh?"

Simon eased away from the cabinet. "No, Joe, I didn't." His pulse raced. He didn't know whether to be glad or mad. The woman was such a contradiction. She kept him in a constant state of alert.

"She bought the old drug store. Plans to put in a boutique. Paid cash and already has the Farmers and Fred Posey working on it." Joe rattled on for several minutes about happenings in town before Simon could ask.

"Do you know where she's staying, Joe?" His heart

skipped a beat. This was a good sign, right?

"Nope, sure don't. But then again, she's got three choices—the Cottonwood, Pink Palace, or the motel on the highway. Which one do you think she'll choose?"

"I don't have a clue."

"I'd bet my bottom dollar she'll be at the Pink Palace what with Helen being the realtor and Fred her plumber. I bet they both put a bug in her ear on where to stay."

"Yeah, you may be right. Thanks for the info, Joe."

"You bet."

Hallie was in town and opening a boutique. Would she be doing so if she didn't want to marry him? Hell. Who knew how a woman's thinking worked. He'd better not get his hopes up.

In the barn he tossed fresh hay in the stalls getting ready for his horses. He'd bring them over tomorrow and then visit a cattle auction the following week. The entire fence line had to be checked for breaks before he put any cattle out to pasture. It felt good to be home again. If Hallie were here with him, his life would be perfect.

* * *

By four o'clock Hallie had done all she could that day. She was pooped. Her stomach grumbled reminding her she hadn't eaten since breakfast. An ice cream soda sounded good and would be enough to hold her until dinnertime. The Cottonwood Bed and Breakfast was above the ice cream shop but she'd decided to stay at the Pink Palace, an Inn a few blocks off the square. Maybe they'd still have a room when she got there.

Refreshed from her soda, she pulled into the visitors parking area at the Pink Palace. It was a charming old Victorian home painted pale pink trimmed in slate gray. A wide porch with gingerbread trim circled the entire house. Wicker furniture and hanging plants added color to the spacious area.

Mrs. Posey, Helen's mother-in-law, met her at the door and showed her to a room on the first floor and waited for her to look around.

The room was large with a massive four-poster bed, chest, desk, love seat and chair. A French door opened onto the front porch. It would allow her to come and go at will without having to go through the hall and out the main entrance. The walls were burgundy with wide dark molding around the floors, ceiling and door. Mauve, and teal blue was used throughout the room with accents of yellow. A vase of fresh yellow tea roses sat on the chest. They released a subtle scent of sweetness throughout the room. She inhaled the delicious smell and peeked into the connecting bathroom. It had a claw-foot bathtub perfect for long soaks.

"This is beautiful, Mrs. Posey."

She beamed. "I heard you were coming so saved it for you. It's my finest room."

"Why, thank you. How'd you know I'd be coming?"

"Helen called and said you'd need a place to stay." She moved to the door. "Let me know if you need anything."

Hallie tossed her suitcase on the bed and unpacked. The room was perfect. She'd be comfortable here while she worked on the store. Should she call Simon, let him know she was in town? No, she wouldn't. For one thing she was chicken and the second, it was best she spend time alone working things through in her mind. His sexy body and steamy kisses would be distracting.

Feeling refreshed from her shower and clean clothes, she stepped out of her room and asked Mrs. Posey the name of a place to eat a light dinner. She suggested the tearoom located a block behind her house. The menu included sandwiches, soups, and salads. "Everything's homemade. No one cooks better than Lola. Try a piece of her coconut pie. It's the best in the county." She reached up and adjusted the silver pins that held her white hair in place. "Best hurry though. She closes at eight o'clock on the dot."

It was several hours before sundown, still steamy outside so she drove the one block rather than walking. No need to get sweaty again after her cool shower. The car, hot from the short time she'd been inside felt like an oven. She started the vehicle, cranked up the air and let the heat escape through the open windows. The interior cooled by the time she reached Lola's Tea Room.

The tearoom was small and crowded. She was shown to a table for two under a window with a view of the back garden. The soup of the day smelled wonderful, but she settled on a chicken salad sandwich and spinach salad. People around the room sent her curious looks and smiles. An older woman wearing a big white apron delivered her food.

"Here you go, hon. Hope you enjoy it." She wiped her hand on the apron and extended it to Hallie. "I'm Lola." Her smile was gracious and infectious.

Hallie shook her hand. "Hello, Lola. I'm so pleased to meet you. I'm Hallie Barron. I'm staying over at the Pink Palace."

Lola leaned in for privacy. "I know. Sue Posey called and told me you were on your way over." She glanced around at her interested customers. "Can I tell them who you are?"

"Well, I…I guess so."

She clapped her hands twice and the place got quiet. "This is Mrs. Hallie Barron. She's the lady opening the boutique downtown on Front Street."

The room echoed with greetings. She heard pieces of conversation "paid cash," "hired the Farmers," and "Simon's girl" float around the room. Hallie blushed to the roots of her hair. Was there nothing these people didn't know? Before she left, stuffed from her dinner and a large piece of Lola's coconut cream pie, she'd had a variety of offers of help. Several mentioned applying for a job when she was ready to hold interviews.

Simon watched Hallie eye his truck as she got out of her car and walk up the path to the house. Dressed in a long slim khaki skirt and white sleeveless blouse tucked in at the waist, she looked good enough to eat. He stood as she climbed the steps.

Her smile was unsure but welcoming. "Hello, Simon."

He reached for her hand and drew her over to the wicker sofa. "Hello, sweetheart." Tilting her chin, he placed a chaste kiss on her lips. "Let's sit down." She sat on the middle cushion, not close enough to suit him. "Come on, move closer so I can put my arm around you." Putting his arm around her shoulders, he leaned in to smell her hair and kiss her temple.

"Does your appearance here mean you've forgiven me for yesterday?" Her hand was linked with the one

224

draped across her shoulder. She rubbed her cheek against it and kissed his knuckles.

"No. It means I love you and want to be near you every chance I get." With any luck it would be for the remainder of his life. He'd have to remember to get a glider or double swing for his front porch. "Why didn't I know you were coming to town, buying a business and causing a general stir around here?"

"I wasn't sure what I was going to do. I looked last week but didn't make a decision until last night." She laid her head against his shoulder and sighed. "You know, I'm not used to informing anyone about my plans. I've become independent since James's death. Old habits are hard to break."

He squeezed her shoulder. "I can understand that, Hallie. I'm independent too."

"How're things at your ranch coming along?"

"It's great to be home but I miss Mama's cooking. It's lonely. I miss Whitney something awful." Thinking, he trailed his fingers up and down her arm. She shivered and he warmed her arm with his palm.

"Hallie, I may have been unfair to you. When I asked you to marry me, I didn't realize how hard it would be to leave Whitney. I want her with me. If you decide to marry me, we come as a package deal."

She was quiet. His heart sank. Then she smiled. "Package deals have more value."

"Phew. You had me worried there for a minute." Tilting her face up to his, he stroked her cheek. "I hope Mama and Justin will agree. I know Justin wants to take over her care, but she needs me. I'm the closest thing she has to a father."

"I always expected her to be with you, anyway.

And, I expect deep down they know that what's best for her. It may take a while for them to come to terms with it."

"I miss Whitney, sugar. But, it's you I ache and long for. You I think of first thing every morning and the last thing every night." Growling, he nipped her ear. "And what I think affects other parts of my body, love."

She laughed. "Shame on you, Simon." Glancing around, "Mrs. Posey could hear what you're saying."

"I doubt it's anything she hasn't heard before." He pulled her up with him. "Walk me to my truck. I've got to get up early in the morning."

Arm-in-arm, they walked down the path. The shade had been pulled down on the small town shutting out sound as well as light. On the corner, the old streetlight cast a dim yellow glow through the branches of the huge oak tree spotlighting a white oleander bush in the yard giving it an ethereal quality. The warm still air was scented with the fragrance of the tea roses and wisteria in Mrs. Posey's garden.

In the dark shadows by his truck, Simon drew Hallie into his arms. His lips claimed hers in a lingering kiss. When he ended it, he laid his forehead against hers. "Goodnight, sweetheart."

* * *

Hallie woke early. Smells of baking bread and coffee seeped under her door making her stomach grumble. Dressing in jeans and old tee shirt, she joined Mrs. Posey in the large kitchen. The older woman squealed when the door squeaked.

Holding her hand over her heart, she exclaimed. "Oh my goodness, dear. You scared me. I seldom see anyone in here before eight o'clock."

"I'm sorry. I'll try to make more noise the next time so you'll be expecting me."

"Have a seat and let me pour you a cup of coffee."

Hallie grabbed a cup off the counter and poured her own cup. "No need to wait on me. You go ahead with what you're doing. It smells wonderful, Mrs. Posey."

The older woman went back to the dough she was rolling up for cinnamon rolls. "Call me Sue, dear."

"I will, if you'll call me Hallie." She took another sip of coffee. "This is delicious. Do you blend your own?"

"Yes, I do." She winked. "But don't ask for my recipe as it's an old family secret." She bent to lift a pan of rolls from the oven. "You want one of these while they're hot. Be careful though. The syrup from the butter, cinnamon and sugar can burn you." At Hallie's nod, she skimmed two off the pan and onto the plate she'd set out for her.

"Ready to get busy on your shop this morning?"

Hallie looked at her in question.

"Honey, nothing's a secret around here for long. People aren't nosy, more like interested." Using a piece of thread, she slipped it under the roll of dough and crossing the ends pulled until she had a perfect cut. She set the roll on a clean baking sheet. "Just like we know Simon's head over heels in love with you."

Hallie could feel the heat rising to her face. Sue gave her a sideways glance. "Appears the feeling might be mutual." She chuckled. "Simon is a fine looking man. Loads of women in town have tried to catch him. You must be something special to have won his esteem."

She poured herself another cup of coffee and gazed

out the kitchen window. "It's so pretty out this morning. If you don't mind, I think I'll take this out on the front porch."

"You go right ahead. I'll be serving breakfast in thirty minutes."

"Don't set a place for me, Sue. This is more than plenty. I want to get to work." She relaxed in one of the rockers while finishing her coffee. Everyone is this little town seemed so nice. She felt welcomed and at home. Sitting here was enjoyable, but she was wasting time. She carried her cup into the kitchen and prepared to leave for the shop.

By noon she had the utilities on, and the Farmers had prepped the ceiling and walls for paint. They were mixing plaster to repair the cracks while she studied the paint samples they'd brought. Fred checked out the plumbing and declared it sound. His electrician friend found a few problems with the wiring but nothing major. He suggested she change out the circuits for heavy duty ones. That way she'd never have to worry about throwing breakers. She sent him to Austin to pick up the supplies he'd need and a new industrial energy efficient furnace and air conditioner. With Fred in tow, she went to the local hardware store. She picked out a toilet and a free standing lavatory for the bathroom. For the break area she'd planned for the back of the store, she found a small sink to be installed in the vintage cabinet she planned to have stripped and refinished. After the sink was in place, there'd still be room for a coffee maker and small microwave oven. She was discussing this with Fred in the back when she heard Johnny Farmer say, "Hi ya, Simon."

"Hey, Johnny, good to see you. Is Hallie still

around?"

"Yeah, she's in the back with Fred."

Hallie left Fred to measure the cabinet. Simon was dressed in his work clothes, worn jeans, shirt and boots. But he was still the best looking man she'd ever seen. "Simon. What're you doing in town?"

"I came to see if you'd go to lunch with me. I couldn't face another cold sandwich." He wiggled his eyebrows making her laugh. "And I needed a kiss or two."

She peeked around him to see if anyone watched them. "They've all left. I guess they went to lunch."

Expression smug, he said, "I guess they're trying to help me in the romance department. Nothing like community effort."

The kiss was long and sweet. Hallie sighed into his mouth. "We better leave." She grabbed her purse. "Don't want to give the town reason to gossip."

Holding hands, they walked across the square to a small *café*. "By the way, Loretta is coming to the barbecue Saturday night. It should be an interesting evening. She hasn't attended one since she and Sidney divorced."

"Why do you think she's coming now?" Hallie didn't know how she felt about meeting Justin and Whitney's mother.

"She's curious. Justin told her about us. I imagine she is anxious to look you over."

"Whatever for?"

"Who knows what goes on in that woman's mind? Don't worry about it though. She's harmless. Don't let her intimidate you. She may try."

Hallie reached across the table and took his hand.

"Don't worry about me, Simon. I can take care of myself." He squeezed her hand and laced his fingers through hers. The people at the next table were smiling at them. She pulled her hand back.

"Are Elise and Ted coming Saturday night?"

"Yes. They'll be here. Ted's fired up to see the ranches. He's not too happy with Justin so I hope he doesn't start something."

"Don't worry about it. Justin can take care of himself."

"That's what I'm worried about."

"Geez, Hallie. You don't think Justin would fight with an eighteen-year-old, do you?"

"How should I know what men do in situations like that? I've not had a lot of experience."

"Justin will not hurt Ted. By the end of the weekend they'll be buddies."

"I hope you're right."

"I better get back to work. Have lots of fencing to check before I buy cattle next week."

By Wednesday afternoon the store was cleaned, painted and new plumbing installed in the bathroom. Fred tried to talk her into buying a cabinet for the break room's sink but she wouldn't budge. The old one had character. Rather than listen to him complain, she drew the hole on top and cut the opening herself. He'd mumbled and fussed but in the end admitted it looked good. Patty Farmer would put a waterproof finish on it tomorrow while her husband Jake finished painting the outside trim.

She glanced around at the walls. They were divided into three sections painted green, burgundy, and chartreuse. The colors were repeated in reverse order on the opposite wall. A big square wood pillar dominated each section. She was pleased with the end product.

This morning she'd interviewed seven women for jobs in the store and would hire four of them. She preferred there always be two clerks in the store at all times. It might be necessary to hire more later on.

It was five o'clock. She had plenty of time to shower and change before Simon picked her up at 6:30. After dinner they'd drive out to see Ruth, Justin and Whitney. Grabbing her purse, she headed for the door. "See you guys Friday. Patty, you've got your key, right?"

"Got it, Hallie. Everything will be fine here. Don't worry about a thing."

* * *

Simon's heart lurched when Hallie came out of her room dressed in the filmy sundress she'd worn at the ranch. It wasn't fancy but feminine and left her shoulders bare for him to caress. Unable to resist, he covered each with his hands. They were soft under his calloused skin. Leaning down, he kissed one shoulder, then the other. He cleared his throat.

"We better get going." Putting his arm around her waist, he led her to the door. Outside she encircled his waist with her arm and leaned in to embrace him. Away from the door, he kissed her. Breathing heavy, he pulled back and nuzzled her neck. "I've missed you, sweetheart."

"Mmmm, Simon. I've missed you too." Her hand reached up to touch his face and traced his lower lip with her thumb. Turning his head, he kissed her palm. "Simon, I love you so much. More each day."

"That makes me happy, love. One thing could

make me happier and you know what it is." She nodded.

"Let's go eat before I try to seduce you in Sue's garden in broad daylight. That cement bench over there doesn't look too comfortable for what I have in mind."

She glanced at the backless slab, then back to him and gave him a wicked wink. "I can guarantee you this, if it happens, I get to be on top."

He blinked at her ribald remark then whooped in joy. Lifting her by the waist, he swung her around in a circle as the laughter rumbled out of him. "You make me happy to be alive, Hallie."

Hallie agreed to eat at Jim Bob's, his favorite steak place. It was dark inside with rustic wooden booths and bare wood floors. When they entered, a group of men at the bar yelled and one hollered, "Hey, Simon. Bring the little lady over here so we can meet her."

"Forget it, guys. I don't want to expose her to riffraff like you bums." They booed as he led her to a back booth away from the bar and rowdier crowd. "Is this alright?"

"It's fine. I'd like to meet your friends."

He looked back at the bar. "Those yahoos? Not tonight, sweetheart. I want you to myself." Instead of moving around the booth to the other seat, he said, "Scoot over so I can sit beside you."

With his arm around her shoulders she studied the menu and decided on a filet. Simon ordered the 16 oz. T-bone. When the food arrived, his steak was hanging over the plate. "Simon, how can you eat so much?"

He looked from his plate to her. "I'm hungry. Been eating my own cooking all week, too." Kissing her, he added, "Don't worry, sugar. I won't get fat on you."

Her filet was delicious, cooked as she liked it and her broccoli was crisp but not hard. "I have to admit, the food here is good."

His eyes crinkled with pleasure. "I knew you were a smart woman."

She eyed the steak, fast disappearing on his plate. "Didn't you say your mother was baking a pie for tonight?"

"Sure did." He ate the remainder of his steak then tossed his napkin down beside his plate. "Darn. I wish I had enough room for that broccoli, but I'm stuffed." He winked then picked up the check.

"You ready? Maybe we'll get there before Whitney goes to bed."

Whitney was up when they arrived. Dressed in her pajamas, she met Simon at the door and jumped into his arms. "Uncle Simon. I've missed you." Her small arms twined around his neck as she planted kisses on his face. With her hair down and washed, the auburn color matched Simon's, the resemblance between the two uncanny.

Bussing her cheek, his face was alive with delight to have her close again. "I've missed you too, sugar."

Hallie exchanged greetings and hugs with Ruth and Justin. Simon turned and approached her. "Look who I brought to see you, Whitney."

"Hi, Hallie." She peered around to see if there was anyone else. "Where's Elise?" She reached out and Hallie took her in her arms for a hug.

"She's at home going to school. She'll be here Saturday for the barbecue."

Ruth stepped in and took Whitney. "Okay, miss. We let you stay up so now it's up to bed with you."

"Here, Mama. Let me take her." Whitney chattered all the way up the stairs. Simon appeared to enjoy her every word.

Ruth brought the coffee pot and pie to the table. "She's missed Simon. I don't know if I'm doing the right thing keeping her here."

Justin laid out plates, napkins and silverware for the pie. He looked at Hallie. "I keep telling her I'd be fine here by myself but she won't have it."

Ruth patted his cheek. "I think Simon can better take care of himself than you can, Justin. Maybe in a year or two."

"Gran, in a year or two? You need to be worrying about yourself right now. Not me, Whitney and Uncle Simon."

Simon came down the stairs. "Did I hear my named being mentioned?"

Ruth spoke up. "I'm not leaving that baby, Justin, until she's a lot older. She needs me. I'm the closest thing she has to a mother right now."

Justin hugged her. "I know, Gran. I hate to see you work so hard. I wish we didn't have this monstrosity of a house that required so much work."

"Don't say that, Justin. One day you'll fill this house with kids." She put slices of pie onto the plates while Justin passed them around. "This house isn't hard to keep clean with help coming in every week. Now that pool is a different story all together, but Whitney enjoys it and I know you do too after a day of hot work."

Simon reached for the coffee pot and poured them all a cup. "She's right, Justin. As much as I dislike this house, you grew up here and it's your home." He cleared his throat. "But I've got to say something here about Whitney." All eyes turned as he paused to take a sip of coffee. "Mama, you're not going to like this but I think Whitney needs to be with me."

"What? You can't take care of a child and run a ranch."

"Yes, I can. She needs me. I'm not leaving her here. As soon as I get settled, get the ranch up running, I'll move her over to my place."

CHAPTER THIRTEEN

Thursday morning Hallie parked in front of her Stepping Up in Georgetown. Gladys was showing evening gowns to a young woman but waved when she walked past. Today marked another step toward making the decision she'd struggled with for a week. She inspected the books while waiting for Gladys.

"Hey, Hallie. What're you doing back so soon? I thought you were staying in Granite Springs until next week." She poured herself a fresh cup of coffee then sat down across from Hallie.

Hallie closed the book and set it aside. "Gladys, how would you like to buy the boutique?"

Gladys, cup halfway to her mouth, froze. "Are you pulling my leg?"

"No. I'm not. There's no one I'd rather sell it to than you." She smiled at her good friend. It felt good to make her happy.

With hands over her mouth, near tears, Gladys said, "Oh my God, girl. You know I want to buy this place but it'll take me a while to come up with the money."

"Don't worry about the money. We'll work out a way for you to buy it without having a large down payment. I'll call my lawyer and have him draw up an agreement. We'll get everything settled by the middle of next week."

Gladys stared at her wide-eyed. "Just like that? It's that easy?" Her brows furrowed, she asked, "What's going on here, Hallie? Are you sick?" A look of worry crossed her face. "Honey, you don't have cancer or some bad disease, do you? Please tell me you don't."

"No, Gladys, no. I'm fine. I promise." Hallie leaned back in her chair and studied the pencil she'd been holding. She cleared her throat. "I'm thinking about getting married."

Gladys dropped her chin and raised her right brow. "Married? To who?" She sucked in a breath and added, "Oh, I see what's going on here. You want a sex life. Nothing wrong with that Hallie, but hell, don't marry the man, have a fling."

Hallie whooped. "Gladys, you're incorrigible." Leave it to Gladys to be as blunt as a nail. "There are a couple of problems though. First, he wants to marry me. The second is I love him something awful."

Her friend studied her for a full minute. "You're sure it's love and not lust, an itch that needs scratching?"

Hallie choked on the sip of coffee. Coughing, she sputtered, "Yes…yes, I'm sure."

"Hummm. And the man, I guess it's Justin's uncle, that rancher, cowboy fella. How do you know he's not fickle like the boy?" She waved her hand. "You know how I feel about men, don't trust the species." She pursed her lips. "I guess some of 'um are decent enough."

Neither spoke, but drifted with memories of the past. Hallie thought back to the evening before. It was so easy for her to make up her mind to start a new business, but so hard to commit to Simon. Yet in a sense, wasn't that what she was doing when she bought the shop and loaned Justin the money? She was putting down roots, investing—in Justin because he was part of Simon, and in Granite Springs because it was Simon's home. In her own way, she was committing. But she couldn't marry Simon without saying "I do." The commitment to him would have to be spoken, and would be an investment of the heart.

"From the way your face is all scrunched up, everything must not be rosy. You don't think he's after your money, do you?"

Startled by the question, Hallie sat straighter in her chair. "No, goodness no. I don't think that." She chewed her lip, wondering if she could discuss her fears with Gladys. "Did you ever think about remarrying after Tom's death?"

"Hell, no. But, I have to say, Hallie, you and James had a happy marriage. Tom and I didn't so don't use me as a comparison gauge." She studied her fingernails. "I hope my negative comments haven't colored your thinking, making you doubt your own judgment."

"I don't think so, Gladys. My problem is I'm afraid to commit, change my life, let someone take James's place, get undressed in front of a man I've known such a short time."

Gladys howled with glee and Hallie joined her. Their laughter brought the other sales lady, Julie, back to the office. "When you two get through having fun, I could use some help out front."

Gladys jumped up. "I'll go help her. But I need to say one more thing." She worried her bottom lip. "Your real fear is of cheating on James. James is dead and buried, Hallie. You had a wonderful life together, but he'd want you to love again. If he didn't, he wouldn't have been worthy of your love all those years." Winking, she added, "Now about getting naked, you don't think for a minute that man doesn't have a damn good idea of what's under those clothes. He knows what he'll be getting. Anyway, he's not marrying you for your body. I'm sure he wants the whole package."

Hallie stood and hugged her good friend. "Thank you, Gladys."

"You're welcome, Hallie. Be happy."

Hallie spent the remainder of the day ordering mannequins, display cabinets, tri-fold mirrors and other items the shop would need. Gladys would set aside part of their present inventory to be delivered in Granite Springs and order additional items to round out the stock in both stores. She didn't expect to open in Granite Springs until early in July.

At home, she and Elise ate a light dinner. Elise was excited about her classes and a possible teaching position in a suburb of Austin in the fall. After eating, Hallie retired to her bedroom. James's dresser still held his dresser set and his jewelry coffer. She lay the grooming set out on Ted's dresser. Opening Ted's top drawer, she pushed things aside to make room for the jewelry chest. There were few items of jewelry, but Ted would cherish each piece. The picture of James she'd kept on her bedside table looked perfect on Elise's dresser. The other pictures, she divided up between the two kids. They could set them out or store them.

She lay awake for a long time, thinking back on life and her many blessings. Her memories with James were precious, never to be forgotten, but it was time to put them away, to make new ones. Looking ahead to the future and what it might bring, she fell into a peaceful sleep.

* * *

Johnny and Patty Farmer were at the store when she arrived. A carpenter friend of theirs had built dressing rooms across the back. It would serve as a divider between the store and break room. The Farmers were busy staining the wood to match the molding and posts. An enclosed area on one end of the kitchen would serve as her office. The second floor would be used for unpacking and storing merchandise. It was accessible by the antique elevator the electrician had deemed safe and reliable. Some day she might restore and convert the third floor into an apartment. The place resembled a boutique more every day.

Satisfied with the stores progress, she left to visit Ruth and see if she could help with barbecue preparations. Ruth's kitchen was filled to capacity with volunteers making potato salad and peach cobblers. Chester, wrapped in a big apron, greeted her with a warm hug.

"We've missed you, gal."

She gave him a kiss on the cheek. "I've missed you too, you old softie."

Caitlyn smiled as Ruth introduced her to Shelia Porter.

"It's good to meet you at last, Hallie. I've met Elise. She's a delightful young woman."

"Thank you, Shelia. So is Caitlyn. You too look enough alike to be sisters."

Shelia laughed. "She does resemble my side of the family. Bless her heart, all she got from her daddy was his temper."

Caitlyn blushed. "Mother. You're not without one yourself, you know." Shelia sputtered then laughed with them.

"Ruth, is there anything I can do to help?"

"Not a thing. Looks like we've got things under control." Ruth surveyed the room and pointed to the large wall oven. "We've got the bunk house oven and these two so we'll bake the pies tomorrow evening so they'll still be warm. Chester will make coleslaw in the morning. He and the boys will make tea and the garnishes that afternoon."

"Okay, if you're sure. I guess I'll go see how Simon's coming along with all his work. Maybe I can help him."

Chester winked and grinned. "You do that, gal. I'm sure he'll be able to find something for you to do."

He "yelped" when Ruth popped him with her dishtowel. "You be nice, you old coot."

"Dang, Ruth. I was."

Hallie closed the door on their laughter.

She found Simon in the barn brushing down Redman. Sadie was in a neighboring stall. Both horses greeted her with a nicker when she entered. Simon's smile of greeting sent a tingle through her body. His kiss left her breathless and happy.

"Hey, I came over to help out, not mess around."

"I need to get out and check more fence line before supper. You want to go with me?"

"Sure." She hadn't thought to wear her boots but did have on jeans. "Have you got an extra hat I can borrow?"

"I'm sure we can find something upstairs that will work. Might find some boots that fit."

Wearing a pair of Ruth's old boots, shirt and hat, they rode out. They found several breaks and by the time they were repaired, it was after five o'clock. At six o'clock, horses dried, brushed and in their stalls, they headed for the house. Hallie started dinner while Simon showered. He came out shaved, smelling and looking too damned sexy for words. She felt dirty but hadn't thought to bring a change of clothes.

"I bet you can find something of mama's upstairs. Check the closets, use what you want. I'll keep an eye on dinner."

Grateful for the offer, she located what she needed and showered upstairs. She came down in fresh jeans and shirt. The jeans were tight across the butt but fit everywhere else.

Dinner consisted of what she could find in the freezer. She'd put on fresh black-eyed peas, green beans and defrosted a small slab of round steak. When she came back from her shower, Simon had put potatoes on to boil and was breading the steak to fry.

Hallie looked at the potatoes. "Does this mean you feel the need for potatoes at every meal?"

He grinned. "No, but I'm mighty hungry tonight and they'll be good with the steak and gravy."

She cocked an eyebrow. "Gravy, huh? I suppose you like gravy at every meal, too."

Hands coated with steak batter he leaned in for a kiss. "As often as I can get it, darlin'."

They washed dishes together. When the last pots and pans were put away, they went outside to sit on the porch.

"I've decided I need a porch swing or glider like the one on your front porch. I don't like not having you close enough to kiss." He held out his hand. "Come sit in my lap."

She put her arms around his neck and leaned her head against his while he rocked them. The rocker didn't have arms so her legs draped across his. Dark out, the cicadas chirped a pleasant tune. The sound was soothing and with the creak of the rocker sounded like nature's symphony.

Hallie cupped Simon's face and kissed his brow, then let her fingers drop to trace his lips. His hand moved from her waist up her side, grazing the fullness of her breast, causing her to shudder. Combing his fingers through her hair he pulled her face down for his kiss. His lips were soft, then hard as he played upon her mouth, drawing, exploring, giving, and taking until she was panting with desire.

"Simon," she moaned as his lips moved to her neck. Simon loosened the top buttons of her shirt and placed his lips on the creamy white mounds above her bra. She was so beautiful and her desire for him roared in his head making his body hard with wanting. Her skin was sensitive to his touch and he reveled in every jerk and shudder of her body. His hand returned to her breast, holding it as he brushed his thumb across the taut nipple. Aching to feel her against his hardness, he lifted her and sat her astride his knees. His eyes locked with hers as he put her arms around his neck. Hands at her waist he pulled her closer until his erection met the juncture of her thighs. He waited, giving her a chance to say no. When she didn't, his hands moved to her breasts to caress and tease. He rocked them back and forth.

As their bodies moved with the rhythm, Hallie thought she'd scream the pleasure was so intense.

Pressing closer, she buried her face in his neck. And then Simon stopped rocking.

She froze. He'd built this fire in her body, made her want him, ache for him. In a strained voice he said, "Sweetheart, we've got to stop." He eased her back from his body and moved her until she sat across his lap. Holding her against his chest, he added, "This isn't fair to you, Hallie. You'll think I'm trying to influence your decision tomorrow by seducing you tonight."

Simon watched the taillights of her car until the red spots got smaller and then disappeared. He released the breath he'd been holding and sat down on the top step of the front porch. Bloody hell, that was the hardest thing he'd done in his life. Mad, she'd said less than two words when she left. He chuckled. Sleep would be impossible tonight, even after a long cold shower. He hoped Hallie couldn't sleep either. That had been his intention. Not that he'd planned the scene in the rocker. It was time she gave him an answer so they could have a normal sex life, one in his bed. However, the rocker had been interesting.

* * *

Hallie was still fuming when she crawled into bed. The cold shower hadn't helped a great deal. Her body still yearned for the feel of his and release. Beating her pillow, she tossed and turned trying to get comfortable. She hoped he was as uncomfortable as she was. *Influence my decision, my ass. He did that on purpose.* A giggle escaped her. The scoundrel.

* * *

The area around Cole Ranch was fast filling with cars. Hoping for a prime spot, Hallie drove around to the back and found a place by the garage. Voices and laughter filled the air along with the scent of barbecue crisping on the grill. Jezebel lay close to the action. She wagged her tail and "woofed" a greeting but wasn't about to give up her location.

Chester saw the exchange and waved. He grabbed a beer and brought it to her. "You'd think we never feed that old dog."

Taking the beer, she laughed. "But you don't feed her barbecue, Chester." The beer was cold and delicious.

"Your kids are here." He pointed toward the pool. "Ted's had a good time today. Justin took him riding and the boy did real good. He's a nice kid, Hallie."

She hugged him. "Thank you, Chester. I'm proud of them both." Her eyes searched the crowd.

"If you're looking for Simon, he's over by the big oak talking to Loretta." He furrowed his brows. "You watch out for that woman, Hallie. She's a barracuda."

Simon listened to Loretta's chatter with half an ear. His attention was on Hallie as she walked toward him. God, she looked good. Town folks called out greetings, and she stopped to chat with them as she made her way over. Tonight she wore a white off the shoulder blouse tucked into a full mid-calf blue skirt. A leather and silver concho belt hung loose at her waist. The hair he loved so much was in its usual style but fuller.

"Simon. Simon! I'm—"

He didn't realize Loretta was trying to get his attention until she tugged at his arm. "Oh, sorry, Loretta. Excuse me for a minute."

Hallie's face lit when he approached her. His heart thundered at the welcome he saw in her face. Grinning, he leaned in and gave her a quick kiss before enfolding her in a hug. "Oh, darlin'. It's good to see you."

She stroked his face. "It's good to see you, too. Now we better get over to that woman behind you. She's shooting daggers our way. The famous Loretta, I assume?"

With his arm around her waist, he led her over to the oak tree. "Loretta, I'd like you to meet Hallie Barron. Hallie, this is my sister-in-law, Loretta Cole."

The beautiful woman smiled. Taking Simon's other arm, she pressed herself against his side. "Your ex sister-in-law, darling." She extended her free hand. "I'm pleased to meet you, Hallie."

"You too, Loretta." Her trim figure encased in designer jeans and boots, could have been an advertisement for Neiman Marcus. But, for all her beauty, she seemed cold.

"Are you staying here tonight, Loretta?"

"Goodness, no. Whitney and I have a room in town at the Cottonwood Bed and Breakfast."

"I'm sorry things didn't work out between Justin and Elise. He's a fine young man."

"Yes, well, me too. Your daughter was what he needed to take his mind off this ranch. This ranch will never be what it once was and I don't want to see it break him like it did his daddy." She smiled but it didn't quite reach her eyes. "As for his raising, I can't take much credit there." Squeezing Simon's arm, she added, "Sidney and Simon are responsible for that."

Simon pulled his arm away from Loretta. He wanted to throttle the woman. "If anything broke Sidney, it wasn't this ranch, it was you, Loretta. You and your money grubbing ways. Now, if you'll excuse us, I'd like Hallie to meet some friends of mine."

Hallie could feel the anger vibrating through Simon's body. He was walking so fast she struggled to keep up. "Simon, slow down." He stopped.

"Sorry, darlin'. That woman is so self-centered. Sometimes I wonder how Justin and Whitney can be related to her."

"The fine Cole blood dominated, that's how. Simon, don't let her ruin the party for you. Put it out of your mind."

He cupped her elbows and put her hands at his waist. "There's only one thing that would ruin this evening for me, Hallie. I think you know what that is."

His beautiful blue eyes gazed at her in question. Emotion filled her chest making her voice croak. "Yes, I know."

He took her arm and almost raced her to the barn. He knelt on one knee in the dust. Sitting on a bale of hay, time stood still for Hallie. Dust bunnies danced in beams of sunlight that divided darkened areas. The rays highlighted Simon's dark auburn hair making it appear gold in places. He took her hand.

"Hallie."

She looked down at the man she loved, the man who wasn't embarrassed to bare his soul in front of his family and friends. Her heart beat like thunder, her chest ached with mounting emotion.

He stroked her hand and brought it to his lips to place a searing kiss in her palm. "I've loved you almost from the moment we met. You're the woman I've dreamed of, searched for, and never hoped to find. I need you in my life, Hallie. If you'll marry me, I'll cherish you for the rest of our lives." Hope radiated from his eyes making them glow with a life of their own. "Will you marry me, Hallie?"

Moisture pooled in her eyes. For the first time in weeks, she had no doubts about her future. Her future was here with this man. Taking his hand, she placed a kiss in the palm and then placed it to her cheek. "I love you too, Simon. Yes, I'll marry you."

Simon tilted his head back and mouthed, "Thank you, God." Then grinning like a fool he clasped her close and kissed her until they heard the roar of approval from the crowd gathered at the barn door. Hallie blushed scarlet, but Simon was nonplused. He waved his hand and said, "Go away, I'm not through, yet."

Hallie looked in awe as they backed off a ways and got quiet. When she turned back, he took her hand and slipped a beautiful three stone ring on her finger.

"Simon, it's beautiful. But I don't need a ring."

He folded her hand over his and brought it to his lips kissing the ring on her finger. "Oh, but I do, sweetheart."

Smiling though her tears, she whispered. "I'll cherish it always, as I will you."

He helped her to her feet. Arm around her waist, he announced to the crowd, "We're getting married."

The minute they walked through the door, they were mobbed. Ruth and Chester, both mopping at their eyes, hugged them hard. Chester muttering, "It's about time you two quit avoiding the inevitable." Justin, Ted and Elise embraced them and expressed their joy. Loretta shook their hands and though she mouthed congratulations, Hallie could see her heart wasn't in it.

Sam Porter and Shelia stood behind them in the food line. He clapped Simon on the back. "We're so happy for you, Simon. Introduce us to your bride-to-be."

Hallie was pleased to meet the man she'd heard so much about. An affectionate man, he hugged her.

"Hallie and I met yesterday morning, Sam. It's good to see you again, Hallie. I'm anxious for your boutique to open," said Shelia. "I've visited your store in Georgetown and love your clothes."

"Great. I hope we'll see you often, then."

While the women talked fashion, Sam leaned toward Simon and lowered his voice. "I hear Justin found an investor for the ranch. I'm glad for him. He deserves a chance to build the place back up."

"Yes, he did. A generous one too, I might add. I'd offered Justin a loan, which he turned down, but I couldn't have advanced him anywhere near the amount he received last week."

The big man wrinkled his brow. Hands in his pockets, he rocked back on his heels. "I don't suppose you'd tell me who this investor is, would you? Joe Booker's being mighty hush-hush about the entire situation." He raised a hand and tilted his head. "Not just being nosy. I have the boy's best interest at heart. Wouldn't want some shyster to come in and take his ranch from him."

Simon clapped him on the back. "I appreciate that, Sam. But, don't worry. I checked it out. He's in good hands."

Hallie and Simon looked for a deserted place to eat and ended up back in the barn sitting on a bale of hay.

"You happy, darlin'?"

"Enough to bust."

He beamed. "Can we get married next week?"

"Next week? There's no way I can get a wedding together in a week."

"Do you want to have it at your church in Georgetown?"

She thought for a minute. "You know, I think I'd like to get married here, in your smaller church. After all, we'll be living here."

"Then it'll be easy to get married in a week. Everyone will pitch in and help. That's the way things are done around here." He grinned. "I'll tell them to send me the bills. The women enjoy spending someone else's money."

"Hmm. We'll see."

He sat their plate aside. "Come here and let me love on you a little."

"Ha. After the way you treated me last night? No way."

He lunged for her and she evaded his grasp. "Well, I had to do something to help you make up your mind."

She brushed the hay from her skirt. "I'd made up my mind before I got in the car Friday morning." With a wink, she added, "I wonder what would have happened if you hadn't stopped rocking." Laughing, at the look of shock on his face, she ran for the door.

"Well, hell," he muttered.

He caught up with her talking to Caitlyn and Elise. While the band warmed up Corbett, Ted, and Justin checked the portable wooden dance floor to make sure it was level. The ranch hands cleared the food and folded the long tables.

The small white lights draped in the big tree and around the pool fence gave enough light to move without bumping into people. Perfect for dancing. Sam walked up with a bag of sawdust and sprinkled it on the floor. Justin appeared at the microphone. "Family, friends, neighbors. The Cole family is pleased to have you with us tonight. To begin this dance, let's have Uncle Simon and his sweetheart, Hallie Barron, lead off." The group clapped and whistled. "Befitting the occasion, the dance will be a country waltz."

Held close in Simon's arms, Hallie reveled in the joy that filled her heart. A good dancer, Simon spun her around the dance floor to their audience's cheers and teasing remarks. He ignored them and looked at her, his happiness evident for all to see.

He squeezed her waist. "I hate to let you go, but think we better get some other folks out here on the dance floor?" She nodded.

They left the floor and returned with another partner, Simon with Elise and Hallie with Justin. Next, Simon chose Ruth and she picked Chester.

His voice gruff with emotion, he spoke. "You've made our boy a happy man. I'd about given up hope he'd find his soul mate."

She laid her cheek against his wrinkled one. "I love him something awful, Chester. I'll take good care of his heart." This man loved Simon like a son. He was more family than employee.

"What about you, Chester? Did you ever meet your soul mate and marry?"

He stopped and kissed her cheek. "No, I never married. She loved someone else. Now, you've danced long enough with this old man. Let's get some of the young folks on the floor."

The exchange continued until Hallie found herself without a partner. She looked around the packed dance floor and spotted Simon with Loretta clinging to his neck. The band started another song and Loretta didn't appear to want to let Simon go.

Smiling, she tapped her on the shoulder. "Excuse me, Loretta, I'm cutting in." Flashing her a hateful glare, Loretta released Simon. They watched her cut in on Sam and Shelia.

"Thank you for rescuing me."

"My pleasure, darling." He smiled at her use of darling. Hallie realized it was the first time she'd used an endearment in place of his name.

"Did you notice Justin and Caitlyn dancing?"

She nodded. "They're smiling. Look at Corbett and Elise. I think something may be going on there." Her gaze continued to roam until it landed on Ruth and Chester. From the expression on Chester's face, it was obvious he loved her. Was she his soul mate? Had he loved her all these years?

"Hmm. And then there's your mother and Chester. Wonder how long that's been going on." How had they not noticed before?

"What're you talking about?" Glancing around, he located them and watched for a while. "Well, I'll be damned. After all these years."

Hallie excused herself and went inside to the bathroom to repair her makeup and hair. When she came out through the den, Loretta was on her way in. "Oh, Hallie. I'm so glad I caught you. Sit down and talk with me a minute."

She hesitated, but didn't want to be rude. "Alright, but just for a minute. I want to get back out to Simon before the band stops playing."

Loretta peered at her watch. "You've got a while

yet." She cleared her throat and toyed with the seams in her jeans. "I don't know how to say this. I don't want to hurt you, but I feel you should know."

"Know what, Loretta?"

"I hate to see you marry Simon without knowing the truth about some things. You might change your mind when you know."

"I doubt there's anything you could tell me to change my mind about Simon." Angry, she stood up. "I'm going out."

Loretta grabbed her arm. "Not until you've heard me out." Expression determined, she blurted, "Sidney was not Whitney's father. Simon is."

A fist closed around Hallie's heart. "You're lying. If that were true, Simon would have told me. You're so miserable you can't stand to see anyone else happy."

"It's the truth. Simon loves me. He always has, that's why he's never married. You'll be a substitute for me."

She shook herself. "If he loves you so much, why isn't he marrying you?"

Hands on her designer clad hips, she mocked. "Because I won't marry him. I have no intention of being a worn out rancher's wife. Plus, you have plenty of money and when he has access to that he'll be back to see me."

All she could do was stand there and shake her head. Her world was being cut apart and this woman wielded the scissors."Yes, it's true. Ask him. I dare you." She looked self-satisfied. "But you don't have to ask, do you? You've seen how much they favor, how he holds her, dotes on her. Would any man be so crazy about a child that wasn't his own?" She laughed and looked at her sculpted nails. "It was a harmless flirtation on my part. But it ended with me being pregnant. The funny thing is, Sidney never knew. Simon is Whitney's father, Hallie. Don't doubt me for a minute." She grabbed Hallie and shook her. Her voice rose. "Do you hear me? Simon is Whitney's father."

Hallie shoved her away and turned toward the door. There was a sound from the balcony above, a cry like a hurt animal. Standing there, above them, was Whitney. The tragic expression on the child's face broke her heart.

"Mommy? Mommy? Why...?" She started to cry, and then a high-pitched keen echoed from her throat ending in a whimper. Then silence.

"Whitney...honey." Hallie ran up the stairs and tried to comfort her, but she backed away.

Loretta knelt before her, "Baby, baby, come to Mommy." Whitney scooted against the wall, cringing away from her.

Frantic, tears blurring her vision, Hallie rushed out the door in search of Simon. He stood talking to several men. She'd left the door open and Whitney's cries, "No, Mommy. No," carried across the night air. He looked up and saw her running toward him. Grabbing her shoulders, he asked. "My God, Hallie. What's wrong?"

Biting back sobs, she choked out. "Loretta informed me that Whitney is your child, not Sidney's. Whitney overheard every word."

"What?" His face registered shock but he didn't deny the words. Then rage took over and he bellowed like a bull. "I'm going to kill that woman. She's unfit to be around the child."

"She needs you, Simon. Whitney needs you."

He nodded. "I'll come to you later, Hallie. I've got to fix this first. I'm sorry." He kissed her and went inside.

The tears fell making it hard for her to see the road—tears for the child and for herself. Brushing them away, she tried to focus on the country road. Simon should have told her Whitney was his. She would have understood. Maybe. Then again, he'd betrayed his brother's trust with his wife. No, she wouldn't have understood. That was unforgivable. The way Loretta talked Simon still loved her. She didn't for a minute believe that. It was evident in his every action he abhorred her. Had Loretta seduced him then taunted him about the pregnancy furthering his guilt and self-loathing?

Thank God Elise had gone home with the Porters. Talk about odd situations. Caitlyn and the Porters seem to like Elise and had invited her over so Ruth would have extra room if needed. Maybe she should go back and get Ted, take him to the Pink Palace with her. Pack her bags and go home. No, that could wait until morning.

Poor Whitney. Without Simon and Ruth, the poor little thing didn't have a chance. As much as she detested what Simon had done, he was a good parent. She hoped Loretta couldn't take her from him. The woman was sick. She needed to be in therapy.

Thank God she had an outside entry. She couldn't face Sue. The phone rang as she slipped inside. She heard Sue talking but not her words. The gossip link was spreading the news.

Tucked in her bed she cried, almost as hard as

she'd cried when James had died, though in many ways, his death had been a release. For him, from the pain, and for her, watching him suffer. She'd had years of memories to look back on, to soften the bittersweet ache. There would be no softening of the blow tonight. She'd loved again, and lost again, not by death, but by deception. Her memories would be painful and ugly because they were lies.

CHAPTER FOURTEEN

"Hallie, my love. I need you so." Thank God they would be married soon. He ached to hold her and be held to soothe his aching soul. The hurt and confusion on Whitney's face would haunt him for a long time. She'd been through so much in her short lifetime. He'd left her, asleep at last tucked in bed with Mama. They'd talked for over an hour, making sure she understood. He was her uncle, not her father. She had clung to him as if her life depended on it and wouldn't let Loretta near her. Loretta was in Whitney's bed now in a brandy-induced sleep. This time her lies had backfired. Maybe she'd learned something. A shame it was at Whitney's expense.

"Don't you think, pumpkin, that if you were my daughter I'd tell you?" She shrugged but didn't speak. "Because if I was your father, I'd shout it to the whole world I'd be so proud. That's what your daddy did. He loved you so much."

"He shouted it to the whole world?" Her lip trembled as she waited for his answer.

"Yes, he did. Every time he took you to town, he'd make the rounds and show you off to his friends." She smiled.

"When your daddy died, I wanted to take care of you because I love you too. We wanted you to grow up here on the ranch. And you've been here with Gran and me ever since. Your mother has talked to you about why you don't live with her, right?"

She nodded. "Yes, cause her lifestyle in uneven."

"Unstable."

"Yeah, unstable." She yawned and rubbed her eyes. "Why did my mama lie about you being my daddy?"

"Your mama is mixed up about many things and has a hard time telling the truth. She lies sometimes to get what she wants. I don't know how to explain it, sugar."

"You punish me when I lie. Did her mama not teach her to tell the truth?"

"No, she didn't. And because of her lies, your mama doesn't have many friends." He tweaked her nose. "You have lots of friends, don't you?"

"Yes." Her head bobbed up and down.

"Are you okay with this now? Do you think you can give your mama a hug in the morning when she leaves to go home?"

"Uh huh. And I'll tell her to not tell any more lies."

"Good." He picked her up and carried her into Ruth's downstairs bedroom. "Your mama is asleep in your little bed upstairs so how about you sleep with Gran tonight?" He helped her undress and slip into pajamas. She brushed her teeth and washed her face. When he tucked her in and kissed her, she whispered, "Uncle Simon, I wished you were my daddy. I want to live with you." He brushed her hair back from her face. Voice gruff with emotion, he whispered, "I wish it, too, pumpkin." She was asleep before the words were out of his mouth.

The Pink Palace was dark, not a light on anywhere.

Why should there be? It was after two in the morning. Where's Hallie's car? He parked and shut off the lights, letting his eyes adjust to the darkness beyond the weak streetlight. It wasn't there.

Dread washed through him. Did she believe Loretta's lies? Please, God, no. How could she leave without talking to him? Giving him a chance to deny what he'd been accused of?

He turned on the lights and headed out of town. Disappointment rose bitter in his throat. Pain filled his chest, squeezing his breath. It hurt. It hurt like hell. He'd given her his heart and she'd stomped the life out of it. He beat his fist against the steering wheel. Good riddance, woman. Enjoy your cold, loveless, celibate life.

As if on autopilot, his truck stopped in front of his house. Bone weary and heart sick, it was all he could do to get out of the truck. He needed to get a dog, something to welcome him when he came home at night. In the house, he stripped off his shirt and unbuttoned his jeans as he made his way toward his bedroom. A sliver of light from the bedside table guided his way. At the door he stopped and stared. His heart in his throat, he groaned, "Hallie."

She lay curled on his bed, her feet pulled up under her long skirt to warm them. He sat down in the chair and dropped his head in his hands. Tears threatened but he shoved them back and whispered, "Thank you, God." Pulling the coverlet over her, he kicked off his boots and slid in beside her. He eased his arm under her head and shoulders, pulling her close. She mumbled something, snuggled in to his side and went back to sleep. He studied her face. It was void of make-up, fresh and clean—beautiful. This was all he needed in life—to come home to this woman and hold her all night long. Smiling, he turned out the light and fell asleep.

Hallie woke to Simon's chest hair tickling her nose. Her skirt, bunched up around her legs, tied her down. She tugged enough from under Simon so she could turn over. He rolled toward her, reached out and tucked her back against his body. Smiling, she closed her eyes and went back to sleep.

* * *

Simon woke to the smell of coffee and frying bacon. Stretching, he blinked and remembered the evening before. Coming home to find Hallie asleep on his bed. Damn, she'd woken before him. This was not at all how he'd intended the morning to go. The clock read nine thirty. After a quick shower, he met her in the kitchen. She stood at the stove, frying eggs. He slipped his arms around her waist and kissed her neck.

"It's about time you woke up and got in here." He turned her in his arms for a thorough good morning kiss.

"Why didn't you wake me before you got up, sweetheart? I had a better way to spend the morning." He wiggled his eyebrows making her laugh.

"I bet you did." She smoothed her hand over his naked chest. He was mighty sexy this morning standing there barefoot wearing nothing but his jeans and a wicked smile. "And, I have to admit I was tempted. But, we have to get to church this morning." She put their plates on the table.

"We could miss this morning. No one would miss us."

"Ha! I got strict orders from Sue. Anyway, if we don't, they might hold a prayer service for us for fornicating on the Sabbath." He whooped with glee. Scooping her up, he twirled her around before setting her back on her feet.

"Hallie, I love you. You're so much fun to be around."

They made it on time. The congregation was seated but many turned to observe their entrance. Chester and both their families sat in one pew and scooted over to make room for them. Jo Beth and Paul sat in the next row up. Simon tapped her on the shoulder.

"I'm glad you're here, Red."

"You think I would miss this? Anyway, I want to help plan your wedding."

He grinned and winked at Hallie. Patting Jo Beth's back, he said, "Thank you, cuz." Squeezing Hallie's hand, he leaned in to whisper. "See, I told you there would be lots of help."

The pastor asked for the visitors to rise. Simon rose and introduced Hallie, Elise and Ted. "Pastor, I'd—"

Pastor John grinned and held up his hand. "Be patient, son. We'll get to that in a minute. "Jo Beth and Paul, it's nice to have you with us today." He studied the congregations to see if he'd missed anyone. "Well, I see the church is packed today." He looked at Simon and Hallie. "I think the Lord and I can thank Simon and his charming *fiancée* for that." He chuckled. "I'm grateful to see they made it." He pulled on his ear. "Was beginning to worry."

The congregation burst into laughter. Hallie felt the blush of heat engulf her face. The comment didn't faze Simon. He laughed with everyone else.

"Now, before Simon starts talking, do we have announcements from anyone else this morning?" No one stood up or raised their hand. He nodded at Simon. "Son, you have five minutes. I've got a sermon to deliver this morning."

Simon got up and pulled Hallie to stand at his side. "Hallie Barron has consented to be my wife." The church roared with applause. Clearing his throat, he went on. "Not being a patient man, I'd like to have the wedding as soon as possible." A few chuckles were heard around the room. "I figure if we get our marriage license in the morning, we should be able to get married Thursday morning."

Hallie shook her head. "Thursday morning?"

Simon grinned and winked. "Sugar, I think I can wait until Saturday afternoon." The laughter was deafening.

Hallie threw up her hands and sat down.

"But, we'll need some help to get this planned. If you're willing to help, you can send me a bill for your expenses." He started to sit down then waved his hand for attention. "And, the whole town is invited."

"I'll plan the reception. We'll have it on the lawn at the Pink Palace." Everyone turned to see Sue Posey standing across the aisle. "After all, she's staying at my place." She looked at Hallie and nodded. "We'll have plenty of time each evening to plan together."

Hallie returned the nod with a smile. "Thank you, Sue."

Lola, sitting in the front pew, stood. "I'll bake the cakes."

"Patty and I'll provide the music," shouted Johnny Farmer.

"I'll decorate the church," said Jo Beth.

Sam Porter added, "We'll provide the champagne."

Offers continued. Simon, voice gruff said, "I told Hallie we'd have help from the congregation, but I had no idea you'd be so generous. Thank you all."

Pastor John beamed at his flock. "What we've seen today is part of what church is all about. Sharing your joys with your church family and pitching in to help each other. I know Simon has been there for many of you when you needed him. It's nice to see him on the receiving end. Hallie, we're so pleased to see the joy you've brought Simon."

He opened his *Bible*. "Today's sermon is on, appropriately so, marriage. It's my custom when we have an upcoming wedding to deliver this sermon. We can never hear it too much." Slipping on his glasses he said, "Turn in your *Bibles* to—."

Lunch at Ruth's was a joyous affair. Hallie enjoyed every minute. Jo Beth kept them laughing by teasing Simon. Elise returned from picking up her things at the Porters with Caitlyn in tow. Chester came in bearing a fresh peach cobbler. He found Corbett about to knock on the back door, brought him in and Ruth insisted he join them. Much to Ted's delight, Whitney had adopted him and become his shadow. She'd expected Loretta to join them but she'd left while they were at church.

On their way to Simon's, Hallie scooted to the center of the bench seat in Simon's pickup. She hooked her arm thorough his and held his hand. His thumb stroked her palm sending goose bumps racing across her skin. They'd not talked about the previous evening's experience.

"Simon?"

"What, sugar?"

"We need to talk about what happened last night."

He put his arm around her. "Yes, we do. But let's wait until we get home and get comfortable."

When she came out of the bathroom, he was stretched out on the bed in a t-shirt and denim shorts. He held out his hand. She lay down beside him, head on his shoulder. He wrapped his arms around her. She fit her body to his with her arm around his waist.

"Loretta was lying last night." He turned to look into her eyes. "When I got to the Pink Palace and you weren't there, I thought you believed her." He stroked her hair. "The drive here was hell. Hurt and heartsick, I stumbled into the house and found you asleep on my bed." Voice thick with emotion, he continued, "I was so grateful, I just sat and watched you. I wanted to wake you and love you but contented myself with holding you while we slept." Giving her a quick kiss, he added, "Thank you for trusting me."

She stroked his jaw. "I have to be honest, Simon. When I left the party, I was broken-hearted, believing Loretta's web of deceit. I kept thinking if you'd only told me, I could have forgiven you. But, betraying a brother is unforgivable. So, I cried and prepared to go home to lick my wounds." Voice choked, she added. "But, I remembered how you longed for children and decided that if Whitney was yours, there was no way in hell you'd let her continue to believe otherwise. So, I got out of bed and dressed. On my way out, I bumped into Sue Posey on the front porch. She was sitting outside my door."

She couldn't help but smile as she relayed the older woman's comments to Simon. The minute she stepped onto the porch, Sue had said "It's about time you came to your senses and went to that boy. Loretta has made another mess for him to clean up." She shook her head and snorted. "This time she's hurt that precious child with her lies."

"I'm sorry I kept you up, Sue. It took a while for me to work through it all."

"At least you did." She stood and started inside. "Do you have clothes for church in the morning? If not, you better get some because I expect to see you two there in the morning."

Hallie hugged the older woman. "Thank you, Sue."

"You're welcome. Now, scoot. Don't give our boy something else to worry about."

Simon chuckled. "Did you get her unspoken message at church this morning?"

"Loud and clear. There will be bed check at the Pink Palace tonight and Hallie better be in hers."

They didn't speak for several minutes. Hallie was almost asleep when he said, "Last night Whitney told me she wished I was her daddy and she could live with me."

"She did? Did you tell her our plans?"

"She fell asleep before I could tell her she'd be living with us."

He eased up on his elbow to look down at her. His rugged face tense, Hallie sensed his inner turmoil. "Are you sure, you won't mind having her with us? You've raised two children and here I'm asking you to take on another. It's asking a lot. I guess I'm selfish. I want you both."

"No, love. I don't mind. That's one of the reasons I love you so. Your devotion to your family and desire to care for Whitney." She stroked his cheek, testing the amount of stubble. "I have to say, I find it macho and sexy."

His eyes jerked to hers to see if she was teasing. "You don't say?"

She grinned and nodded. "It's going to work out, Simon. When school starts, I can drop her at school on my way to the shop. In the afternoons she can stay with me until time to come home."

He sighed and dropped his head to hers. "God, Hallie. What did I do to deserve you?" Laying back down, he pulled her close and kissed her forehead. "You know, we haven't talked about birth control." His fingers trailed up and down her arm causing a delicious tingle. She shivered. He wrapped both arms around her.

"No, we haven't."

"I don't want you to take birth control pills. I've read they're not safe for women over thirty. How about if we use condoms?"

"We could do that. Or we could not use birth control and see what happens."

His body froze. She could feel his tense alertness. "What if you get pregnant?"

"I guess we'd have a baby."

In less than a second she was on her back pinned beneath his body. Elbows below the pillow, his hands cradled her face. His eyes searched hers. "Would it be dangerous for you to have a baby at your age?"

She gave him a playful slap on his side. "I'm not ancient, you know." Then she wrapped her arms around his waist and squeezed. "I don't think it would be dangerous. The Dr. might want to do special tests to make sure the baby was alright."

Voice choked, he asked. "Would you want a baby at this time in your life? With Whitney, and your boutique, would it be too much for you?"

"No, Simon. Nothing would make me happier than having a baby with you. As far as the boutique goes, I can work from home if need be."

He rolled to his side taking her with him, settling her head under his chin, arms locking her close. She stroked his side and back in comfort, and she'd glimpsed the smile on his lips.

* * *

The wedding march began. The church doors opened and Ted escorted her down the aisle as if he'd done it numerous times. Filled with people and fresh flowers, a low buzz followed her path. The scent of roses and day lilies teased her nose, their beautiful scent adding to her joy of the day. People greeted her as she walked by, easing some of her nervousness.

Then she saw him. Tall and handsome, watching her as she walked toward him. Hands clasped in front, his eyes locked with hers and he smiled. Her smile answered his and echoed the happiness she felt. Tears pricked her eyes and as he placed her hand on his arm, she saw the sparkle in his.

"Dearly beloved, we are gathered today in the sight of God and these witnesses…"

When Pastor John pronounced them husband and wife, the room exploded with applause and cheering.

"Oh Lord, you're beautiful, Hallie." Simon felt pretty smug. He'd coaxed her into her room at the Pink Palace for a quick kiss. It was too crowded outside. "I'll remember you in this dress 'til the day I die." She was exquisite. The dress fit her curves, the low neck showing off the creamy globes of her breasts. He ran his hand from her waist up to cup them then leaned down to kiss the exposed flesh.

She curled her arms around his neck. Her lips were swollen from his kisses. "Umm, Simon. We have guests outside."

He pulled her close, fitting her to his arousal. "Do you think they'd miss us if we stayed in here a while longer."

"You don't want Sue searching for us, do you?"

He groaned. "Hell, no. We better get out there."

The band played during dinner. They cut the three tier cake, toasted each other with champagne and danced with every person in town, from the youngest to the oldest. At long last Hallie was in his arms again.

"Have I told you how sexy you look in those high heels?"

She grinned up at him. "Three times at least."

He growled. "I guess you know I mean it."

"Wait until we get home tonight and you see what I'm wearing with them."

He stopped dancing and gazed around. "I don't think anyone would miss us if we leave now."

"Curious, are you?"

"Damned straight. I've waited long enough." He took her hand and started toward the side of the house.

"Wait, Simon. What about my bags?"

"Elise put them in your car earlier." She couldn't walk fast in the spike heels. They kept sinking into the grass. He whipped her up into his arms and made for their escape.

When they reached home, Simon tossed her suitcase into the front room. "Come here, bride." He carried her across the threshold, kicking the door closed with his foot. "Welcome to our home, Mrs. Cole." In the bedroom, he set her on her feet.

"Do you have any idea how happy I am?" He stoked her cheek, his hand reaching into her hair.

"Yes, I do, Mr. Cole. As happy as I am, I hope."

He kissed her long and deep, teasing and tasting her mouth. Cupping her breast, he stroked the nipple. She moaned into his mouth. He broke the kiss and stepped back.

Faking a yawn, he glanced at his watch. "My goodness, look at the time. It's almost eight o'clock. I'm ready for bed. How about you?"

She grinned and stretched. "It has been a long day."

He started unbuttoning his shirt.

Taking his hand, she said, "Here, let me help you out of this." His breath caught at her touch as she worked the buttons loose. He shrugged out of the shirt and tossed it on a chair. She ran her hands across his bare chest, twining her fingers in the curly hair. "I've wondered how this would feel. It's so soft." She rubbed her cheek across his chest hair then planted a kiss between his biceps.

Voice thick with yearning, he said, "Turn around, Hallie. Let me help you out of this dress." Fingers clumsy, he managed the tiny hook, then eased the zipper down below her waist. The dress slid off her arms into a puddle at her feet. Leaning down, she caught it, stepped out, and hung it on the bedpost.

When she turned around, he looked his fill. The longline strapless bra ended above the lacy bikini panties and pushed her breasts up to overflowing.

Garters held up sheer hose treating him to a small expanse of creamy flesh. His eyes moved down the hose to her small feet in the sexy heels, then back up to her face.

"My God, Hallie. You're beautiful." Kicking his shoes off, he stepped closer and trailed his fingers across the cleavage of her breasts then around their fullness before dipping beneath the bra to stroke the sensitive flesh hidden from his view. With his tongue, he retraced his path. She moaned and ran her hands down his chest to reach his belt buckle. He brushed her hand aside and made fast work of his slacks, leaving them in a heap on the floor. Setting her on the edge of the bed he knelt to remove her shoes. Taking his time, he removed a stocking, planting kisses on her leg as he uncovered her skin. He kissed the sole of her foot and moved to the other leg.

Her face was flushed with passion, her breathing rapid. His heart swelled with the knowledge she wanted him. His hands spanned her waist then moved up to her breasts again. "What do you call this piece of underwear? It looks like it may take a knife to get you out of it."

"It's called a *bustier*. Do you like it?"

"I love it, but right now I want you out of it."

She started undoing the small hooks and eyes at the top.

"I see now. Here, let me." He wanted to watch as his hands exposed her beautiful breasts. She started working on the ones from the bottom then stopped to let him do the last one.

The *bustier* fell away. As it did, her breasts filled his hands. A low moan filled the room. Beautiful, full

270

and ripe, the aureoles pink, the nipples taunt with wanting. His breathing was rapid and jerky. He buried his face in her fullness and raked his tongue over her each tip.

Hands fisted in his hair, she moaned. "Simon, Simon."

He stood, taking her up with him, and yanked back the covers. He rolled onto the bed taking her with him. She landed on top. Thank God it was a sturdy bed. Grabbing his face between her hands, she seduced his lips with her mouth. Rolling to his side, he positioned them facing each other. Stripping off his shorts he tossed them across the room. He reached down for her bikinis, eyes locked on hers. Sliding them down her legs, he teased her inner thighs on his way to her feet and then back again.

She reached for his fullness, stroked it while he gasped for breath. Her hands slipped over his hip to his buttock. She stroked then followed the path of his spine to explore his back and around to his chest. When she started back down his stomach, he grabbed her hand and put it around his neck.

"Simon, your body is beautiful." His heart lurched at her appraisal. He gathered her close reveling in the feel of her breasts against his chest. Running his hand down her back, he cupped her buttocks and pulled her closer to his arousal. She opened her legs and moved one across his hip. "I want you, Simon. I want you now. Love me, please."

* * *

"Uncle Simon, Jo Beth said I could hold Ashley for a minute." Whitney hopped onto the sofa beside Simon. Having her with him and Hallie had been a joy. She seemed happy and her teacher said she was doing well in school. Blue eyes serious, she coaxed. "I'll be real careful. She's delicate."

Simon lay Ashley in Whitney's arms and watched her as they discussed how beautiful she was. Whitney ran her fingers over the fine downy hair on the baby's head. "She's so soft. Do you think her hair will be red like Jo Beth's?"

"It's hard to tell, pumpkin. We'll know in a month or two." Ashley started to fuss. Simon took her, put her on his shoulder, and applied gentle pats in case she had an air bubble.

Hallie watched, heart constricting at the beauty of this big, beautiful man holding the tiny baby. So gentle and expert, as if he did it every day. His auburn hair against the baby's blond head, he turned his face to nuzzle and kiss the sweet neck. Tears sprang to her eyes. No man on earth deserved children more than Simon.

Justin and Caitlyn demanded their turn with the baby. They would marry in May. At Sam and Shelia's insistence, Caitlyn had returned to college and graduated in January. She was so happy for them. Simon put Ashley in Justin's arms.

Hallie pulled Simon to his feet. "She's precious, isn't she?"

He smiled down at the baby. "Yes, she is. New life is so amazing."

"Listen up, everybody. Elise and I have an announcement to make." Corbett, tall and dark with a smile stretched across his face, held Elise at his side. Almost as tall as Corbett, her blonde beauty complimented his ruggedness. She looked at her mother, giving her a radiant smile.

Hallie grabbed Simon's arm. He gazed down. Seeing the mist in her eyes, he hugged her close.

"Elise and I are engaged." As he turned and kissed his *fiancée*, the room echoed with cheers.

After hugs and congratulations, Hallie grabbed a sweater and Simon's jacket. "Let's go for a walk."

It was warm for early April. Signs of spring poked through the grass. It wouldn't be long until the fields would be carpeted in shades of blue and red—blue bonnets and Indian paintbrush in full bloom. They walked toward the barn, arms around each other, hips bumping every few steps. One of the mares had a new foal and they stopped to look. She leaned against the stall, Simon's arm around her shoulder. Reaching up, she pulled his face down for her kiss.

"Simon. I'm pregnant."

He closed his eyes and froze, then dropped his forehead to hers. Voice choked, he asked, "Are you sure?"

She hugged him close. "If the pregnancy tests are as reliable as they advertise, I'm sure. I've had other symptoms."

"Why didn't you tell me?"

"Because I didn't want you to get your hopes up and it not be true."

His face was radiant. "A baby. Our baby. I can't tell you how happy this makes me." Tears swam in his beautiful blue eyes. His brow furrowed. "What about you, Hallie? How do you feel?"

She smoothed the wrinkles from his forehead. "Great."

"Thank you, God." He kissed her. She wiped the

moisture from his eyes. "Thank you, Hallie, for your love and the chance to be a father." He whooped with joy, slinging his hat into the air. The mare squealed and stomped her dislike of the noise. Hidden behind his mother, the foal peeked around in fright.

"Oh, I'm sorry, girl."

Grabbing Hallie's hand, he kissed it and looked down into her eyes. "I never believed I'd be a father. How can a man be so fortunate?"

Hallie kissed him. "Simon, you're a good man. After all the love you've invested in your family, you more than deserve a child of your own."

About the Author

Linda LaRoque is a Texas girl, but the first time she got on a horse, it tossed her in the road dislocating her right shoulder. Forty years passed before she got on another, but it was older, slower, and she was wiser. Plus, her students looked on and it was important to save face.

A retired teacher who loves West Texas, its flora and fauna, and its people, Linda's stories paint pictures of life, love, and learning set against the raw landscape of ranches and rural communities in Texas and the Midwest. She is a member of RWA, her local chapter of HOTRWA, NTRWA and Texas Mountain Trail Writers.

Linda writes contemporary western romances, time travel historical romances, women's fiction and futuristic romances.

~ * ~

Visit Linda at these locations:

www.lindalaroque.com

http://www.lindalaroqueauthor.blogspot.com

https://www.facebook.com/linda.laroque

http://www.goodreads.com/author/show/649259.Linda_
LaRoque

Other Books by Linda LaRoque

Contemporary Westerns
Forever Faithful
When the Ocotillo Bloom

Futuristic
Born in Ice

Time Travel
My Heart Will Find Yours—The Turquoise Legacy
Book 1
Flames on the Sky—The Turquoise Legacy Book 2
A Way Back
Desires of the Heart—novella
A Law of Her Own—novella
A Marshal of Her Own—novella
A Love of His Own—novella
A Time of Their Own—an anthology containing A Law
of Her Own, A Marshal of Her Own, and A Love of His
Own
Birdie's Nest

Women's Fiction
Shattered Vows
Wounded Hearts—novella